I0657073

Benjamin Charles Jones

One Hundred Lectures on the Ancient and Modern Dramatic Poets

Benjamin Charles Jones

One Hundred Lectures on the Ancient and Modern Dramatic Poets

ISBN/EAN: 9783337412968

Printed in Europe, USA, Canada, Australia, Japan

Cover: Foto ©Andreas Hilbeck / pixelio.de

More available books at **www.hansebooks.com**

ONE HUNDRED LECTURES

ON THE

ANCIENT AND MODERN DRAMATIC POETS,

THE HEATHEN MYTHOLOGY,

ORATORY AND ELOCUTION,

DOWN TO THE NINETEENTH CENTURY,

COMMENCING WITH THESPIS, THE FOUNDER OF THE DRAMATIC ART,

SIXTH CENTURY B.C.

———◆———

BY

B. C. JONES.

FIRST SERIES, CONTAINING IX. LECTURES.

LONDON:

W. H. ALLEN & CO., WATERLOO PLACE.

1862.

Price 8s 6d.

PREFACE.

WE do not expect men in affluent circumstances to trouble themselves much in devoting their time to produce literary works. Some few exceptions there are to this rule, and posterity will not forget to honour the names of those who may thus labour for the benefit of society. Not finding many of this class of writers, we necessarily look to those requiring our support for their exertions to enlighten us. This being the case (and public support being essential), I venture to throw my humble labours into the scale of public opinion, anticipating nothing but a just balance of public favour. I am not vain enough to imagine that I shall immortalise myself by my attempt to eclaircise the drama and dramatic poets to your capacities, but I am ambitious enough to seek the praise and approbation of my fellow-men ; therefore, if I can produce anything of merit deserving your good opinion, accord it freely, or if I twaddle and waste good paper, why! deal with me in the same spirit. If the food I produce is worth your feeding upon, digest

it well and I will afford you a fresh repast every week ; or
if it does not agree with your taste, you can eschew it altogether.   I must confess I'd rather have your support than
otherwise, for it will encourage me to exert my genius and
to try if I cannot be agreeably useful to my fellow citizens ;
and, furthermore, if I do succeed, how glorious it will be
to think I shall not be altogether forgotten to posterity.
'Tis the natural vanity of mankind to desire this : life, 'tis said,
is all vanity—some people add that a little vexation of spirit
is sometimes commingled with it.   How generous then, my
friends, it will be on your part to encourage my vanity by
making me believe I am amusing and enlightening you, and
how gratifying it will be to you to know you are not occa-
sioning me any vexation of spirit in not disappointing my
hopes.   I candidly confess and freely admit that I want
your support—how else will I be incited to proceed to the
issue of what I contemplate ?   This will depend upon the
extent of support I receive : by that I will have to decide if
I venture to issue these numbers, which I ask you to purchase
to edify yourselves and 'replenish my exchequer' or not.
"Money's the thing," they say, "that makes the mare to go,"
and as the song says, " I want money, I want money;" spend
a little of your spare cash, and don't despair of an adequate
requital.   *Quid sit futurum cras fuge querere carpe diem*
—this being my motto, I will proceed now to tell you what
I purpose offering you.   I propose to collect all the information in my power and render it unto you, relative to

the dramatic poets and dramatic productions of all ages, but you must not expect from me impossibilities—all the talent that ever existed is not within my reach. I am already in possession of sufficient material to write upon for the next year or two, therefore if you as vividly grasp at the enlightening flashes that I purpose electrifying you with, as I cause them to appear, I'll promise you not to disorganise your gastric capacities, but give you such food as you shall digest with pleasure; yet you must not expect from me too much, lest I disappoint you and bring your maledictions on to my own unfortunate noddle. Let us go on smoothly; be you moderate in your demands and I'll be as prolific in my effusions as nature will allow me.

The first series of my lectures, will be upon the Greek tragedies. I purpose going through the whole of the works of the three great masters, Æschylus, Euripides, and Sophocles, " whose characters appeared bathed in tears, with murderous weapon in hand, terror and pity on either side, preceded by despair and followed by woe." After these my province will be to search for more material of same character by other hands and to be followed by the comedies which were produced about same period. My present plan is to finish these two series with Seneca, whose birth took place the same year as the Christian Era commenced. I will then collect what matter I can for you that was produced in this era previous to Shakspeare's time (some I have already in my possession of rather an interesting character),

and when I come to the great poet himself, I hope to lay
before you such lucid definitions of his various impressions
as may, perhaps, gain me your confidence and entitle my
works to your regard with favour and esteem. The works of
the great poet last named to you may be fairly considered as
forming a part of the riches of the kingdom, traditional and
everlasting—it has been said that " they are her estate in
fame, that fame which letters confer upon her ; the worth
and value of which or sinks or raises her in the opinion of
foreign nations, and she takes her rank among them according to the esteem which these are held in." Talk of enthusiasm in favour of our Shakspeare! this, I think, beats all
the rest hollow—it actually goes so far as to say that the
whole world judge the standard of our position in the scale
of nations as is only to be balanced by those who can produce a poet of equal merit ; or another interpretation of it
may be that in accordance with the estimation this poet is held
in by the various nations of the earth, so is the worth and
greatness of our nation esteemed by them. I revere the
genius and memory of our sweet bard as much as any one
in the world, but I cannot go quite so far as " Capell " does,
particularly whilst we know that there are nations in the
world (yea! and civilised nations to) that know very little
about Shakspeare at all, and the little they are acquainted
with of him they scarcely comprehend. We know very well
that his works have been translated into almost every living
language, but whilst we are aware that the whole of Shak-

speare's language is but very sparsely comprehended amongst our own people, what a stupendous error it is to suppose that all nations are so entirely acquainted with him as to set up their opinions of us by virtue of his writing !

I must here break off dilating upon our immortal bard, or my preface may be construed as a prefix to his works. That opportunity has not yet arrived with me, and I must reserve further remarks on this head for a future occasion, particularly as I contemplate bringing before your notice the following list of names, all of them authors of more or less talent, excepting a few who were actors of much distinction and considerable renown :—Æschylus, Euripides, Sophocles, Aristides, Simonides, Prodieus, Anaxagoras, Pericles, Socrates, Aristophanes, Epicarmus, Dionysius, Lycophron, Plautus, Terence, Pratinas, Hesychius, and Seneca, also Cid, Bedford, Boiardo, Ariosto, Bale, Buchanan, Ferreira, Cervantes, Chapman, Daniel, Lope de Vega, Alleyne, Jonson (Ben.), Guevara, Fletcher, Beaumont, Massinger, Ford, Browne, Marlowe, Marston, Calderon de la Barca, Davenant (Sir William), Carey, Cartwright, Denham, Cowley, Cavendish (Duchess of), Banister, Moliere, Cotton, Dryden, Quinault, Betterton, Etherege (Sir George), Racine, Shadwell, Collier, Otway, Tate, Campistron, Dennis, Zeno, Southern, Dancourt, Baron, Centlivre, Le Sage, Congreve, Steele (Sir Richard), Cibber, Addison, Vanbrugh (Sir John), Motte, Crebillon, Phillips, Farquhar, Destouches, Booth, Roger (Earl of Orrery), Boyle (Charles), Boyle

(John), Young, Fenton, Oldfield (Ann), Holberg (Baron),
Ramsay, Marivaux, Gay, Pope, Piron, Macklin, Chaussee,
Brown (Sir William), Lillo, Quin, Voltaire, Savage, Carey
(Henry), Moore, Thomson, Phillips (Ambrose), Chiari,
Dodsley, Arno, Goldoni, Fielding, Johnson (Dr. Samuel),
Colle, Hill, Favart, Whitehead, Clairion, Legris, Clive
(Catherine), Rousseau, Hanmer, Carlin, Fielding (Sarah),
Diderot, Whitehead (William), Gellert, Baretti, Garrick,
Carmontelli, Walpole, Barry, Montague, Sheridan (Thomas
and wife), Foote, Mason, Belloy, Murphy, Lessing, Mossop,
Cuningham, Cesarotti, Chabonon, Churchill, Beaumarchais,
Cumberland, Crawfurd (Ann), my friend Capell (before
alluded to in this preface), Laharpe, More (Hannah), Bur-
goyne, Stevens, Boswell, Boswell (James), Bartelemon,
Cowley (Hannah), Chalmers, Holcroft, Daschkoff, Macken-
zie, Dudley, Jones (Sir William), Dibdin, Edwin, Alfieri,
Goethe, Anderson, Jordan (Mrs.), Collin, Douce, Fergus-
son, Sheridan (Richard Brinsley), Feith, Pindermonte,
Bingley, Fabre, Cimarosa, Siddons (Mrs.), Inchbald, Cook,
Capnist, Cobb, Candettini, Holme, Kemble (J. P.), Devon-
shire (Duchess), Schiller, Derby (Countess), Iffland, Moore
(Edward), Bloomfield, Talma, Steevens, Constant de Re-
beque, Vestris, Picard, Kotzebue, Kempelen, Scott (Sir
Walter), Lewis, Elliston, Foscolo, Emery, Nicolo, Banti,
Benger, Kean (Edmund), Byron, Banks, Shelley, Lucan,
Miller, Drake, Aristotle, Dunster, Dante, Flaxman, Berges,
Falieri, Carew, Carlos, Clarke, Chesterfield, Chiabrera,

Clive, Combreare, Cowper, Crawshaw, Devereux, Roscoe, Smith, Hazlitt, Webster, Ancourt, Bowle, Sheridan Knowles, Talfourd, Douglas Jerrold, Bulwer, Bourcicault, Baliol, Amot, Bartholomew, Scarrion, Memoravila, Wycherly, Behn, Bettinelli, Blondell, Blood, Buxton, Bruton, Malone, &c. This list must not be taken all as authors; some were actors and some few of them will be introduced into my lectures merely by way of examples, but more or less, they will all be noticed and the works of many of them will be entirely investigated and treated upon ; yet it cannot be expected that the whole of their productions will be reviewed, nor will a complete history of their lives be compiled, yet I will tell you sufficient concerning them to interest and amuse you.

LECTURE I.

LET me communicate to you a few facts. Notwithstanding all the pains that have been bestowed upon the subject, the information we possess relative to the dramatic poets and eminent actors who preceded Shakspeare is exceedingly scanty; yet, scanty as it is, but few people of the present generation have made themselves acquainted with it. We are accustomed to look upon Shakspeare as the Alpha, yea! and many of his admirers have considered him also the Omega of dramatic literature—the first and the last—all before his time they deem but as a chaos, all since but as feeble shadows of the past. My sentiments respecting the great poet being well known, I need not repeat them here; yet, however much I admire him, I am not disposed to go this length—the greatest, let us grant him to be, both before and after his time, but do not let us shut all other clever men out of the pale of our memories; it will not be depriving our Shakspeare of a single laurel that adorns his brow our affording others the meed of praise their talents entitle them to. There were many who preceded Shakspeare possessed of highly cultivated minds and of no mean share of poetical genius; their numbers were doubtless much greater than we are aware of, for it is a fact well known that

many plays were written before Shakspeare's time the names
of which are lost, and many names of authors have reached
us whose writings are entirely missing; besides which, some
plays have reached us the writers of them never having been
satisfactorily authenticated.   Mr. Collier has justly observed:
" It is probable that prior to the year 1592 the copyright
of plays was little understood and less recognised;" various
companies were performing the same drama at the same
time, although they had been brought out by special companies for their own exclusive use.   Collier accounts for this
by stating that it was not the practice to print the plays,
consequently by far the greater number of what were
written have never reached us, and some that have come to us
are imperfect.   My province is to give but a cursory glance
at the dramatic poets of this era previous to Shakspeare, for
this reason : I am quite certain, let me take however much
trouble I may, I cannot light upon sufficient matter of
importance to make my lectures interesting to you—not
such as may be relied upon as regards its accuracy.   I
might, I know, overcome the difficulty by introducing fiction
and some of my own compositions, but fiction I am determined to avoid, and I have not yet summoned up sufficient
courage

> To bring the angels, demons, furies and the spright
> Of my own imagination " to the world's light."
> How can one who to commerce has been devoted
> In literature e'er expect to be noted ?
> 'Tis not our fate in looking for public favour
> To find response (unless cautious in behaviour).
> So caution here with me shall mark my guarded way,
> Ere I produce my Tragedy for public play.

—Yet, though I do not intend dilating upon the doubtful period
alluded to, it is nevertheless my intention to go back to the

sixth century before the birth of Christ, to Thespis, the founder of the dramatic art. Some have given Homer this credit; mentally, perhaps, no man more deserves it, but practically to Thespis I say the honour is due. I propose bringing before your notice the names of many authors of great repute and high merit, including a few of the sex we delight to look upon, also many actors whose combined talents shed a lustre upon the age they adorned. Yes, it is when we meet with the higher orders of talents combined with virtue apparent in the souls of our sisterhood that we may truly say they add a brilliancy to that lustre that shall reflect honour and renown on their memories. I have said that I purpose introducing to your attention the names of some of our leading actors, which I will do, both of the past and the present period; for be it borne in mind that without good actors to bring good writings before the world in their intended light many of our greatest authors would have remained in comparative oblivion. I may also have occasion to make allusions to the names of individuals who were neither dramatic authors nor actors. In doing this it will be but to diversify my remarks to you.

In going back to the rise of the drama in the world, I commence with Thespis. He lived at a village near Athens, about 530 years before the birth of Christ. The reason his name is mentioned in many old books, as well as in several modern works as being the founder of tragedy is, because at the feasts of Bacchus, where they used to indulge in dithyrambic choruses, Thespis introduced between the parts mythological stories which he used to recite; but why the title of founder of tragedy is awarded him on this account I am somewhat slow to comprehend, unless it was that these representations on Thespis's part were enthusiastic in their character, and perhaps sometimes produced rather tragical effects upon his audiences. There is nothing that I can find to show that these recitations were either tragic or comic in their tendencies, only that they were speaking parts. I therefore prefer giving Thespis the credit of being the founder of melodramatic representations. It is said that upon one occasion he received for his reward a male goat. It was the custom at these entertainments to reward those who distinguished themselves, some say with a male goat, others his skin, and again, others say a skin of wine (some of them often had their skins too full of this commodity—poor Æschylus has been condemned for the practice). The fact is Bacchus was the original planter of the vine, and it being ascertained that the goat did some mischief to the plant by eating the leaves, it was thought necessary to destroy the animal; from this it became a religious ceremony.

The first name (he being really the first tragedian) that I have upon my list is Æschylus. He was born at Athens in the year 519 before the Christian Era. He was the son of Euphorion and of good birth; he had a brother named Cynægirus, another Ameinias—of both these history speaks favourably, and of Æschylus it tells of his greatness as a soldier and a poet. We are told that he fought at the battles of Salamis, Marathon and Platæa in the Athenian army, but it is to his writings we look for his fame. He is said by some to have written seventy, by others ninety tragedies, and to him is attributed the origin of writing pieces in which more than one character is introduced upon the stage at the time; he also introduced the custom of clothing his characters in dresses pertaining and suitable to the parts they were representing. Although we are told that he wrote seventy or ninety tragedies, and that he received thirteen public prizes, only seven of his productions have come down to us; these are the Eumenides, Surplices, Cheopliore, the Persæ, Agamemnon, Prometheus Vinctus, and Septem Duces apud Thebas. In one of his tragedies, the Eumenides, we are told that he represented some of his characters with such ghastly masks on their heads that the effect was to frighten several children to death and many women into premature labour. His style of writing is rather abstruse and somewhat disconnected, but it shows the author to have been wonderfully imaginative, also prodigious and vigorous in his conceptions. It has been observed that his writings are the most difficult to comprehend of all the Greek classics, but I do not entirely accord in this idea. He was once condemned to death for inserting a few passages into one of his tragedies said to have been of an impious character, but his brother Amyneas, who defended him, saved him by uncovering his arm from which he had lost his hand at the battle of Salamis,* in defence of his country—the effect was a reversal of the sentence, the poet was pardoned. Some of the ancient writers have reported that this extraordinary man only composed when in a state of intoxication. He died at the age of sixty-nine, just 450 years before the birth of Christ.

Buckley makes it appear that Æschylus was born six years earlier and died six years sooner. The author of a very clever work called " The Theatre of the Greeks," gives the period of Æschylus's birth five years sooner than I

---

* The battle of Salamis was fought between the Athenians and Persians near the island of Ægina, situate in the Ægean Sea, about twenty-two miles in circumference. It was formerly called Œnopia, but afterwards bore its name from Æquia, daughter of Asopus, who was married to Actor, son of Myrmidon. Jupiter visited her in the shape of a flame of fire and turned her into the island. The island itself was infested by swarms of ants, which Jupiter changed into men ; they became a powerful nation, but ultimately they were subdued by Darius and finally driven from the island by Pericles.

have stated, and makes his death two years later than Buckley. If this be correct Æschylus must have been seventy-two years old when he died, instead of sixty-nine according to Buckley's statement and my opinion. Having now given you my own remarks upon this poet, I think I cannot do better than confirm them by reading to you an opinion of the author of the "Theatre of the Greeks." He says: "Æschylus must be considered as the creator of tragedy ; it sprang forth from his head in complete armour, like Minerva from the brain of Jove." This just confirms the opinion I expressed to you at starting respecting Thespis. There is no proof whatever that Thespis was the founder of tragedy, but we have ample conviction that Æschylus's tragedies are the first upon record, and now extant; therefore in absence of other proof his name stands first.

In our general impressions respecting philosophy and oratory we invariably go back to the Greeks for our models, frequently citing Homer for poetry, Demosthenes for oratory, and Xenophon for history. The works of these are to be met with in good schools and in the libraries of scholastic individuals; but it is an extraordinary fact that even in the present day you may go into public libraries and into those connected with literary institutions without meeting with them. Certainly, such books as the ancient dramatic poets are seldom to be seen at these places : the only way I can account for it is that the general public is not acquainted with the heathen mythology, and this being the general foundation upon which these great authors based their productions, they are not frequently inquired for, consequently are seldom seen in the catalogues of these institutions. Franklin tells us that "the information we have of ancient tragedy is merely verbal criticisms and readings, trite exclamations and undistinguishing applause made by dull and phlegmatic commentators." He says, " The old tragedians have been shamefully disguised and misrepresented," that " its real and intrinsic merits have never been thoroughly known nor enquired into." I believe this to be a fact, and I attribute it to what I have just told you—the public not being acquainted with the theory upon which the ancient dramatic works are based. Franklin says, " To place the spectator in a position to comprehend it, some able writer may possibly lay the foundation for a complete history of it." Now, I do not profess myself to be an " able writer," nor am I assuming credit for arranging a complete history of the ancient drama; but I am sanguine enough to imagine I am laying the foundation for a more general enquiry into its details and merits by supplying a copious description and a few illustrations, combined with a lucid definition of those parts I attempt to treat upon, my great object being to explain to my hearers the leading incidents relating to the writers' ideas and to convey to you by such language as you may easily comprehend what the authors' thoughts were, and the impressions they were intended to convey. By this method I am enabled to explain to you the abstruse passages according to the little talent Providence has been pleased to endow me with, and if I am fortunate enough to carry you with me into the spirit of my subject (which I shall do by your generously giving me your attention) I do not fear succeeding in affording you some little instruction.

I have told you at the beginning of this lecture that Thespis was the first who introduced speaking or dramatic parts between the choruses; these recitations were called episodes. An episode is a narrative; a narrative is a relation of an incident; incidents are the foundations upon which representations are based; therefore the reciting these episodes renders them dramatic representations; thus am I

B

confirmed that we owe the origin of the dramatic art to
Thespis and the foundation of tragedy to Æschylus.   After
Thespis there were written what were called the fifty plays
of Licyonian and Pratinas; then Phrynicus (who was a
pupil of Thespis) wrote nine plays.   There was another poet
about same period of same name—he wrote two plays; then
there were Alcæus, Phormus, Chœrilus.   This last-named
individual is said to have written no less than one hundred
and twenty tragedies.   Then again there was Apollophanes,
and Cephisodorus, who wrote the Amazons, and probably
the tragedy called Daulis.   All these were comparatively of
minor consideration, for real and pure tragedy can scarcely be
considered on a sound footing until the poet Æschylus issued
and represented his sublime productions.   The two great
masters in Greek tragedy after Æschylus were Sophocles
and Euripides; the former of these we are told wrote 130
tragedies, but seven of these only have come down to us.
Euripides has credit for having written from 75 to 92
tragedies; of his productions we have 18 extant and translated into English.   I purpose treating upon the productions
of these two poets, as well as Æschylus, in full, that is to
say, I will go through the whole 32 tragedies and explain to
you the characters introduced; also the plots and arguments
associating each with a dissertation upon their respective
merits and tendencies, but as the time is now getting on I
must begin my actual work by introducing, first, the Pro-
' metheus Chained, of Æschylus.

The Grecian authors based their productions almost
entirely upon the fabulous belief of their own age and that
antecedent to it, mainly drawing their characters or guiding
influences of them from the heathen mythology, the theory
of which was that Chaos was the first god of all.   This may
be very easily imagined, Chaos meaning empty space, or, as

Hesiod called it, "a shapeless mass of matter." I suppose he meant the clouds, or floating vapours, but it matters little which it was—the empty clear blue space we are sometimes apt to try to mentally penetrate, or the clouds that intervene between that and us: 'tis enough to know it means indefinitism. Then there was Terra; from her sprang Japetus; he was son of Cœlus. Cœlus and Uranus, or Ouranus, are the same. Japetus was the father of Prometheus. We also have it that Prometheus was the son of Japetus and Clymene—she of the Oceanides—so that he had two mothers, earth and water, like Shakspeare's bubbles.

Then we have two more characters represented—which two we will explain, if you please, as meaning the will and determination of Jove, these are forced upon Vulcan to perform the task of making the chain and fastening Prometheus to the Scythian rock.

In the opening speech of the tragedy, Strength calls Prometheus " the artificer of man ;" this alludes to what Apollodorus tells us of Prometheus. He says he made the first man and woman on this earth out of clay; that he stole fire from heaven (another version is from the chariot of the sun) and infusing the fire into his models he animated them and they became human beings. We have heard of another strange thing of a similar character but this is most strange ; yet, if you, my friends, choose to harbour the stranger, why, let us say, with Shakspeare, " As a stranger give it welcome."

Prometheus was a very cunning god indeed, up to all sorts of knowing things; so shrewd in fact, that he even deceived Jove himself. He outwitted the chief god but he was too knowing to be entrapped by Jove's attempt upon him through Pandora and her box. The work of chaining Prometheus to the rock has been attributed to Mercury, but as Vulcan

was the first who erected a forge on earth, I think Æschylus
has very properly assigned the work to his hands.   The re-
luctance of this god to execute his master's commands is
finely pourtrayed in the following passage :—

" VULCAN.

" Stern Pow'rs, your harsh commands have here an end,
" Nor find resistance !   My less hardy mind,
" Averse to violence, shrinks back, and dreads
" To bind a kindred god to this wild cliff."

The first line of this passage—

" Stern Pow'rs, your harsh commands have here an end."

means, Unchangeable Pow'r! you are now inflicting your
worst punishment, you cannot do more.   Æschylus gives
the term of Prometheus' bondage as 30,000 years, but the
divine Hercules released him after he had been bound 30
years.

Prometheus had the credit of being a prophet, for Jove
himself had been known to consult him.   Here is Æschylus's
allusion to this tradition ; he makes him say, in the ninth
page of the play,

————————" My clear sight
" Looks through the future ; unforeseen no ill
" Shall come on me :"

By this it would seem that he knew beforehand what was
coming to him, and I suppose by the same foresight he knew
'twas useless attempting to avert his doom ; therefore he
goes quietly with Strength and Vulcan to the rock.   But
we must not forget that Æschylus introduces Force as well
to assist the other two, so that if Prometheus had attempted

to put Jove's Strength out, Mr. Force would have stepped
in and by a little pressure no doubt brought Prometheus to a proper sense of feeling. He knew very well his
liver was going to be worried by the Vulture sent by Jove,
and he saw no policy in straining his lungs or wasting his
gall to boot; he says,

> —————————————————" For favours shown
> " To mortal man I bear this weight of woe."

This means, " For having given fire to mortal man, to enable him to fabricate various arts, am I thus punished. We
are not told why Jove took fire from the earth, but we may
conjecture that he did so to prevent the human beings Prometheus had made the use of it. Perhaps this is to be conceived
in a similar light as Adam and Eve being interdicted the use
of the fruit from the tree of knowledge, the difference being
that the one rests upon mere conjecture whilst the other is
stated to be a recorded fact. Prometheus was not like some
cruel parents—he never deserted his progeny, but like a
good father, he taught them the use of metals, the nature of
plants, how to tame horses and how to cultivate the earth.

Now, my friend, having thus far given you the nature
and character of Prometheus, I will proceed to read to you
his pathetic exclamations after he is chained to the rock and
left there by Vulcan, Strength and Force.

> " Ætherial air, and ye swift-winged winds,
> " Ye rivers springing from fresh founts, ye waves
> " That o'er th' interminable ocean wreath
> " Your crisped smiles, thou all-producing earth,
> " And thee, bright sun, I call, whose flaming orb
> " Views the wide world beneath, see what, a god,
> " I suffer from the gods ; with what fierce pains,
> " Behold, what tortures for revolving ages
> " Here I must struggle ; such unseemly chains

" This new-rais'd ruler of the gods devis'd.

" Ah me! That groan bursts from my anguish'd heart,

" My present woes and future to bemoan.

" When shall these suff'rings find their destin'd end ?

" But why that vain enquiry ?   My clear sight

" Looks through the future ; unforeseen no ill

" Shall come on me : behoves me then to bear

" Patient my destin'd fate, knowing how vain

" To struggle with necessity's strong pow'r.

" But to complain, or not complain, alike

" Is unavailable.   For favours shown

" To mortal man I bear this weight of woe ;

" Hid in an hollow cane the fount of fire

" I privately convey'd, of ev'ry art

" Productive, and the noblest gift to men.

" And for this slight offence, woe, woe is me!

" I bear these chains, fixed to this savage rock,

" Unshelter'd from the inclemencies of th'air.

" Ah me ! what sound, what softly-breathing odour

" Steals on my sense ?   Be you immortal gods,

" Or mortal men, or of th'heroic race,

" Whoe'er have reached this wild rock's extreme cliff,

" Spectators of my woes, or what your purpose,

" Ye see me bound, a wretched god, abhor'd

" By Jove, and ev'ry god that treads his courts,

" For my fond love to man.   Ah me! again

" I hear the sound of flutt'ring nigh ; the air

" Pants to the soft beat of light-moving wings :

" All that approaches now, is dreadful to me.

" CHORUS.

" Forbear thy fears : a friendly train

" On busy pennons flutt'ring light,

" We come, our sire not ask'd in vain,

" And reach this promontory's height.

" The clanging iron's horrid sound

" Re-echo'd thro' our caves profound ;

" And tho' my cheek glows with shame's crimson dye,

" Thus with unsandal'd foot with winged speed I fly.

" PROMETHEUS.

" Ah me ! Ah me!
" Ye virgin sisters, who derive your race
" From fruitful Thetis, and th' embrace
" Of old Oceanus, your sire, that rolls
" Around the wide world his unquiet waves,
" This way turn your eyes, behold
" With what a chain fix'd to this rugged steep
" Th' unenvied station of the rock I keep.

" CHORUS.

" I see, I see ; and o'er my eyes,
" Surcharg'd with sorrow's tearful rain,
" Dark'ning the misty clouds arise ;
" I see thy adamantine chain ;
" In its strong grasp thy limbs confin'd,
" And withering in the parching wind :
" Such the stern pow'r of heav'n's new-sceptred lord,
" And law-controlling Jove's irrevocable word.

" PROMETHEUS

" Beneath the earth,
" Beneath the gulfs of Tartarus, that spread
" Interminable o'er the dead,
" Had his stern fury fix'd this rigid chain,
" Nor gods, nor men had triumph'd in my pain.
" But pendent in th' ætherial air,
" The pageant gratifies my ruthless foes,
" That gaze, insult, and glory in my woes.

" CHORUS.

" Is there a god, whose sullen soul
" Feels a stern joy in thy despair ?
" Owns he not pity's soft controul,
" And drops in sympathy the tear ?
" All, all, save Jove ; with fury driv'n
" Severe he tames the sons of heav'n ;
" And he will tame them, till some pow'r arise
" To wrest from his strong hand the sceptre of the skies.

" PROMETHEUS.

" Yet he, e'en he,
" That o'er the gods holds his despotic reign,
" And fixes this disgraceful chain,
" Shall need my aid, the counsils to disclose
" Destructive to his honour and his throne.
" But not the honied blandishments, that flows
" From his alluring lips, shall ought avail ;
" His rigid menaces shall fail ;
" Nor will I make the fatal secret known,
" Till his proud hands this galling chain unbind,
" And his remorse sooth's my indignant mind.

" CHORUS.

" Bold and intrepid is thy soul,
" Fir'd with resentment's warmest glow ;
" And thy free voice disdains controul,
" Disdains the tort'ring curb of woe.
" My softer bosom, thrill'd with fear
" Lest heavier ills await thee here,
" By milder counsils wishes thee repose:
" For Jove's relentless rage no tender pity knows.

" PROMETHEUS.

" Stern tho' he be,
" And, in the pride of pow'r terrific drest,
" Rears o'er insulted right his crest,
" Yet gentler thoughts shall mitigate his soul,
" When o'er his head this storm shall roll ;
" Then shall his stubborn indignation bend,
" Submit to sue, and court me for a friend.

" CHORUS.

" But say, relate at large for what offence
" Committed doth the wrath of Jove iuflict
" This punishment so shameful, so severe:
" Instruct us, if the tale shocks not thy soul.

" PROMETHEUS.

" 'Tis painful to relate it, to be silent
" Is pain : each circumstance is full of woe.
" When stern debate amongst the gods appear'd,
" And discord in the courts of heav'n was rous'd ;
" Whilst against Saturn some conspiring will'd
" To pluck him from the throne, that Jove might reign ;
" And some, averse, with ardent zeal oppos'd
" Jove's rising pow'r and empire o'er the gods ;
" My counsils, tho' discreetest, wisest, best,
" Mov'd not the Titans, those impetuous sons
" Of Ouranus and Terra, whose high spirits,
" Disdaining milder measures, proudly ween'd
" To seize by force the sceptre of the sky.
" Oft did my goddess mother, Themis now,
" Now Gaia, under various names design'd,
" Herself the same, foretell me the event,
" That not by violence, that not by pow'r,
" But gentler arts, the royalty of heav'n
" Must be obtained. . Whilst thus my voice advis'd,
" Their headlong rage deign'd me not e'en a look.
" What then could wisdom dictate, but to take
" My mother, and, with voluntary aid
" Abet the cause of Jove ? Thus by my counsils
" In the dark deep Tartarean gulph enclos'd
" Old Saturn lies, and his confederate pow'rs.
" For these good deeds the tyrant of the skies
" Repays me with these dreadful punishments.
" For foul mistrust of those that serve them best
" Breathes its black poison in each tyrant's heart.
" Ask you the cause for which he tortures me ?
" I will declare it. On his father's throne
" Scarce was he seated, on the chiefs of heav'n
" He show'r'd his various honours ; thus confirming
" His royalty ; but for unhappy mortals
" Had no regard, and all the present race
" Will'd to extirpate, and to form anew.
" None, save myself oppos'd his will ; I dar'd ;

" And boldly pleading sav'd them from destruction,
" Sav'd them from sinking to the realms of night.
" For this offence I bend beneath these pains,
" Dreadful to suffer, piteous to behold :
" For mercy to mankind I am not deem'd
" Worthy of mercy ; but with ruthless hate
" In this uncouth appointment am fix'd here
" A spectacle dishonourable to Jove."

To finish my explanation to you of what I have been reading, I will call your attention to that given by Prometheus to the water nymphs, the daughters of Oceanus. He says, It will yet come to pass that he who holds this despotic sway shall need my advice to save his honour and his throne from destruction, but neither his blandishments nor his menaces shall move me till he first releases me from these sufferings—he shall express his sorrow to me for hurling this indignity on me and he shall soothe me by expressing his regrets—I have the secret in my mind that may prove fatal to him or otherwise, and I'll not make it known until he does this. The nymphs tell him he is bold and intrepid, daring with resentment towards Jove, speaks too freely and contemptuously of the great power ; they think 'twere better not to treat his own sufferings so lightly and with so much disdain, he had much better curb his temper. I advise you this, one of them says, I who am calm and not agitated as you are, therefore take my advice—be patient lest greater ills be inflicted on you, for Jove, once roused, knows no pity nor ever relents. Prometheus replies, I care not though he be stern and his power most terrific, for though he now carries his head high and haughtily he shall humble himself by seeking my advice when he finds his throne in jeopardy : yea! then he shall sue to me and court me as a friend.

Tell us, say the nymphs, what have you done to bring this wrath of Jove on you? I'll tell you, replies Prometheus; When there arose a conspiracy in heaven to dethrone Saturn and place Jove, his son, in his stead, my advice was first asked, and had it been taken things would have been arranged better than they have been, for I am most discreet and wiser than them all. I recommended mild measures, but the impetuous Titans would not be moved by me, and they seized the throne from their father Saturn by force; I then gave Jove my advice how to rule the gods—not by force, but by gentle arts—I told him to use the royalty of heaven with gentleness. I also advised him how to send Saturn and his confederates where they now are—in the deep gulf of Tartarus. For these services he now rewards me as you see. Soon as he ascended the throne he treated the gods in a right royal manner, but for poor mortals he had no regard and he willed that all should be destroyed of the present race and a new one formed. None opposed his will excepting myself, and by my bold pleadings I saved them; it is for this offence I suffer—for being merciful to mankind I am not deemed worthy of mercy by the gods.

I will now read to you a few lines I have composed applicable to the origin of the subject I have just alluded to. You will understand that Jove and Jupiter is the same impersonation; hitherto I have called him Jove, in my lines I mostly designate him Jupiter. If you find any tendency in what I am about reading to you to humour, you will please to understand that I have thrown such touches into it purposely, with a view of relieving the general tenor of my discourse :—

Uranus* and Terra†, 'tis said, did wed ;
Their offsprings as follows quickly were bred,
Mnemosyne‡, Briareus§, also Creus‖,
Giges¶, Phœbe**, Oceanus††, Cœus‡‡,

---

* *Uranus*, or Ouranus, the most ancient god next to Chaos. He was married to Terra or Tithea. His children rebelled against him because he kept them confined. One of them, Saturn, succeeded him on the throne of heaven.

† *Terra*, married to Uranus, by whom she had offsprings Oceanus, the Giants, the Titans, the Cyclops, Saturn, Hyperion, Cœus, Creus, Gottus, Themis, Phœbe, Tethys, Thea, and Mnemosyne. She was also married to the soft zephyrs and gentle breezes, by them she had the following deities : Mourning, Vengeance, Grief and Oblivion.

‡ *Mnemosyne*, daughter of the former, mother of the nine Muses ; her name signifies mentality.

§ *Briareus*, son of the first two before named. He was a giant and visited this world ; here he went by the name of Ægeon. He had fifty heads and a hundred hands. He led the war between the giants and the gods, and when the former were defeated, he was thrown into the crater of Mount Ætna.

‖ *Creus*, one of the sons of Uranus.

¶ *Giges*, another son of Uranus.

** *Phœbe*. Same as Diana, a daughter of Uranus and Terra. She married her brother Cœus. Her children were Latona and Asteria. As Phœbus was considered the sun, so was Phœbe believed to be the moon.

†† *Oceanus*, the sea. A description of him is incorporated in the line themselves.

‡‡ *Cœus*, husband and brother of Phœbe, father of Latona and Asteria.

Gottus,* Tethys†, renowned Saturn‡ bold.
And Hyperion§ with his curls of gold.
Hyperion and Thea wedded soon
And begat Aurora‖, the Sun and Moon ;
Oceanus, god of the waters wide,
Was second son of Uranus and bride.
Then Saturn, he of majestic form,
From this consorted union was born.
They were Titans call'd after Terra's race,
Got by affection redundant in grace.

---

* *Gottus*, another son of Uranus and Terra.

† *Tethys*. Married her brother Oceanus. They were parent to the following rivers : Mæander, Evenus, the Nile, Simois, Schamander, Peneus, Alpheus, Strymon ; also the Oceanides, supposed to be about 3,000 in number (these were all daughters). They are frequently designated the water nymphs.

‡ *Saturn* or *Saturnus*, one of the Titans, son of Uranus and Terra, afterwards ascended the throne of heaven by consent of his brothers with the understanding that he would not let any of his male children live ; he therefore made a practice of swallowing them as soon as they were born, but Rhea, getting tired of so much trouble for nothing, gave Saturn some great stones, which he devoured, believing her that these were her offspring, by which ruse she saved Neptune, Pluto, and Jupiter ; these three were afterwards kings, Jupiter of heaven, Pluto of hell, and Neptune of the ocean, Saturn's brothers, hearing of these male children being in existence, rebell'd against and overpower'd him, but he was released by his son Jupiter, who was twelve months old. Jupiter afterwards dethron'd Saturn and ascended the throne of heaven.

§ Hyperion married his sister Thea ; he was supposed to be the father of Aurora, the Sun and the Moon. Thea is often call'd Thia, Titæa, and frequently (very erroneously) Tethys.

‖ Aurora was mother of the winds and stars, also of Memnon and Ænathion, besides these, Phaeton. She carried off Arion to the island of Delos. Aurora may be consider'd, in the heathen mythology, in similar light to Hrimfaxi in the Scandinavian mythology, the source of dews. In the former she is represented pouring dew upon the earth to make the flowers grow. Hrimfaxi in the latter is represented as the night-horse when, relieved from his harness at day-break, he shakes his long mane, which sprinkles the earth with dew, and cultivates the soil.

These were the gods most godlike to the view,·
But nature shrinks to think what gods will do.
Uranus, the sire, in tyrannic mood,
Kept close his sons confin'd, depriv'd of food,
Till Terra, their mother, who always fair,
Brought food and weapons with maternal care.
Alas ! had she but food only given
These gods had not sinn'd against high heaven,
But being confin'd, they with rage were fired
And hence against the sire the sons conspir'd.
Saturn was first to lead the rebel host—
He deep in sin was compromis'd the most.
Saturn's scythe— O act of deep damnation—
Deprived Uranus of generation ;
Cast to sea of what Uranus was shorn
And from the contact was great Venus born.
Still more was caused by these great defiants,•
Uranus' blood bred furies and giants.
The Nymphs were created in many forms
To govern the waters, the tides and storms.
Oceanus, father of all waters,
Married Tethys, who begat him daughters.
Strymon* and Alpheus† were rivers bright,
Ripling their pure waters by day and night ;
Peneus‡ another—and many more
Whose waters o'er rocks in torrents did pour ;

---

* The river which separates Thrace from Macedonia and falls into the Ægean sea.

† This river rises in Arcadia and falls into the sea after traversing Elis. We are told that in its deification it fell in love with the nymph Arethusa. The goddess Diana changed Arethusa into a fountain and located it in Ortygia, an island near Syracuse. According to some of the ancient writings this river is said to pass under the sea at a certain point in Peloponnesus, re-appears in the island of Ortygia, and there joins another stream called the Arethusa. With a view of confirming this hypothesis we are told that if a buoyant article be thrown into the Alpheus in Elis, it will sink with the river at the point before named under the sea and re-appear in the river Arethusa.

‡ The Peneus rises on Mount Pindus and falls into the Thermæan

Through vales, through valleys o'er plains are now led
Rivers and streams from Oceanus' bed.
Seasons occasion the alternate tides
In Oceanus and Oceanides.
All rivers are Oceanus' daughters,
For he is god of the flowing waters.
To Saturn let me once more turn my muse
And show how gods their powers will abuse.
Some say that Saturn's was a golden reign,
But with his father's blood his hand was stain ;
Ever after this wicked god was curs'd—
He ate a stone which by Rhea* was nurs'd.
Rhea would not have Jupiter perish,
So gave Saturn a stone for a relish.
Thus also by a profound deception
She preserved to the world her son Neptune,
And mighty Jupiter, also Pluto—
Don't you think Rhea was right (ladies) to do so ?
To Saturn she was a devoted wife
Till the rogue deprived her offspring of life.
His word was pledged when he rose to power,
That all his male children he would devour.
Uranus' kingdom 'twas which Saturn gaiu'd ;
Thus o'er gods and goddesses Saturn reign'd
Till Titan and till Titan's brothers saw
That Saturn's word was not the strictest law,—
For through information 'twas discover'd
That Saturn's children were not all smother'd.
The Titans rose—Saturn was overpower'd :
('Twas well his children were not all devour'd.)

Gulph. Its course is very circuitous, passing between the Mounts
Olympus and Ossa, then through the plains of Tempe. Its banks in
many parts are profuse in the growth of laurels, one of which was originally the nymph Daphne, daughter of the god or River Peneus, she being
changed into this indignant form for some naughty act repugnant to her
associates

* Saturn's wife, in addition to the three gods I named to you in my

For Saturn was vanquished, in prison chain'd,
And for a period the Titans reign'd ;
'Till Jupiter, who was then one year old,
Of his sire's incarceration was told ;
Then, like the son of a belovèd sire,
Rose Jupiter in arms 'gainst news so dire.
Now Gods in arms wage sanguinary strife ;
Once more Saturn return'd to active life.
Now Jupiter's pow'r by Saturn was fear'd,
For no more his sire Jupiter revered,
But thought of himself and throne of the skies.
What I tell you is truth—none of it ——

The next character I will have to continue with will be Oceanus, who also pays Prometheus a visit. Then I will have to treat upon a scene between Io and Prometheus, which perhaps will be the most interesting part of my discourse on this Tragedy. Besides which I will, upon our next meeting, be able to proceed with one other of Æschylus's Tragedies. The reason I have not got far into his works upon this occasion is, because this being the beginning of a long series of Lectures, I have considered it necessary to be somewhat more prolific in my introductory remarks than will be necessary on future occasions. Until next we meet, allow me to thank you for your attention, and bid you farewell.

---

lines, she succeeded in saving her children Ceres, Vesta, and Juno. Juno was afterwards Queen of heaven, Vesta the goddess of fire, and Ceres, the goddess of harvests.

LECTURE II.

THE lecture I am about giving places me rather at a disadvantage at the commencement, for this reason, it being a continuation of that which I gave on a previous occasion. The principal part of my introductory remarks was made at the commencement, but I have reserved for this occasion a description of two of the characters, Io and Mercury, as well as the meaning of Strophe, Antistrophe, and Epode. I think an explanation of the three words last named is quite necessary, for few people (even those partially acquainted with classic works) know the meaning of them. Almost invariably the first question I have been ask'd by persons I have advised to read the Greek plays, and who have taken my advice, has been—what is the meaning of Stroph, Antis, and Epod, which I see printed in the margin of these plays; and, as it is more than probable I may have the pleasure at some future period of meeting in private some of my friends now present, I will save them the trouble of asking this question by explaining the meaning now, and I hope what is left for me to describe of "Prometheus Chained," may be deemed enough to interest you for this occasion. I could not get through the whole in one lecture in a manner to satisfy myself, therefore no course was left open to me but either

to divide it into two parts, or make it so long as to tire
your patience and my own lungs, or I must have slurred
it over, and perhaps left some of the most necessary parts
unexplained. Let me at the same time assure you that
although this has occurred in the first instance, it is not likely
to transpire again, or if it does, at all events not frequently.

My first lecture necessarily took up a great part of the time
allotted in introducing my subject fairly before the public;
it being the beginning of one hundred which I have undertaken to publish. This may, perhaps, seem a great many to
contemplate upon one subject; but when we take into consideration the period from which I commence, between five
and six hundred years before the birth of Christ, and
reflect not only upon the variety, but also upon the great
interest of the subject, one hundred lectures are of no great
extent. Why, there is one poet with whose works every one
present, I am sure, is more or less acquainted, upon which I
think I could write a thousand lectures. Ay! ten thousand, and then begin again, finding new matter for another
thousand or two, and experience fresh delight every time
I applied myself to the work. Yes, and you would do the
same, were you to take the trouble of thoroughly inves-
tigating him as I have. Need I mention the name? No!
I can see young ladies shaking their luxuriant tresses, and
old men their hoary locks, brushing up their spirits at the
mere anticipation of it. I mean William Shakspeare, of
glorious and immortal memory, peace to his manes, and
everlasting salvation to his mighty soul! Well! I must
not proceed quite so fast, I am now only at the Shakspeare
of the Grecian school, Æschylus. Respecting our own balmy
and dew'y bard, from whose ambrosial breath I will at some
future period extract for you such odoriferous fragrance as
shall remunerate you well for your attention; but that

time is not yet come, I must first get through with the ancients before I touch upon the poets of the more recent period.

Let me now explain to you as much as I can of Æschylus, then on to Sophocles and Euripides, with a few remarks upon some of the other Greek and Latin poets; not forgetting Aristophanes, 'Dionysius, Epicarmus, Lycophron, Plautus, and the African Terence. The chorus of the ancients was the most essential part of their Tragedies; having originated from religious ceremonies, it was venerated, and looked upon as an inseparable part of the representation. The principal duty these actors had to fulfil was to explain to the audience the meaning of the plays as they proceeded. Perhaps part of the work I have undertaken to perform myself, may be considered in the light of echo of chorus, poet, actors, and all. How much, then, it behoves me to be careful not to jar in my music, lest I put my audience out of tune, and lose the sound of their applause, notes and all, the latter, I assure you, not the least essential part of my interest in you. You see I am candid as well as explicit in my remarks. Shakspeare says "the labour we delight in physics pain." So it does, but a pill sometimes sticks in our throat and requires a pleasant draught to wash it down.

As regards choruses, they are rarely or ever introduced into modern representations ; it is now the fashion to put soliloquies in their place. These answer the same purpose, and (with all due deference to those who may think differently) I prefer the modern usage in this respect to the ancient ; doubtless, there was as much reason in one as there is in the other. In addition to the actors constituting the choruses, there was a leader whom they called the

Choriphæuse. This person's duty was to direct the rest and speak the dialogues and soliloquies himself. The ancients looked upon their theatre as a philosophic school. I may here remark that Euripides was designated the theatrical philosopher, for the reason that he was in the habit of delivering a kind of moral lecture to his audience during the performance of his tragedies. The songs and odes, so profusely introduced into the ancient plays, were sang or recited by the actors constituting the chorus; the usual number of individuals introduced into the choruses being twelve. But Sophocles deviated from this rule, his choruses were frequently composed of fifteen people; these stood or sat in rows, one part of their number in advance of the other, and as their turn came to speak, they passed from right to left. This was called Strophe. As they returned to their places, left to right, they were executing the movement denominated Antistrophe, and when they all stood still, this was designated Epode. I have now explained to you the meaning of these words, therefore, as you read any edition with them printed, you'll understand the movements of the actors constituting the chorus of the representation.

To such friends as were not present on the first occasion I made my appearance here, I will just remark to them that Prometheus is chained to the Scythian rock by Jove's order, for disobedience in having climbed the heavens by the assistance of Minerva, and stolen fire from the sun, which he handed to mortals on earth for their benefit. It seems strange that Jove should have been so vindictive towards poor Prometheus for this generous act, particularly as Minerva assisted him, she being Jove's favourite goddess in all his counsels, and was bred out of his own brain, for we are told that she came out of his head dressed in a full suit of armour and of mature age, besides which she was privileged in prolonging the life of mortals. This looks very much like an injudicious parent chastising one child partly for the acts of a more favoured pet.

I will now read to you a part of the tragedy. Prometheus being still chained to the rock, Oceanus visits him, and addresses him as follows:— .

" Oceanus.

" Far distant, thro' the vast expanse of air,
" To thee, Prometheus, on this swift-winged steed,·
" Whose neck unrein'd obeys my will, I come,
" In social sorrow sympathising with thee.
" To this the near affinity of blood
" Moves me ; and be assured, that tie apart,
" There is not who can tax my dear regard
" Deeper than thou : believe me, this is truth,
" Not the false glozings of a flatt'ring tongue.
" Instruct me then in what my pow'r may serve thee,
" For never shalt thou say thou hast a friend
" More firm, more constant than Oceanus.

" Prometheus.

" Ah me ! What draws thee hither ? art thou come
" Spectator of my toils ? How hast thou ventur'd
" To leave the ocean waves, from thee so call'd,
" Thy rock roof'd grottos arch'd by nature's hand,
" And land upon this iron-teeming earth ?
" Comest thou to visit and bewail my ills ?
" Behold this sight, behold this friend of Jove,
" Th' assertor of his empire, bending here
" Beneath a weight of woes by him inflicted.

" Oceanus.

" I see it all, and wish to counsil thee,
" Wise as thou art, to milder measures : learn
" To know thyself; new model thy behaviour,
" As the new monarch of the gods requires.
" What if thy harsh and pointed speech shou'd reach

" The ear of Jove, tho' on his distant throne
" High-seated, might they not inflame his rage
" T'inflict such tortures, that thy present pains
" Might seem a recreation and a sport?
" Cease then, unhappy sufferer, cease thy braves,
" And meditate the means of thy deliverance.
" To thee perchance this seems the cold advice
" Of doting age ; yet, trust me, woes like these
" Are earnings of the lofty-sounding tongue.
" But thy unbending spirit disdains to yield
" E'en to afflictions, to the present rather
" Ambitious to add more.   Yet shalt thou not,
" If my voice may be heard, lift up thy heel
" And kick against the pricks ; so rough, thou seest,
" So uncontroul'd the monarch of the skies.
" But now I go, and will exert my pow'r,
" If haply I may free thee from thy pains.
" Mean while be calm; forbear thy haughty tone :
" Has not thy copious wisdom taught thee this,
" That mischief still attends the petulant tongue?

" PROMETHEUS.

" I gratulate thy fortune, that on thee
" No blame hath lighted, tho' associate with me
" In all, and daring equally.   But now
" Forbear, of my condition take no care ;
" Thou wilt not move him ; nothing moves his rigor :
"Take heed, then, lest to go brings harm on thee.

" OCEANUS.

" Wiser for others than thyself I find
" Thy thoughts ; yet shalt thou not withhold my speed.
" And I have hopes, with pride I speak it, hopes
" T'obtain this grace, and free thee from thy sufferings.

" PROMETHEUS.

" For this thou hast my thanks ; thy courtesy
"With grateful memory ever shall be honour'd.
" But think not of it, the attempt were vain,
" Nor wou'd thy labour profit me ; cease then,

" And leave me to my fate : however wretched,
" I wish not to impart my woes to others.
" Thou art not inexperienced, nor hast need
" Of my instruction ; save thyself, how best
" Thy wisdom shall direct thee.   I will bea
" My present fate, till Jove's harsh wrath relents."

Oceanus tells Prometheus that he has left his grotto in the sea to visit him and sympathize with his sorrows ; he is moved to this, independently of the consanguinity existing between them.   He says, there is not one whom I regard more, I tell you this in all sincerity, not with any view of flattering you.   Tell me, is there anything in my power I can do to serve you, I am firmly and constantly your friend. Prometheus replies,—Have you come to view my toils, why have you left the ocean, look at me, behold this sight, 'tis the work of Jove, crushing me beneath this weight of woe. I see it all, says Oceanus, therefore I wish to counsel you and advise you to alter your behaviour towards the omnipotent monarch.   Take my advice, be more guarded in your speech, lest you offend him further and he inflict greater tortures upon you.   He may even make a sport of your sufferings, therefore rather meditate some means of escape from what you are now enduring, than continue setting him at defiance.   There is no use kicking against the pricks : the meaning of these words I take to be, 'tis useless striking your heels against the spikes, for they will only cause fresh wounds. Prometheus replies,—I congratulate you that Jove has not inflicted any punishment on you, although you have been as daring as I have been.   But forbear, for your own sake don't interfere, you'll not move him to pity.   Oceanus answers,—You can reason for my safety, but you do not follow out the same course for your own welfare.   I thank you for your courtesy, replies Prometheus, your kindness

will live in my memory, and I honour you; but leave me
to my fate, I don't desire you shall run any risk on my
account.   Then the chorus of water-nymphs addresses
Prometheus as follows —

" For thee I heave the heart-felt sigh,
" My bosom melting at thy woes ;
" For thee my tear-distilling eye
" In streams of tender sorrow flows :
" For Jove's imperious ruthless soul,
" That scorns the pow'r of mild controul,
" Chastens with horrid tort'ring pain
" Not known to gods, before his iron reign.
" E'en yet this ample region o'er
" Hoarse strains of sullen woe resound,
" Thy state, thy brother's state deplore,
" Age-honour'd glories ruin'd round.
" Thy woes, beneath the sacred shade
" Of Asia's pastur'd forests laid,
" The chaste inhabitant bewails
" Thy groans re-echoing thro' his plaintive vales.

" PROMETHEUS.

" It is not pride; deem nobler of me, virgins;
" It is not pride, that held me silent thus ;
" The thought of these harsh chains, that hang me here
" Cuts to my heart.   Yet who, like me, advanc'd
" To their high dignity our new rais'd gods ?
" But let me spare the tale, to you well known.
" The ills of man you've heard : I form'd his mind,
" And thro' the cloud of barb'rous ignorance
" Diffus'd the beams of knowledge. I will speak,
" Not taxing them with blame, but my own gifts
" Displaying, and benevolence to them.
" They saw indeed, they heard ; but what avail'd
" Or sight, or sense of hearing, all things rolling
" Like the unreal imagery of dreams,
" In wild confusion mix'd ? The lightsome wall

" Of finer masonry, the rafter'd roof
" They knew not ; but, like ants still buried, delv'd
" Deep in the earth, and scoop'd their sunless caves.
" Unmark'd the seasons chang'd, the biting winter,
" The flow'r perfumed spring, the ripening summer
" Fertile of fruits.   At random all their works,
" Till I instructed them to mark the stars,
" Their rising, and, an harder science yet,
" Their setting, the rich train of marshall'd numbers
" I taught them, and the meet array of letters.
" T'impress these precepts on their hearts I sent
" Memory, the active mother of all wisdom.
" I taught the patient steer to bear the yoke,
" In all his toils joint-labourer with man.
" By me the harness'd steed was train'd to whirl
" The rapid car, and grace the pride of wealth.
" The tall bark, lightly bounding o'er the waves,
" I taught its course, and wing'd its flying sail.
" To man I gave these arts ; with all my wisdom
" Yet want I now one art, that usefull art
" To free myself from these afflicting chains.

" Chorus.

" Unseemly are thy sufferings, sprung from error
" And impotence of mind.   And now inclos'd
" With all these ills, as some unskillful leach
" That sinks beneath his malady, thy soul
" Desponds, nor seek medicinal releaf.

" Prometheus.

" Hear my whole story, thou wilt wonder more,
" What usefull arts, what science I invented.
" This first and greatest : when the fell disease
" Prey'd on the human frame, relief was none,
" Nor healing drug, nor cool refreshing draught,
" Nor pain-assuaging unguent ; but they pin'd
" Without redress, and wasted, till I taught them
" To mix the balmy medicine, of pow'r

" To chase each pale disease, and soften pain.

" I taught the various modes of prophecy,

" What truth the dream portends, the omen what

" Of nice distinction, what the casual sight

" That meets us on the way ; the flight of birds,

" When to the right, when to the left they take

" Their airy course, their various ways of life,   .

" Their feuds, their foudnesses, their social flocks.

" I taught th' Haruspex* to inspect the entrails,

" Their smoothuess, and their colour to the gods

" Grateful, the gall, the liver streak'd with veins,

" The limbs involv'd in fat, and the long chine

" Plac'd on the blazing altar ; from the smoak

" And mounting flame to mark th' unerring omen.

" These arts I taught. And all the secret treasures

" Deep buried in the bowels of the earth,

" Brass, iron, silver, gold, their use to man,

" Let the vain tongue make what high vaunts it may,

" Are my inventions all ; and, in a word,

" Prometheus taught each useful art to man."

Prometheus's reply means you mistake me virgins, it is not pride in me that I have not replied to you sooner, it is my present woes that cut me to the very heart, and have kept me silent, for who like me, a God of high repute, could suffer such indignity and be in a mood to converse. It is necessary for me to relate to you the cause of all this : the ills of mankind are known to you, but I enlightened his mind, and brought him from a state of ignorance to knowledge. It is not man's fault, he is not to be blamed, 'twas I, from benevolent motives, taught him the art of masonry, and to build houses ; for until I did this he burrowed into the earth like the ant, and dug holes in the ground for his

---

* Haruspex means, to view. The word is taken from the Latin Specio, and applies to the Oracles of Greece, who pretended to prognosticate future events by inspecting the entrails of animals.

habitation. He knew no change of seasons, nor knew he the value of flowers, nor fruits, until I discovered to him their properties and nutritious qualities; everything was rude and unmeaning till I taught their uses. I instructed him in the science of astronomy, I taught him to read, I impressed upon him moral precepts, and I endowed him with wisdom. I taught him how to yoke the oxen, to till the land, and to train horses, also to build ships and how to use their sails; yet, for all this I am deficient in one art, that is, how to free myself from these afflicting chains. The nymphs say: Your sufferings are dreadful to behold, but they have come upon you through your own impetuosity, there's no doctor can cure you, nor is there any medicine that will relieve you. I know it all, says Prometheus; but hear me out, and you will wonder at the useful arts and sciences I have taught mankind. I have shown them the use of medicinal drugs, how to mix healing salves, and make cooling draughts: if I had not done all this to chase away from them pale disease, and to relieve their pains, they would have pined away in desolation. I have shown them how to foretel events, to anticipate the weather, which is indicated by the flight of birds, the causes of strife and love, the rules of social intercourse, the science of anatomy, and the uses of fire; besides all these advantages I have shown them how to delve the earth, and extract the treasures therefrom—iron, brass, silver, and gold—all this have I done; and I have taught them the uses of these materials. And he sums up all his bounties by saying: I it was who taught them all they know.

I have promised you I would describe to you the character of Io. I will do so sufficiently for you to comprehend the meaning of the poet's introducing her into this tragedy, which I conceive to have been with the

intention of teaching us the moral reflection, not to look
upon our troubles too seriously, for however great our afflictions, we are not singular in this respect.   But I think the
manner in which she is treated by the poet not a happy
one for the tragedy.   It occurs to me that the dramatic effect
would have been much better produced had she •merely
passed before the view of the audience, and her sufferings
been described by Oceanus to Prometheus as an example to
him not to dwell too much upon his tortures, as being
greater than others were liable to.   Then, as regards the
character of Io herself, I think she is contemplated by the
poet more in the light of a loose-minded woman than as a
creature of virtuous habits.   She says that nightly visions
appeared to her and told her she would be matched to a
husband of the noblest nature, but it does not appear that
she contemplated much of a marriage ceremony in the
matter.   She told her father by what she was beset; this, to
some extent, may be deemed a prudent caution, but it does
not alter the fact of her desires.   Her father, alarmed at her
prognostications, sent to Pytho and to Donono to ascertain
the meaning of her visions from the oracles.   Their interpretation was that she was beset by loose propensities, and they
ordered Inachus* to turn her out of his house; very harsh
treatment this, most certainly, but herein the moral exists,
that virgins should not only be pure in fact, but also in
thought.   She says :

> " Straight was my sense disorder'd, my fair form
> " Chang'd as you see."

She was transformed into a heifer.   I think the moral
here to be drawn is, that being loose in mind and turned
adrift, she becomes a mere animal,—

---

* Inachus was Io's father.

" Wild with my pain with frantic speed I hurried."

Here again is the moral upon the abandoned woman's character; once loose she goes headlong into sin and iniquity.
She says :—

" And tortur'd with the bryzes horrid sting."

Why may not this mean the sting of conscience? I
think the moral goes quite as far. Now Argus is introduced, who is typically represented as the hundred-eyed
monster, pursuing her from place to place, permitting her
no rest nor peaceful habitation. This completes the moral,
showing that the eyes of all the world are upon abandoned
women, and that they are entirely lost to society. I know
very well some people may put this down as a flight of fancy
on my part, nevertheless, I am quite prepared to prove that
here exists the moral; but supposing for argument's sake
this is a flight of fancy, I am quite satisfied leaving it so
interpreted; for at least it must be admitted, that I have
occupied your attention to a good end, by reciting to you a
moral theory rather than an absurd tale. Mine are lectures,
and if I can delineate a good precept as I proceed, I cannot,
I think, be guilty of any great error in propounding it to
you. You are not bound to take this from me as my *ipse
dixit*. You may receive it if you like merely as an idea.

I will now conclude this tragedy by reading to you
the scene between Prometheus and Mercury. First let me
tell you that Mr. Mercurius was a great thief, and, as Prometheus knew everything beforehand, as well as what had
passed, there cannot be a doubt but he was acquainted with
the character of Jove's messenger; and, I suppose, in some
measure to this, we may attribute Prometheus treating
Mercury so contumaciously as he does. You'll be shocked

to learn the depravity of the character I am introducing to you, and when I tell you that he commenced thieving the very day he was born, you may well wonder at his precociousness—mind you, I won't be certain if it was the actual day of his birth, or the day after, that he stole some oxen from Apollo, which belonged to Admetus, King of Pheræ. He also took Apollo's quiver and arrows. After this he robbed Neptune of his trident, Mars of his sword, Vulcan of the tools he worked with, Jupiter of his sceptre, and Venus of her girdle. I have recently received a communication from this goddess; here is her note. She displays a very neat hand indeed. With much regret she informs me that, through the pilfering propensity of Master Mercury, she cannot, for decency's sake, leave the house, or she would have been here to-night to attend my lecture. Only think of that, ladies, to know that the goddess of beauty contemplated paying us a visit here to-night, and had it not been for the tricks of that thieving rascal, Mercury, she might have been here now. Ah! methinks I see her there just entering at the door. Don't look gentlemen; first permit the goddess to pass into my private room and robe herself, and until she returns look around you, and see if you can't in the meantime admire some beauties of more modest mien.

You see this fellow, Mercury, was able to pursue his predatory practices with impunity, for he was possessed of the power of transforming himself into any shape, or of making himself entirely invisible. He had wings on his feet, and the very cup he sipped his nectar from had wings to it. So we need not wonder at his being a flighty character. He could go to any part of the universe he pleased (as Paddy says) in the twinkling of a bedpost. He had many other names besides Mercurius and Mercury. He was called Cyllenius, Acacesius, Arcas, Caduceator, Ageneus, Acacetos, Delius, Camillus, Tricephalos, and Triplex. He had several sweethearts, whose names were Cleobula, Antianava, Isia, Chione, Creusa, Libya, Polimela, Dryope, Penelope, and the young lady I was before talking to you about, Miss Venus. I wish he'd bring her girdle back, that she might honour us with her company here now. I thought of enumerating to you the names of his children, but they were so numerous that I fear I cannot spare the time, besides, I'm sure you'd not remember half of them. He was the patron god of a variety of beliefs. Statues were erected to him in all sorts of forms, and offerings were made to him of milk and honey, for the reason that his voice was so sweet, melodious, and persuasive, that he was considered the god of eloquence.

Now, I think I have sufficiently described this god to you, so I will read you the scene between him and Prometheus; but first I will relate to you the extraordinary manner in which Æschylus came by his death. This was rather fabulous, and very remarkable. It was as follows:—

When he was advancing into years, he went into Sicily, where he was told by an oracle (this tribe must have been as prolific as the gipsies of the present time) that he would be killed by the falling of a house. In order to avoid such a destiny, he determined to reside in an open field, where, having taken his seat, he was killed by a tortoise falling on to his head, which had been borne aloft by an eagle, and dropped during its flight. The statement, as we read it from the ancient books is, that the eagle took Æschylus's head for a stone, and dropped the tortoise purposely on to it to break its shell. I suppose poor Æschylus's head was bald, at all events his unfortunate sconce was cracked; although we have no information whether the tortoise came out of its shell or no.

" MERCURY.

" To thee grown old in craft, deep drench'd in gall,

" Disgustfull to the gods, too prodigal

" Of interdicted gifts to mortal man,

" Thief of the fire of heav'n, to thee my message.

" My father bids thee say what nuptials these

" Thy tongue thus vaunts as threat'ning his high pow'r ;

" And clearly say, couch'd in no riddling phrase,

" Each several circumstance ; propound not to me

" Ambiguous terms, Prometheus ; for thou seest

" Jove brooks not such, unfit to win his favours.

" PROMETHEUS.

" Thou doest thy message proudly, in high terms,

" Becoming well the servant of such lords.

" Your youthfull pow'r is new ; yet vainly deem ye

" Your high-raised tow'rs impregnable to pain :

" Have I not seen two sovereigns of the sky

" Sink from their glorious state ? And I shall see

" A third, this present lord, with sudden ruin

" Dishonourably fall.   What, seem I now

" To dread, to tremble at these new-rais'd gods ?

" That never shall their force extort from me.

" Hence then, the way thou camest return with speed :

" Thy vain inquiries get no other answer.

" MERCURY.

" Such insolence before, so fiery fierce,

" Drew on thy head this dreadful punishment.

" PROMETHEUS.

" My miseries, be assur'd, I would not change

" For thy gay servitude, but rather chuse

" To live a vassal to this dreary rock,

" Than Lacquey the proud heels of Jove.   These words,

" If insolent, your insolence extorts.

" MERCURY.

" I think thou art delighted with thy woes.

" PROMETHEUS.

" Delighted ! Might I see mine enemies
" Delighted thus ! And thee I hold among them.

" MERCURY.

" And why blame me for thy calamities ?

" PROMETHEUS.

" To tell thee in a word, I hate them all,
" These gods ; of them I deserv'd well, and they
" Ungrateful and unjust work me these ills.

" MERCURY.

" Thy malady, I find, is no small madness.

" PROMETHEUS.

" If to detest my enemies be madness,
" It is a malady I wish to have.

" MERCURY.

" Were it well with thee, who cou'd brook thy pride ?

" PROMETHEUS.

" Ah me !

" MERCURY.

" That sound of grief Jove doth not know.

" PROMETHEUS.

" Time, as its age advanceth, teaches all things.

" MERCURY.

" All its advances have not taught thee wisdom.

D

" PROMETHEUS,

" I should not else waste words on thee, a vassal.

" MERCURY.

" Naught wilt thou answer then to what Jove asks.

" PROMETHEUS.

" If due, I wou'd repay his courtesy.

" MERCURY.

' Why am I check'd, why rated as a boy ?

" PROMETHEUS.

" A boy thou art, more simple than a boy,
" If thou hast hopes to be inform'd by me.
" Not all his tortures, all his arts shall move me
" T'unlock my lips, till this curs'd chain be loos'd.
" No, let him hurl his flaming lightnings, wing
" His whitening snows, and with his thunders shake
" The rocking earth, they move not me to say
" What force shall wrest the sceptre from his hand.

" MERCURY.

" Weigh these things well, will these unloose thy chains?

" PROMETHEUS.

" Well have they long been weigh'd, and well consider'd.

" MERCURY.

" Subdue, vain fool, subdue thy insolence,
" And let thy miseries teach thee juster thoughts.

" PROMETHEUS.

" Thy counsils, like the waves that dash against
" The rock's firm base, disquiet but not move me.
" Conceive not of me that, thro' fear what Jove
" May in his rage inflict, my fix'd disdain
" Shall e'er relent, e'er suffer my firm mind

" To sink to womanish softness, to fall prostrate,
" To stretch my supplicating hands, intreating
" My hated foe to free me from these chains.
" Far be that shame, that abject weakness from me.

" MERCURY.

" I see thou art implacable, unsoften'd
" By all the mild entreaties I can urge ;
" But like a young steed rein'd, that proudly struggles,
" And champs his iron curb, thy haughty soul
" Abates not of its unavailing fierceness.
" But pride, disdaining to be rul'd by reason,
" Sinks weak and valueless. But mark me well,
" If not obedient to my words, a storm,
" A fiery and inevitable deluge
" Shall burst in threefold vengeance on thy head.
" First, his fierce thunder wing'd with lightnings flame
" Shall rend this rugged rock, and cover thee
" With hideous ruin : long time shalt thou lie
" Astonied in its rifted sides, till drag'd
" Again to light ; then shall the bird of Jove,
" The rav'ning eagle, lur'd with scent of blood,
" Mangle thy body, and each day returning,
" An uninvited guest, plunge his fell beak,
" And feast and riot on thy black'ning liver.
" Expect no pause, no respite, till some God
" Comes to relieve thy pains, willing to pass
" The dreary realms of ever-during night
" The dark descent of Tartarus profound.
" Weigh these things well ; this is no fiction drest
" In vaunting terms, but words of serious truth.
" The mouth of Jove knows not to utter falsehood,
" But what he speaks is fate. Be cautious then,
" Regard thyself ; let not o'erweening pride
" Despise the friendly voice of prudent counsil;

" CHORUS.

" Nothing amiss we deem his words, but fraught

" With reason, who but wills thee to relax

" Thy haughty spirit, and by prudent counsils

" Pursue thy peace : be then advis'd ; what shame

" For one so wise to persevere in error ?

" PROMETHEUS.

" All this I knew e'er he declar'd his message.

" That enemy from enemy should suffer

" Extreme indignity is nothing strange.

" Let him then work his horrible pleasure on me ;

" Wreath his black curling flames, tempest the air

" With vollied thunders and wild warring winds,

" Rend from its roots the firm earth's solid base,

" Heave from the roaring main its boisterous waves,

" And dash them to the stars ; me let him hurl,

" Caught in the fiery tempest, to the gloom

" Of deepest Tartarus ; not all his pow'r

" Can quench th' ethereal breath of life in me.

" MERCURY.

" Such ravings, such wild counsels might you hear,

" From moon-struck madness. What is this but madness ?

" Were he at ease, wou'd he abate his frenzy ?

" But you, whose gentle hearts with social sorrow

" Melt at his suff'rings, from this place remove,

" Remove with speed, lest the tempestuous roar

" Of his fierce thunder strike your souls with horror.

" CHORUS.

" To other themes, to other counsils turn

" Thy voice, where pleaded reason may prevail :

" This is ill urg'd and may not be admitted.

" Wou'dst thou sollicit me to deeds of baseness ?

" Whate'er betides, with him will I endure it.

" The vile betrayer I have learn'd to hate ;

" There is no fouler stain, my soul abhors it.

" Mercury.

" Remember you are warn'd ; if ill o'ertake you
" Accuse not fortune, lay not the blame on Jove,
" As by his hand sunk in calamities
" Unthought of, unforeseen : no, let the blame
" Light on yourselves ; your folly not unwarn'd,
" Not unawares, but 'gainst your better knowledge,
" Involv'd you in th' inextricable toils.

" Prometheus.

" He fables not ; I feel in very deed
" The firm earth rock ; the thunder's deep'ning roar
" Rolls with redoubled rage ; the bick'ring flames
" Flash thick ; the eddying sands are whirl'd on high
" In dreadfull opposition to wild winds
" Rend the vex'd air : the boist'rous billows rise
" Confounding sea and sky ; th' impetuous storm
" Rolls all its terrible fury on my head.
" See'st thou this, awful Themis ; and thou, Ether,
" Through whose pure azure floats the general stream
" Of liquid light, see you what wrongs I suffer.

Mercury says, to thee I speak, to thee of splenetic nature whose disposition is embittered against Jove; yea, to thee who have disobeyed my father's commands,* I am bid ask

---

* This alludes to Jupiter's love for Thetis, by whom the Fates had foretold he would soon have a son of greater power and perfection than himself. The decree was known only to Prometheus, he being gifted by the Fates with the divine power of foreseeing everything. The circumstance is frequently alluded by Æschylus in this tragedy. Thetis was one of the sea deities. Her parents were Nereus and Doris. She was the granddaughter of Oceanus and Tethys (not the daughter of these two deities, as stated by Dr. Potter). It would seem by the account of her that both Jupiter and Neptune were rivals for her love ; but although Prometheus resolved not to inform Jupiter of what the Fates had decreed, and although we have no information by Æschylus other than that Prometheus only was cognisant of the decree of the Fates, yet the sequel of the history of Thetis shows that both Jupiter and Neptune became acquainted

you what nuptials you allude to that shall shake his power. Tell me clearly every circumstance, and not ambiguously, for Jove will not put up with it, if you do so, this is not the way to gain his favour. Prometheus answers: Well done, you assume a proud position, young man, lofty language this, but its just like you, a vassal of a proud lord, you are young in power, yet your vanity carries you to a towering height. You'll tumble yet and find your pain when you fall, like your master. I have seen two sovereigns of the sky sink from their high station, and I shall yet see the third. This Jove whom you are serving I shall see fall suddenly, and dishonourably. What occasion have I to fear, not likely, I'll not humble myself to *this* new raised god, he shall never force me to tell him anything. Hence then, go back quickly from whence you came. You need not ask me any more questions, you'll get no clearer answer from me. Mercury replies: It was just such insolence as this on your part that drew your present punishment upon you. Never mind that, says Prometheus, my miseries are nothing to you, I'd rather endure these, than be as you are, a

---

with the fact, and they both discontinued their addresses to her in conse- quence. She was afterwards married to Peleus, son of Æacus. At their wedding, which took place on Mount Pelion, a great festival was pro- claimed, at which all the deities attended, excepting only the goddess of discord. She was called Discordia, queen of contention. At this gathering of the deities she threw amongst them a golden apple, designing it to be given to her who was fairest amongst the goddesses (you may be sure there was contention enough for this prize, and much scramble). Thetis had several children, and in experimentalising upon them to ascer- tain if they were immortal or no, she entirely consumed them by the fire she used in the operations. The great Achilles was one of her children ; he was saved by his father, Peleus, from sharing the same fate by Thetis's hands, and he was rendered invulnerable by his mother ; leaving only one part of his body unprotected, that being the heel she held in her hand whilst performing the operation of plunging him in the River Styx.

lackey at Jove's heels. If you consider my remarks insolent,
it has been your rudeness to me that has induced them.
Quoth Mercury: Upon my word one would think by the
tone of your remarks that you are delighted with your
present situation. O yes, certainly, of course I am, replies
Prometheus. I'd like to see my enemies accommodated in
like manner, yourself amongst them. I hate you all. I
deserved your gratitude, but I endure this injustice instead.
Ha! I see, says Mercury, you are scarcely aware what you
are saying—you are mad. Yes, indeed, I am mad, says
Prometheus, if it be madness to hate mine enemies. Ah
me! On Prometheus's making this sorrowful exclamation,
Ah me! Mercury says, that sound of grief Jove doth not
know of. There is much more meant in Mercury's remark
than at first appears. The fair inference to be drawn from
the poet's meaning is, ha! for all you show so much bravado,
you cannot help giving utterance to sorrowful tones. Jove
is not aware that you are afflicted to this extent, or I am of
opinion he would rebate some of his rigour. Prometheus
(still implacable), Ah! well, he'll know of it by-and-bye;
time discovers everything. Yes, but time does not seem to
make you wise—what is best to do for your own welfare.
You can rate me as a boy, and you will not give me an
answer to Jove's message, says Mercury. If he were worthy
of a reply from me, says Prometheus, I'd send him a courteous one. But why do I waste words on you—a servant, a
mere boy. Let me tell you, don't try to get any information from me; for not all the tortures that Jove can inflict
shall induce me to give utterance to what I know, until he
first unbinds me from this rock. He may hurl his lightnings, snow, and thunder, at me, and rock the earth to atoms,
yet he shall not force me to tell him what shall cause the
sceptre to be wrested from his hand. You had better think

again, says Mercury, will this defiance loose your chains?
Subdue your insolence; be not so fool-hardy.   One would
think your miseries would teach you more consistent conduct.
I have reflected, retorts Prometheus, and weighed my actions
well; and I know I can't gain much from your counsels.
Your talk may fidget me, but it won't induce me to alter
my determination.   Don't imagine that I am at all afraid
of Jove, or the inflictions he may perpetrate on me.   I disdain them all.   I am not a weak woman, to entreat and
supplicate for mercy from mine enemy.   I see, says
Mercury, I cannot move you—you are implacable.   My
gentle persuasion is useless.   You are haughty and un-
yielding, proud and ungovernable; but take heed, if you
do not obey Jove's injunction, you'll find such a storm come
upon you, that you'll be deluged in fire, thunder, and lightning, and the very rock you are chained to shall crumble
and bury you beneath its ruins.   Your body shall be
rolled about with its debris until in course of time it comes
again to the light, when the ravenous eagles shall feast on
your mangled carcase.   This shall be your fate,   unless
some one offers himself to be sent to the dark descent of
Tartarus, to reprieve you.   This is no fiction on my part;
'tis a truth.   Jove has decreed it, and you know he utters
no falsehoods.   Now the nymphs interpose: they say they
think Mercury's remarks are reasonable, he only wishes you
to be more humble, be advised.   What a pity it is, you,
who are so wise, should still be so obstinate.   You are very
good, says Prometheus to the nymphs, but I knew all he
has told me before he uttered a word.   'Tis nothing more
than the common order of things ; one enemy in the power
of another must, perforce, suffer.   I am prepared for it,
" Let him do his spite," for all this he shall not move me, do
what he will he has not the power to kill me.   Why, the

fellow's mad, says Mercury; probably, were his mind at ease, he'd not be so furious. But you nymphs, who have gentle hearts, associating yourselves with his sorrows, take warning, remove speedily from this place, lest you be enveloped within the sphere of his afflictions. The nymphs spurn Mercury's caution, and declare they will not be so base as to desert him, for they hate his foul betrayer. Upon which, Mercury very consistently says, remember, I have warned you, don't complain afterwards against fate. In conclusion, Prometheus says he feels the earth rocking, 'tis true he utters no fables, already I feel my pangs doubled. The roaring thunder shakes the very base of this rock. The lightning rends it asunder, and its fragments, with the sands from the sea-shore, are whirl'd aloft into a terrific hurricane. The sea is so disturbed that 'tis impossible to discern where the water's margin commences, or the sky terminates. All this is done to afflict me. See you this, justice and freedom, what wrongs I suffer?

Here terminates my Second Lecture. I thank you for your attention.

LECTURE III.

THERE is an old saying, and often a true one, that there is but one step from the sublime to the ridiculous: so is it with Æschylus, from his "Prometheus Chained" to his "Supplicants." To call this latter production a tragedy is simply ridiculous; I will, therefore, merely consider it in the light of a pamphlet, and treat it accordingly. The word "Supplicants" has been perverted by Buckley into "Suppliants." "Suppliant" is a contraction taken from the Latin (*supplico*), whilst "Supplicants" is a full, euphonious word, with a substantial Latin foundation (*supplicans*). I therefore think that Buckley has made a great mistake in substituting the contraction for the full word. Euripides has also produced a tragedy called the "Supplicants;" but his work is of very different material to this I am now upon. The subject is different, the plot is different, and the play is altogether widely different in every respect. The one has much merit in it as a tragedy; whilst the other is, as Buckley very properly designates it, "a mass of hopeless absurdity." With this view of its merits I do not deem it prudent to waste our time in dilating upon it, further than to relate to you the tale upon which it is based, and to point out to you where our author has differed from the original.

Of course, you clearly understand I am not condemning
Æschylus because he has made this one mistake, for we
must not forget the words of Cowell: "That which a man
saith well is not to be rejected because he hath some errors.
No man, no book, is void of imperfections." This great
mistake of Æschylus's puts me in mind of a tapeworm—a
number of joints upon insecure ligaments, and an end
without a finish. The story is as follows :—

Ægyptus and Danaus were sons of Belus. At their
father's death they agreed to reign conjointly on the throne
of Egypt—they did so; but ultimately disagreed and parted.
Ægyptus had fifty sons, and Danaus had fifty daughters.
Danaus with his daughters left Egypt, and went to Argos,
where he was generously received by Gelanor, the king, who,
finding himself not popular with his subjects, abdicated his
throne in favour of Danaus (Æschylus has substituted
Pelasgus for Gelanor. The mythology is, that when Danaus
settled in Argos he invited his fifty nephews to his court
to visit him. They arrived at Argos, were affianced to the
fifty princesses, and most probably everything would have
gone on comfortably enough had not the young gentlemen
been so anxious about the matter. Their pertinacity excited
Danaus's suspicion, and he consulted the oracle upon the
subject. As these people were fatalists, their prophets'
prognostications were taken as incontrovertible facts. They
told Danaus that he would be murdered by one of his sons-in-
law. This, of course, put the old gentleman upon his guard,
and (naturally enough) he tried to subvert the dreadful
decree. He, first of all, raised an objection to the nuptials
taking place, on account (as he said) of the near relationship
existing between the young people; but Ægyptus pressed the
matter with such earnestness that Danaus yielded, but he
did not do so without an ulterior intention in his mind; and

immediately on the marriage of his daughters, he called them to him, and, giving them each a sharp-pointed sword, he told them to murder their husbands. You must understand that daughters in those days were daughters, and sons were sons. The first duty they had to perform, was to be dutiful to their parents, particularly to their papas. They knew what the consequences would be were they not to obey the injunctions imposed upon them, at all events, up to a certain age; consequently, it became, as 'twere, a part of their belief. It was perhaps thought religiously in these cases, that the parent was responsible for the children's actions ; so the young ladies all assented to Danaus's proposal.

Pardon me, if you please, I am constrained here to break off, just to relate to you the state of agitation I fell into when I was writing this part of my lecture. Goodness gracious! you cannot imagine how I shuddered at the idea of fifty lovely-looking Princesses steeling their hearts so as to rub up brass enough, by the light of the silver moon, to rob their precious jewels of the remainder of their golden days. 'Tis quite clear Danaus put them upon their metal, and they as readily wrought the deed to a deep and everlasting die. These were the iron-hearted daughters of Danaus. King of Argos. They did their work in one " fell swoop. The lights burned blue, my knees trembled, and my hair stood on end like " quills upon the fretful porcupine." I felt a chill creeping all over me as the ghastly spectres of the " blood boltered" Princes flitted before my " fear surprised eyes;" they minded me of Banquo's progeny, and I expected every minute to see their father rise from the earth (as he does at the Theatres) " and push" me " from my stool." The sight " scar'd my very eye balls ;" and as their debilitated trunks toppled over one after another, methought I saw the young ladies carefully pack up the bearded excrescences they had shorn from them, and quite unconcernedly march off to the tune of "Trip trop tro"—"Here we go"—"All of a row." Would you believe it that some of these girls, with the greatest *sang-froid* imaginable, carried the heads of their husbands by the hair, some by the beard, exposing the horrid visages of their victims as they passed by my visual organs. This was a most horrid sight, and as the coral drops of blood like beads fell to the earth, they became coagulated, and made the very grass crisp over which the heads had been borne. The ladies arrived at their papa's house just in time for breakfast, and having divested themselves of their superabundant incum-brances, they proceeded to relate to Danaus how very amusingly they had passed the commencement of their honeymoon. But what is this? 47, 48, 49, who is absent? 'Tis Miss Hypermnestra and Master Lynceus. Ha! escaped. "Then comes my fit again." The fact is, these two were the juniors of the number, and Hypermnestra being rather nervous, put off the sword business for the morning; but when the dawn approached, her resolution had vanished with the shades of night; in fact, she found Lynceus a far more agreeable companion with his vital spark extant, than his vitality extinct. This dereliction of duty could not of course be allowed to pass, so little Hyper was had before her papa, and would have been condemned to death, only that the people took her part, and Danaus in consequence was afraid to put his threat into execution. It has been suggested to me that had some of the other young ladies acted as Hyper-mnestra did, they might have come to a similar conclusion to what she determined upon. But stop a bit; I forgot to tell you the sequel of the fantastic illusion I suffer'd under. You must please to understand that when the ghosts of these young gentlemen appeared before me, there were only forty-

nine of them with their heads off; the fiftieth seemed a
full-blown Patlander chanting the following lines :—

> Och, murther and thieves !
> This tale it so grieves
> My heart, and much it doth tase me,
> I'll niver believe—
> So say what you plase—
> No, niver believe it to plase ye !
>> Tol de rol lol de rol de ri idderdy,
>> Tol de rol idderty, tol de rol lay !

Danaus now took it into his head to persecute his
daughter and son-in-law, which he did in every way he
possibly could ;. but, ultimately, they were reconciled, and
Danaus named them to succeed him on his throne. It would
also appear that one of the young ladies killed Ægyptus,
their uncle, but for all this they all received absolution by
Jupiter's order, and by the sanction of Mercury and
Minerva, the heads of the forty-nine Princes were buried at
Argos, but their bodies were left at Lerna, where the
murders had taken place. This is the tale as it originally
stood, but in the play as related by Æschylus, old Danaus
goes to Argos with his daughters and seeks protection
for them at the altars. Pelasgus then affords them an
asylum at his palace, and the Argive people fight Ægyptus
and his army, they having follow'd the damsels and their
paternal papa, and so the play ends anyhow and no-
how. There's a great deal of boasting in this play about
the high connections of the parties, particularly as regards
Danaus and his family. They boast descent from Io (the
Cow), I will, therefore, explain to you the lineage : Io's first
calf was Epaphus, Epaphus begat Lybia, Lybia begat
Belus. Belus was father to Danaus, and the Danaides,
these hopeful young ladies were Danaus's daughters.

My plan at first was to go through the whole of Æschylus's works before beginning either Euripides or Sophocles;
but finding a subject that has been written upon by them all
three, I think I cannot do better than arrange them consecutively.   In no instance throughout the whole collection
of these Grecian tragedies does a more convenient opportunity occur for carrying on one story treated upon by three
different authors, than in this instance which I am about
adopting.   I have gone through " Prometheus Chained," I
have given you an outline of the tale upon which Æschylus's
production called the " Suppliants " is based, and I have
mentioned to you that Euripides has written a tragedy bearing
the same title, but of quite a different character in every
respect—plot, foundation, and execution, all are different.   I
have now done with the "Suppliants" of Æschylus ; but the
"Suppliants" of Euripides will be taken after I have treated
upon—first, Sophocles's "Œdipus, King of Thebes ;" second,
" Œdipus at Colonus," by same author; third, Euripides's
" Phœnician Virgins ;" fourth, Æschylus's " Seven Chiefs
against Thebes ;" fifth, "Antigone," by Sophocles; and sixth,
the " Suppliants," by Euripides.   In this order they will be
taken.   The original cause of all the misfortunes that are
represented in these six tragedies was born under the direst
calamity that could possibly befall humanity.   Polynices
and Eteocles were the sons of their own brother.   For
you to understand this clearly, it is necessary to tell you
that their mother was Jocasta; she was first married to
Laius, King of Thebes, but for a long time they occupied
separate apartments, for the following reason : Laius was
told (by an oracle, of course,) that he would be assassinated
by his own son, upon which he very naturally thought that,
if the fates prognosticated such a mishap should befall him,
he would not, at all events, contribute towards its consum-

mation himself, he said, I will not have any sons, and he formed the resolution I before named to you. But it so occurred that having been to a feast, and being one of those jolly dogs, devotees of the God Bacchus, he became rather comfortable; he might have been only a bit muzzy, or slightly inebriated; or perhaps he was tipsy; or he might have been downright intoxicated, in common parlance, dead drunk. I cannot tell you for certain which it was, because I had not the pleasure of being at the jollification myself. At all events, it is quite clear Laius was in that state which, if any of us were now in, he would lay him down to rest, and act most wisely by so doing. It would seem that Laius adopted this course, but we have no specific information whether Jocasta administered to her husband's comforts or no; yet it is quite certain that Laius, being in a state of happy obliviousness, forgot his former resolution and the oracle's decree, for just three months less than a year from this very period he found himself the father of a bouncing boy. The infant was no sooner born than it was resolved upon to have recourse to a deed too cruel to name without shuddering. The little innocent prince was handed to a servant, with instructions to destroy its life; but whether it was from the fact of the creature being a prince, or from a feeling of genuine pity, the result must speak for itself; the servant did not carry out the orders given him. This compassionate individual merely bored a hole in the child's heels, inserted a sort of twig through them, and hung him up to the boughs of a tree to take his chance on Mount Cithæron. A shepherd found him, and took him to his master, Pollybus, King of Corinth, at whose court the child was educated, and named Œdipus; this name was given him on account of his feet being swollen. We need not wonder at his having swollen feet, considering the humane course that had been resorted to—viz., hanging him up by his heels. The reason so much care was taken of the infant by Pollybus, is to be attributed to the fact that his wife, Periboea, had no children, and she having taken a fancy to Œdipus, the King permitted her to adopt him. In course of time young Œdipus grew to be a young man, but unfortunately, as he grew to manhood, his misfortunes kept pace with his years, and not only grew with him, but descended to his offspring. Amongst these was Polynices, the cause of the war which I will relate to you. Polynices and his family were descendants of Venus on the father's side, and Juno having made up her mind to vent her spleen on all the race of the Goddess of Beauty, they came in for a share of her notice.

Now to return to Œdipus. In due course of events he grew to manhood; he was the idol of the kind lady who had adopted him; he was a very good-looking young fellow, and he was much regarded by his companions, not, however, without creating a little jealousy amongst some of them. It now came to pass that certain insinuations were bruited about respecting the legitimacy of his birth, which, of course, wounded his pride, and induced him to resolve upon going to Delphi, to consult the oracle. He did so, and was told not to return home, for if he did he would be the cause of his father's death, and be married to his own mother. Such an augury, of course, alarmed him, and he made up his mind not to go back to Corinth. Therefore, taking a contrary direction, he met a chariot in the narrow part of the road; the chariot was occupied by Laius, a herald, three attendants, and an outrider. They, in an authoritative tone, commanded Œdipus to make way, which induced the young man's hot blood to rebel, and they came to blows, the result being that Œdipus slew them all excepting one attendant, who made his escape. Of course Œdipus was ignorant who the persons were whom he had slain, nor did Laius know Œdipus was his son. Here was one part of the prediction fulfilled.

Now, Laius being dead, and Jocasta a blooming widow in the prime of life, Creon, her brother (who ascended the throne) gave out that whoever would destroy the Sphinx should have the crown of Thebes, and the hand of Jocasta into the bargain. The Sphinx was a monster sent by Juno into Thebes, to destroy the people and lay the country waste. To kill this brute it was necessary to answer the following enigma :—" What animal in the morning walks upon four feet, at noon upon two, and in the evening upon three ?" Œdipus explained that it meant Man : since in the morning of life, he crawls upon his hands and feet ; in manhood he walks erect upon two feet ; and in old age he moves upon three, for he is compelled to have a staff to help him on his way. This having solved the enigma correctly, the Sphinx, enraged at its defeat, dashed its own brains out against a rock, and Œdipus succeeded to the throne of Thebes, and the hand of Jocasta. Jocasta and Œdipus had four children, Polynices, Eteocles, Antigone and Ismene.

Now, having gone through this part of the history of Laius and Œdipus, down to the next generation, I will take up my narrative with Polynices and Eteocles. These two brothers, when the unfortunate circumstances connected with their father's life were discovered, drove him from Thebes, and ascended the throne upon the following arrangement :—They agreed to reign one year, alternately. Eteocles (although the junior) took first turn, and when his time expired he refused to resign, consequently, Polynices, fearing violence as well as injustice, left Thebes and went to

Argos. Here he was well received by Adrastus, the King, and he married Argia, Adrastus's daughter. Here they raised a large army, and Polynices marched at the head of the troops against Thebes. He selected seven of his most famous generals, and apportioning his troops into as many divisions, he arranged that all should attack the seven gates simultaneously. This was done; but being met by Eteocles, and the Thebans, they were defeated; six of the seven chiefs were killed, and the two brothers, Eteocles and Polynices, meeting in single combat, slew each other.

The two brothers now being dead, Creon again ascended the throne of Thebes, and to avenge the invasion that had taken place, he issued a decree prohibiting the Argives removing their slain, amongst which were the bodies of Polynices, and some of the chiefs. Creon declared they should lie exposed to birds of prey, and should not receive the sacred rights of sepulture; he also ordered that whosoever transgressed this edict should be buried alive. Antigone, sister to Polynices, setting the tyrant at defiance, sought Polynices' body and buried it. In consequence of this praiseworthy act, she was adjudged to undergo the punishment decreed by Creon; but she nobly defeated his cruelty by destroying herself. Hæman, Creon's son, who was devotedly attached to Antigone, sued in vain for her pardon, and in consequence sacrificed himself on her grave in despair. This is one statement; another is that she was immured in a cave, and that it was here she destroyed herself. Hæman here also killed himself in despair, and threw himself upon her body. I think it is not at all improbable that it was from this statement that Shakespeare took his idea of the tomb scene in " Romeo and Juliet." This, of course, is merely a conjecture on my part. It is rather difficult to reconcile this statement of Antigone's death, when we read of her being afterwards with Œdipus, in his banishment, up to the time of his death; but I can only give you such information as history affords me, it is for you to decide which statement you prefer. Ultimately Creon was killed in a battle, undertaken by Theseus, King of Athens. Theseus invaded Thebes through the solicitations of Adrastus, King of Argos, the mothers of the seven chiefs and his own mother, Æthra, all imploring him to avenge the outrage upon humanity which Creon had perpetrated. It is from these seven dames, the mothers of the chiefs, supplicating Theseus, that the title of Euripides' Tragedy of the "Supplicants" is taken.

We are told that the tragedy of "Œdipus, King of Thebes," by Sophocles, was esteemed by the Athenians as the most perfect composition that ever graced their stage. I am myself disposed to coincide as far as I know with this opinion. If acted now-a-days, it certainly would be most appreciated by an English audience, it being what is termed a good acting play, containing many bold strokes of dramatic excellence, affording fine variety for acting if put well upon the stage. Some have attributed passion, violence, and pride, to Œdipus: I think suspicion and meanness may be added to these vices. His behaviour to Creon, in suspecting him of conspiring with Tiresias, fully justifies me in putting this construction upon the character, and Creon's retaliation is entirely consistent. It is true that Œdipus is impelled to his misfortunes by the decrees of Fate, for in those days matters were carried to extremes in this respect. We may well say so in this instance, as Œdipus's destiny was prognosticated before his birth by Apollo, the great sky-high magician.

The scene opens in the temple of Jupiter, where the priests and people of the city have congregated, supplicating

the god to allay the plague that is raging in the country.
Œdipus enters, and says to his sons, who are present—

> " Why have you here your seats,
> Holding these suppliant boughs ?"

" I have not sent a menial messenger to discover you, but
I have sought you myself. Tell me what reverend priest
art thou, whom my sons are attending—of what rank are
you? speak ! Tell me what afflictions are you seeking to
alleviate ('tis strange the king should ask this question,
whilst around him were blights, pestilence, and plague)—tell
me what fresh misfortunes are you seeking the gods to redress ? Let me know and I'll assist you all in my power."
The Priest says : " Great king, you see what we are; here,
before thy altars, are children of unripe years, and aged
people ; also we, the priests of Jupiter. Some here amongst
us are sons of the nobility, true Theban blood. The rest of the
people are at prayers round the Forum, congregated there also
with suppliant boughs in their hands, and at the other
temples there are more people supplicating like ourselves.
Do you not see that the state is in a storm, unsettled, and
oppressed, because she is not able to discover the stain of
blood she is afflicted with (this alludes to the murder of
Laius). Her herds perish, the crops are scorched and
burnt up; our infants die in their birth, and the whole
country is devastated, and becoming desolate with pestilence and ruin. Pluto is being enriched, our deaths
are so numerous. We come to your altars because we consider you are inspired to do good. You have already freed
us from the fierce ravages of the monstrous Sphinx, and
we hope to see you restore us to life and healthfulness.
Before thee, O King, we prostrate ourselves, imploring thy

aid. O thou best of men, go see the affliction in the city, and guide us with thy wisdom. Your country hails you as her preserver. With this in our memory let us not see a sad reverse, and our country sink into ruin. Restore the state once more, for which our people will glorify your reign. To rule thus is better than by protection of ships of war, or armed batteries."

It must be taken into consideration to account for this language, which is in reality a worship, that Œdipus having killed the Sphinx, he was looked upon as a miracle, and almost deified; in fact, some accounts of him state that he was taken up to heaven and made a god of; but he has also been represented as being in hell; so you see there's a slight difference of opinion respecting his spiritual disposition. We are told that the earth opened, and that he disappeared at the very spot he pointed out himself he would die upon. This I will explain to you more fully at the end of this tragedy. It is right I should name to you, that, although the three poets, Æschylus, Euripides, and Sophocles, treat the children of Œdipus as being by Jocasta, some of the ancient statements go to show that Jocasta destroyed herself immediately after she found out her unfortunate position with her husband, and that this occurred much sooner than is shown by either of our poets. In fact all their writing tends to induce a probability to this effect, for, in all the tragedies written upon the subject, we see that there is a considerable blank, or dearth of matter relative to the period of Œdipus's marriage with Jocasta, and the manhood or maturity of the children. The statement I allude to is, that Œdipus married Euriganea, a daughter of Periphas, soon after Jocasta's death, and that the children were all by his second wife. I shall have to allude to this subject again by-and-bye, because Euripides

introduces them into his tragedy of " The Phœnician Virgins,"
after Jocasta is dead, and when Œdipus is at Colonus in
banishment. According to Sophocles, the encampment before
Thebes must have lasted longer ere the attack was made
than is stated by either Euripides or Æschylus, for
Sophocles tells us, that Polynices journeys to Colonus, to
have an interview with his father, whilst the encampment is
before the Theban walls. The others represent him as having
charge of one of the divisions of the army, and he is recognised there at his post by Antigone, from the tower by one
poet, and by the other, through his agent, the soldier.

Œdipus says :

> " O my lamented sons, for ills well known
> " To me you seek redress ; I know that grief
> " Hangs heavy on you all, but most on me :
> " His private sufferings each bewails ; but I
> " Mourn for the city, for myself, and you.
> " I want no voice to rouse me ; many tears
> " These eyes have pour'd, with many anxious thoughts
> " My breast has labour'd, tracing various ways
> " For your relief. That, which alone could give
> " Hope of success, I follow'd ; I have sent
> " Creon, whose veins are rich with royal blood,
> " Son of Menœceus, to the Pythian shrine
> " Of Phœbus, to inquire what I must do
> " To save the city. As I number back
> " The days since past, I marvel ; for his stay
> " Exceeds just expectation. When he comes,
> " If I perform not what the god directs,
> " May I be deem'd the vilest of mankind."

" My good people, I lament with you, I feel this grief
most ; it hangs heavier on me than on any one else. Each
man has his share of suffering, but I mourn for you all.
'Tis not necessary to remind me, I have shed many tears, felt

the greatest anxiety, and I have been constantly thinking
how to relieve you. The only chance left I have adopted.
I have sent Creon to the shrine of Phœbus, to inquire from
the oracle there what I am to do to save the city. I am
wondering at his delay; but when I know what the gods
direct, if I do not perform the office, deem me unworthy.
Ah! here approaches Creon; his head is wreathed in laurel,
denoting cheerful success. What answer bring'st thou,
Creon? Good news say'st thou! say all will be well, and
end happily." Creon says, All may be well if we direct our
course properly. Do you wish me to speak publicly, or in
private with you? You say, here, publicly! Then Phœbus's
commands are "to drive hence the pollution of the realm,
that which is now nourished in the bosom of the land;"
we are not to "cherish an incurable ill." This must be
done by exile or death, for now "their blood desolates this
suffering land."

The poet shows good judgment in sending Creon to the
shrine of Phœbus, for Apollo knew what was to occur previous to Œdipus's birth. Œdipus asks Creon to whom does
the injunction point; to which Creon replies: Once, ere you
were king, Laius reigned in Thebes. He was murdered, and
we are commanded to hunt up the assassins (either Creon
must have misunderstood the oracle, or the oracle did not
know if Laius was attacked by one or more people; the
impression was that he was attacked by a band of
ruffians; probably this belief being on Creon's mind, he
did not distinctly understand if the oracle told him murderer or murderers). If they are pursued they'll be discovered, but if we neglect our duty, they'll escape. Laius
was on his way to consult the oracle, but he never
returned home. He and his attendants were all killed
but one, and he flew away in fear; they were oppressed by

a numerous band (the fellow who escaped must have been the early spirit of Falstaff, for he magnified one into a numerous band); there have been people suspected, but no proof has ever arisen. About same period we were troubled here with the Sphinx, which took our attention, consequently we neglected to seek the murderers of Laius. Taking into consideration that Œdipus conquered the Sphinx immediately after he had slain Laius, their search after Laius's assassin could not have been very rigorous. Œdipus says :

    " But I will bring them into light again
    " From their first cause. Of Phœbus for the dead
    " This zeal is worthy, worthy too of thee ;
    " And we confederate in the same just cause
    " You shall behold ; this country and the god
    " I will avenge. Not for some distant friend, *
    " But for myself, this execrable guilt
    " Be it my care to crush : for the same hand,
    " That murder'd him, may soon be raised to plunge
    " With the same rage the falchion in my breast ;
    " Therefore avenging him I guard myself.
    " But rise, my children, from your lowly seats
    " With speed, and bear these suppliant branches hence.
    " Hither th' assembled sons of Thebes convene :
    " My pow'r shall be exerted ; and once more
    " Will we, confiding in the favouring god,
    " Together prosper, or together fall."

---

* Dr. Potter makes a long note on this sentence, and he concludes by remarking that it is obscure. I do not think so, the meaning being I will not act indifferently in the matter, as if for a person I have no interest in, but I will proceed as if the cause were mine own, for some near relative : it cannot mean for himself, for, if he were murdered, he, of course, could not act at all in the matter ; the obscurity (what little there is) exists in the sentence " But for myself :" that which Dr. Potter quotes, " some distant friend," is clear enough.

I will bring the matter to light. Our showing zeal in this will be creditable to us both; so assist me, and you shall see I will avenge the god and Laius. It will not be working for a stranger, but for myself; for the same hand that destroyed Laius may plunge the dagger into my breast; therefore, by punishing the perpetrator of the dark deed, I protect myself. The last line of this speech—

" Together prosper, or together fall"

is what we seldom meet with in the Greek plays. It is what people of the theatrical profession call a climax, giving an actor (if he have the ability to use it properly) an opportunity of leaving the stage with eclat —

" Together prosper, or together fall."

Some of the lines sang by the chorus are very poetical, and well worth your attention. I will read a few of them to you. I cannot sing them, because I have not got their score to know what music they were set to :—

" Chorus.

" Thou oracle of Jove, what fate
" From Pytho's golden shrine
" Brings to th' illustrious Theban state
" Thy sweet-breathed voice divine ?
" My trembling heart what terror rends,
" While dread suspense on thee attends.
" O Delian Pæan, healing pow'r !
" Daughter of golden hope, to me,
" Blest voice, What now dost thou decree,
" Or in time's future hour ?

" Daughter of heav'n's almighty lord,
" Immortal Pallas, hear !
" And thou, Diana, queen ador'd,
" Whose tutelary care

" Protects these walls, this favour'd state,
" Amidst the forum 'round whose seat
    " Sublime encircling pillars stand !
    " God of the distant-wounding bow,
    " Apollo, hear ; avert our woe,
      " And save the sick'ning land !

    " This realm when former ills opprest
      " If your propitious pow'r
    " In mercy crush'd the baleful pest
      " Outrageous to devour ;
" In mercy now extend your care,
" For all is misery and despair,
    " And vain the counsils of the wise.
    " No fruit, no grain to ripeness grows ;
    " The matron feels untimely throes,
      " The birth abortive dies.

    " The shades, as birds of rapid flight,
      " In quick succession go,
    " Quick as the flames that flash through night,
      " To Pluto's realms below.
" Th' unpeopled town beholds the dead
" Wide o'er her putrid pavement spread,
    " Nor graced with tear or obsequy.
    " The altars round a mournful band,
    " The wives, the hoary matrons, stand,
      " And heave the suppliant sigh.

    " With deep sighs mix'd the hallow'd strain
      " Bursts fervent to the skies :
    " Deign then, O radiant Pallas, deign
      " In all thy might to rise.
" From this fierce pow'r, which raging round
" Unarm'd inflicts the fiery wound,
    " Daughter of Jove, my country save ;
    " Hence, goddess, hence the fury sweep
    " To Amphitrite's chamber deep,
      " On the rough Euxine wave !

" Doth aught the Night from ruin spare ?
" The Morning's sickly ray,
" Pregnant with death, inflames the air,
" And gives disease its prey.
" Father of gods, whose matchless force
" Wings the red lightning's vengeful course,
" With all thy thunders crush this foe !
" Potent to aid, Lycian king,
" Thy shafts secure of conquest wing,
" And bend thy golden bow !

" Thy beams around, Diana, throw,
" And pierce this gloom of night,
" As on Lycæum's moss-clad brow
" Thou pour'st thy silver light !
" Thy nymphs, O Theban Bacchus, lead,
" The golden mitre round thy head,
" Grief-soothing god of wine and joy ;
" Wave thy bright torch, and with it flame
" This god, to gods an odious name,
" This lurid pest destroy !

"Delian Pæan " alludes to the festival of Delia. A
particular hymn was chanted here in honour of Apollo.
This festival was held at Delos, and it is stated that the excellent
King Theseus first established it. Ariadne was daughter
of Minos, first King of Crete. She fell in love with Theseus,
and gave him a statue; the statue was covered with
wreaths of flowers ; then the music proceeded, and the people
went through a variety of evolutions indicative of a maze.
From such a place Ariadne had released Theseus. The
word Delia takes its rise from the Island of Delos. It
was here that Latona rested, after having been driven all
over the world ; here also Apollo and Diana were born.
The altar raised here in honour of Apollo was considered one of the seven wonders of the world. We are
told that he built it himself when he was only four years old,

and that the material he used consisted of goats' horns
which he collected on Mount Cynthus, one day after
Diana had had a chase there. The Persians never sacrificed
flesh at this altar, as it had to be kept free from blood. The
oracles propounded here were simple, concise, and clear; in
fact, it was an establishment for manufacturing moral
proverbs. No dogs were permitted on any of the Cyclade
Islands, and they neither allowed children to be born there,
nor people to die (we are not told if they were able to carry
out these two last regulations or not.) As regards the birth
part of the business, it is most strange, for the island itself
came into existence (being raised out of the sea by Neptune)
purposely, to enable Latona to give birth to Apollo and
Diana—she did so whilst leaning against a palm tree.
This was another piece of persecution through Jupiter's
amours and Juno's jealousies; for when Juno found out
that Jupiter had been philandering with Latona, she sent
the serpent Python to torment her wherever she went:
Juno drove her from heaven. Terra was so terrified by
Juno, as to induce her to drive Latona off the earth, and
goodness knows where the poor goddess would have fluttered
her wings, had not good old Neptune taken pity on her,
and raised this little island out of the sea purposely for
her to perch upon.

The line—

" Immortal Pallas, hear !"

does not allude to Pallas, son of King Evander, but
(although it is a man's name) to Minerva, who assumed it,
she having killed, in single combat, one of the giants begot
of Tartarus and Terra, whose name was Pallas. The line—

" Deign then, O radiant Pallas, deign"

alludes to the same deity, and the line—

" Potent to aid, Lycean King"

is applied to Apollo, as one of the names he bore was Lycius, from which a festival was held at Argos, called Lycæus, and presided over by Apollo.

I will now read to you one of the finest acting scenes of all the ancient writers. In the hands of two good actors, much might be made of it. It is rather long, and developes a great deal of Œdipus's real character, widely differing from the generous and considerate Tiresias. The chorus is introduced in the original, but I will abandon it, as it is not important to the scene, and I will be better able to recite the parts as a dialogue between the two characters to some effect than by introducing a third. When I have finished this scene it will be time to break off this lecture, deferring the remainder of the play for the next occasion I may have the pleasure of meeting you. I cannot avoid this sometimes, as the subject I am now upon runs into six different tragedies by three separate authors, and I am compelled to arrange my explanations so as to enable me to elucidate the whole of them. In the meantime, you will be able to get the fourth number of my work for a small shilling, and I hope it may afford you an hour's amusement in your boudoir.

" ŒDIPUS.

" Well are thy vows address'd ; nor vain those vows,
" But of much force, and lenient of our ills,
" Wou'dst thou with deep regard attend my words,
" Which I, to each related circumstance
" A stranger, and a stranger to the deed,
" Shall speak ; for far my search could not extend,
" Having no marks to guide my steps. But now
" A Theban tale enroll'd, to all of Thebes
" I give this charge. Whoe'er among you knows

" By whom the son of Labdacus was slain,
" Him I command t' unfold the whole to me.
" But if, through conscious guilt, he fears t' avow
" The deed, and charge himself ; no harsher doom
" Awaits him, than to leave this land, unhurt.
" But if among you be a man, who knows
" Another, of another realm, whose hand
" Was with this blood polluted, let him speak,
" And not conceal the murderer ; for from me
" Ample shall be his recompence, and thanks
" Added besides.   But if ye will not speak,
" If fearing for himself, or for a friend,
" There be a man that disregards my words,
" What then shall be my solemn mandate hear.
" That man let none within this realm, whose throne,
" Whose empire I command, beneath his roof
" Receive, let none hold converse with him, none
" Admit him at the altars of the gods,
" His vows, his offerings to partake, or share
" The cleansing laver ; from your houses all
" Chase this pollution of our land ; for thus
" To me the Pythian oracle declared
" Its will ; thus therefore with the god I join
" Confederate, and the dead.   But on the wretch
" Who did the deed, whether he lies conceal'd
" A single ruffian, or with many leagued,'
" I imprecate this curse ; his wretched days,
" Cut off from all the social joys of life,
" Let him wear out in misery.   In my house
" If I protect him, conscious of the deed,
" May all these curses fall on me.   The same
" I charge on you ; make you these solemn vows,
" In zeal for me, for Phœbus, and this land
" Thus of its fruits, and its protecting gods
" Bereft.   Nor ought we, though no voice divine
" Impell'd us, unattoned to leave the blood
" Of one so noble, of a monarch slain.
" To trace this murderous deed my fortune now
" Assigns to me, for mine the regal pow'r

" Which once was his ; his bed, his wife is mine ;
" Our children too, but that the adverse gods
" Denied him children, had in common ties
" Been close conjoin'd : but now disastrous fate
" Hath burst upon his head.   Therefore for him,
" As for my father, vengeful will I rise,
" Unwearied in th' attempt to find the man
" That slew the son of Labdacus, whose blood
" From Polydorus its illustrious stream
" Derived, from Cadmus, and Agenor old.
" To those who act not thus, I pray the gods
" That the till'd earth may never yield its fruits,
" And barren be their bed ; beneath the ills,
" Which now oppress us, let them waste, and feel
" A fate yet more severe.   But to the sons
" Of Thebes, who with applause these things receive,
" May justice join her aid, and all the gods
" Be present always, with propitious pow'r !
" O sage Tiresias, whose enlighten'd mind
" Notes all things, whether such as may be taught
" To mortals, or require the sacred seal
" Of silence, things of heav'n, or things of earth,
" Though quench'd thy visual beam, yet not unknown
" To thee the baleful pestilence that wastes
" The city ; from whose rage our soul relief,
" Our soul defence, illustrious seer, is found
" In thee ; for Phœbus, though perchance thine ear
" His mandate hath not reach'd, thus gave response
" To our inquiries, that this pest shall hence
" Alone its ravage cease, if, clearly known
" The murderers of Laius, we avenge
" On them, by exile or by death, his blood.
" Refuse not then, from what of augury
" From birds on wing thou draw'st, or from aught else
" Of thy prophetic art, to save thyself,
" To save the city ; save me too, and put
" All the pollution of the dead away.
" In thee are all our hopes : t' exert his pow'r
" In doing good is man's most glorious task.

D

" Tiresias.

" Alas, alas, how dreadful to be wise,
" From wisdom when no profit is derived !
" Mine is this knowledge, fatal to thy peace.
" I should not then have come.

" Œdipus.

" What may this mean ?
" And why this gloomy sadness on thy brow ?

" Tiresias.

" Dismiss me to my house ; thy ills more light
" Wilt thou sustain, I mine, this grace obtain'd.

" Œdipus.

" Nor just, nor friendly to thy country thou,
" Thus to deprive her of thy sage advice.

" Tiresias.

" Nothing of good to thee thy speech, I see,
" Portends : of ill productive be not mine.

" Chorus.

" Now by the gods, whate'er thy wisdom knows,
" Suppress it not, we suppliant all implore.

" Tiresias.

" For you are all unwise.   Ne'er shall my voice
" For this find utterance, nor disclose thy ills.

" Œdipus.

" To know, and not to speak ! Implies not this
" Treachery to us, and ruin to the realm ?

" Tiresias.

" My peace I will not hurt, nor thine.   In vain
" Why wilt thou urge ?   From me thou shalt not know.

" ŒDIPUS.

" Thou vilest of the vile—for thou wou'dst raise
" Th' insensate rock to rage—wilt thou not speak,
" But show thyself unfeeling and unmoved ?
' Who would not be enraged to hear thy words,
" Which cast dishonour on this injured state !

" TIRESIAS.

" These things will come, though silent be my voice.

" ŒDIPUS.

" Then what will come, to me thou should'st disclose.

" TIRESIAS.

" Further I will not speak ; so let thy rage,
" If such thy will, in all its fierceness rise.

" ŒDIPUS.

" Then I will speak as anger prompts my tongue,
" Without reserve whate'er my thoughts suggest.
" Know then I deem thee complice in this act ;
" I deem the deed was thine, save that thy hand
" Struck not the blow : hadst thou enjoy'd thy sight,
" I should pronounce the act were thine alone.

" TIRESIAS.

" Indeed ! Nay then I warn thee to abide
" By thine own solemn charge, and from this day
" Hold converse nor with these, nor me ; for thou
" Art the accurs'd polluter of this land.

Potter makes a long note upon this scene, in which he states that Tiresias " is dreadfully obscure." His meaning and intentions are surely clear
enough ; he is a prophet, and knows that it was Œdipus who killed
Laius.   He loves him and is loyal to him, therefore he is reluctant to
disclose his knowledge.   Potter further states that " Eustathias ingeni-
ously supposes that Tiresias alludes to Jocasta ;" he says, further, " this
perhaps is too great a refinement :" he should have said absurdity.

" ŒDIPUS.

" Hast thou no sense of shame, that thou hast dared
" Utter such taunt ?   How think'st thou to escape ?

" TIRESIAS.

" I have escaped, e'en by the potent truth
" Which I maintain.

" ŒDIPUS.

" By whom hast thou been taught ?
" Not by thy art divine.

" TIRESIAS.

" By thee constrain'd
" Unwillingly to speak.

" ŒDIPUS.

" What ?   Speak the words
" Again ; my knowledge so will be more clear.

" TIRESIAS.

" Were they abstruse ?   Or dost thou bid me speak
" To try me ?

" ŒDIPUS.

" Not to speak it as a thing
' Known ; yet repeat thy words.

" TIRESIAS.

" Again I say
" Thou art the much-sought murderer of the King.

" ŒDIPUS.

" Thou shalt not triumph for this second taunt.

" TIRESIAS.

" More shall I speak then, and enrage thee more ?

" ŒDIPUS.

" Say what thou wilt, it will be said in vain.

" TIRESIAS.

" I say flagitious is thy intercourse
" With those most dear to thee; thou know'st not this
" Nor seest the ills in which thou art involved.

" ŒDIPUS.

" Think'st thou no vengeance such reproach awaits?

" TIRESIAS.

" I have no fear, if truth hath aught of pow'r.

" ŒDIPUS.

" It hath, but not for thee; it is not thine;
" Thy ears, thy soul, e'en as thine eyes, are blind.

" TIRESIAS.

" Unhappy thou in thus reproaching me
" For soon on thee the same reproach shall fall.

" ŒDIPUS.

" Confiding in thy blindness thou from me,
" Or any that have eyes, no vengeance fearest.

" TIRESIAS.

" To fall by thee is not my fate; those things
" Belong to Phœbus; ample is his pow'r.

" ŒDIPUS.

" The fiction this of Creon, or thine own?

" TIRESIAS.

" Creon ne'er wrought thee ill: the work is thine.

"ŒDIPUS.

' O greatness, empire, and thou noblest art*
" That giv'st to life its glory most desired,
" What baleful envy on your splendor waits,
" Since for this royal pow'r by me unsought,
" But by the state presented a free gift,
" The faithful Creon, who the first appear'd
" My friend, with dark and secret malice works,
" Wishing my ruin, and suborns this wretch,
" This sorcerer, this artificer of wiles,
" Whose trains delude the people, sharp of sight
" To lucre only, to his science blind.
" Where hast thou e'er display'd a prophet's skill?†
" Why, when the ravening hound of hell her charm
" Mysterious chanted,‡ for thy country wise
" Didst thou not solve it? Of no vulgar mind
" Was this the task ; the prophet this required.
" No knowledge then from birds didst thou receive,
" None from the gods t' unfold it : but I came,
" This nothing-knowing Œdipus, and quell'd
" The monster, piercing through her dark device
" By reason's force, not taught by flight of birds.
" Yet dost thou now assay to drive me out,
" Weening to have thy stand next Creon's throne.
" But thou, and he who form'd this base design
" With thee, shall feel my power : but that thine age
" Some reverence claims, thou shou'dst e'en now be taught ;
" And feel the madness of thine enterprise.

---

* This is truly a Shaksperian speech, in which is developed the perverseness of Œdipus's character : either it is so or immediately preceding this part of the scene he must have been dissembling. I think the character of Œdipus perverse throughout.

† Here he commences mean taunting, and acts the tyrant : it would be the repeated instances of this description, in the character of Œdipus, that would destroy all sympathy for his misfortunes, were the tragedy acted now-a-days.

‡ This alludes to the enigma which was chanted by the Sphinx.

" TIRESIAS.

" Thou art a King ; yet I have equal right
" To answer thee ; this pow'r is mine ; to thee
" I am no vassal ; Phœbus is my lord :
" Nor will I be enroll'd 'mongst those who wait
" On Creon for support.   I tell thee then,
" Me since with taunts thou hast reviled as blind,
" Thou hast indeed thine eyes, yet canst not see
" What ills disclose thee round, nor where thou hast
" Thy habitation, nor with whom thou livest.
" Know'st thou who gave thee birth ? Thou art a foe,
" And know'st it not, to those allied to thee
" Most closely, whom the realms beneath contain,
" And who behold the light of heav'n.   The curse
" Of father and mother on each side
" With dreadful steps pursue thee, and ere long
" Will chase thee from this land, now blest with sight,
" Then blind.   How will Cithæron, how each strand
" Ere long re-echo to thy mournful cries,
" When thou shalt know that, driv'n by swelling gales,
" The port of marriage thou hast gain'd, thy bark
" Where anchor cannot hold !   The numerous train
" Of other ills thou see'st not, which will rank
" In the same line thee and thy sons alike.
" Go to ; with foul revilings Creon taunt,
" And my voice ; yet things more vile than thou
" Is not 'mong mortals that shall e'er be crush'd.

" ŒDIPUS.

" From him these piercing insults must I bear ?
" Perdition on thee ! hence, away, begone.

" TIRESIAS.

" I had not come, hadst thou not sent for me.

" ŒDIPUS.

" I knew thee not in speech so void of sense,
" Or here thy presence I had scarce required.

" TIRESIAS.

" Such thou may'st deem my spirit, void of sense :
" But they, who gave thee birth, esteem'd me wise.

" ŒDIPUS.

" Who are they ?   Stay.   Of those that breathe to whom
" Owe I my birth ?

" TIRESIAS.

                " Thy birth this day will show,
" This day will show the horrors of thy fate.

" ŒDIPUS.

" How dark, how full of mystery all thy words !

" TIRESIAS.

" Such to unfold well suits thy piercing mind.*

" ŒDIPUS.

" My glory thou wou'dst turn to my reproach.

" TIRESIAS.

" That glory hath brought ruin on thy head.

" ŒDIPUS.

" If I have saved this realm, I reck not that.

" TIRESIAS.

" Well then, I now depart.   Boy, lead me hence.

" ŒDIPUS.

" Ay, let him lead thee ; for thy presence throws
" Confusion on th' affairs that now engage
" Our care : begone, and trouble us no more.

---

* Now comes Tiresias's turn to taunt : he means you insinuated that
your piercing mind was more cunning than mine in discovering the
Sphinx's enigma, why, then, do you not discover my meaning ?

" TIRESIAS.

" I go : but first will speak for what I came,
" Nor dread thy frown ; thy vengeance hath no pow'r
" To touch my life.   I tell thee that the man
" Whom thou hast sought, 'gainst whom thy solemn charge,
" Thy threats have been proclaim'd, that man is here ;
" Of foreign birth now deem'd, his residence
" Here fixing ; but full soon he shall be found
" A Theban born, nor in his fortune long
" Rejoice ; his visual ray in darkness quench'd,
" His high state sunk to beggary, a staff
" Shall to a foreign land his steps direct.
" A brother and a father to his sons
" Shall he appear ; to her that gave him birth,
" A son and husband ; to his father found
" A rival and murderer.   Go thou in ;
" Muse on these things ; say, if thou find them false,
" No portion of a prophet's skill is mine."

The next part of this scene is an interview between
Œdipus and Creon, in which the King pursues his accusation of Creon and Tiresias, attempting to get up a manœuvre
to lay the murder of Laius on his shoulders, and so deprive
him of his crown and authority.   I would willingly give
you an explanation here of the part I have been reading of
this scene, but there are two reasons why I do not do so
now; in the first place, the scene is not finished, as the
same description of conversation continues with Creon as
was transpiring with Tiresias ; and until the whole of it is
read to you, I choose to defer the point ; besides which the
usual time allotted to each of these lectures has already considerably expired, and I doubt not but you have listened so
attentively to what I have said that you will sleep upon it,
and favour me with another visit, so that I may have the
pleasure of renewing this same subject to you, which I expect will occupy the full scope of my next lecture.

LECTURE IV.

I WAS compelled to conclude my last lecture in the middle of a scene, and before I renew it, let me offer a few remarks upon the subjects of elocution, oratory, and modulating the voice; which latter quality I take to be the great essential necessary to render us harmonious and agreeable in speaking. It is not a science, nor do I believe it can be taught, unless it be in such a set manner so as to make it painful to the correct ear to listen to.

No person having the natural gift of modulating the voice, in the truly passionate sense, ever recites a part exactly the same upon two separate occasions. I grant you will find a similarity in all three essentials, voice, action, and gesture, yet the natural actor is sure to differ, every time you listen to him, at some point or other in his modulation. This goes to prove that although you may, to some extent, make a science of elocution, you cannot make a man a true orator, unless he have the inspiration of modulation in his soul—this is a fact every day portrayed. You may meet with people of the highest education, including many of our clerical orators, whose expressions and sentences frequently seem to scratch our nervous systems by their abrupt harshness in attempting to be impressive. I have heard some,

when they have strained to do that which nature never
intended they should accomplish, so rant and roar, that I
have thought with Hamlet "they imitated humanity abomin-
ably," just as if " some of nature's journeymen had made
men, and not made them well." I am aware that constant
study, and the advantage of good society may work wonders;
but nature does more, and try all you may, you cannot
infuse oratorical inspirations into mortals' souls, unless the
vital spark be there to receive the impression. Attempts
may be made to make displays, but they are sure to be like
costermongers' calls, more noise than harmony.

To you who aspire to the sublime accomplishment of
elocution, I venture advice. In the first place, throw off
all nervousness, assume confidence, though you die for
it, for if you do not you'll never live to get through your
first chapter without palling your audience. In the second
place, be modest in your demeanour, begin slowly, and let
your voice rise and fall with your words, as your language
denotes important or subordinate matter. Do not affect
mannerism, nor let your manners degenerate into affecta-
tion; if you do, you will be laughed at for insipidity, and
condemned as a coxcomb. I know very well that such namby-
pamby creatures are often courted by young ladies' mammas,
because they are " such nice young men;" yet, spite of this
advantage, I fervently recommend you not to assume these
effeminate vices; where they exist as natural defects, they
are to be deplored, particularly if there be any latent talent
to be displayed. I conscientiously advise aspirants of this
class, whomsoever they may be, rather to hold forth to their
mammas' select tea parties at home, than to harangue public
audiences abroad. The true spirit of elocution may be often
found under a battered greasy hat, and covered by threadbare garments, whilst elegant broadcloth of the finest tex-

ture, and the smartest brimmed chapeau that Paris may bring to the pinnacle of fashion, may not create an inspiration in the dullards who wear them. Our stomachs, too, have a great deal to do with the matter, for if they be not in proper order, our spirits flag, our voices fail us, effective enunciations are not obtained, and in our efforts to overcome these deficiencies, we become noisy by the harshness of our endeavours. Therefore, you, who purpose holding forth, do not overtax your gastric capacities, for if you do you may strain at, or distrain upon, your capabilities, and produce but little profitable execution to your summons.

I have met with men whose voices were so execrable that when they have spoken it has been something like a noise between a screech and a howl; yet for all this I have listened to them with some degree of pleasure—why? I'll tell you—they possessed the natural gift of modulation, and by judicious usage, they rendered their speeches not only agreeable, but edifying. Now, "look here, upon this picture, and on this." I have also met with men enjoying the advantages of attractive personal appearances, full, melodious voices, and blessed with sound education, yet when they attempted to make a speech, it was more like a bull roaring, than an oratorical display. And what was it they lacked, forsooth? Why, I'll tell you—intonation and modulation, and being minus proper cadences, they were harsh and boisterous in their declamation. I have, therefore, felt relief in quitting their company, even in ordinary conversation.

I like to hear people impressive, provided always they be not noisy nor dogmatical: the voice must be modulated to speak correctly; this is done by varying the accentuation, but care must be taken not to vitiate the sentences you are delivering. A good practice when reading (if alone) is to intone your words as you utter them, and by so trying the effect upon your own ear you will soon discover if you have any melody in your utterance or not. To use the word melody in this sense, to some people may seem inappropriate, as it is often thought applicable only to set music, but that is a mistake; there is melody in modulation and in intonation; in fact, these qualifications may be deemed the soul of elocution. The tones and semi-tones can only be measured by the ear, for there is no possible method of drumming it into people. You must understand that although I suggest to you to practise intoning your words when you read, I do not mean you to do so in a sing-song manner, but in measured cadences, so as to produce melody. This eventually becomes a science of your own making, and is the nearest approach to natural modulation that can be produced, and in your oral discourse it will pass for the natural element, provided you use a little caution and some prudence. The greatest point of all to be observed is not to appear mechanical in your utterance, for if you do, all your efforts will fail, and you will expose yourself in the attempt. Our voices are governed as our corn laws were, before our friends, Cobden and Bright, commenced their oratorical displays upon the question—viz., upon a sliding scale, upwards and downwards; upwards we may designate ascension, and downwards descension. The voice has naturally only these two courses to travel, and according to the impetus the speaker gives it at starting, so will it ascend or descend in declamation or cadence. It is not by theory, nor by set rules that the art of modulating the voice can be accomplished, it must be by example, nature, and practice. An emphasis may be said to be an allusive force of modulation, to be used only when you wish to be impressive in your remarks, but not as a practice in general colloquial conversation; for how-

ever correct it may be in an oratorical display, such im-
pressiveness in your ordinary discourse is sure to make you
enemies, inasmuch as men of quiet dispositions will take
exception, and cite you as labouring under excitement,
and ladies will be inclined to consider it abrupt; therefore,
be explicit, but persuasive, rather than obtrusive, emphatic,
or dictatorial.

Perhaps, in introducing the subject I have just been
dilating upon, it may be considered by some that I have
gone out of my avowed course. That may be to a certain
extent, but as my speaking has been upon an art essential
to the subject I have in hand, I think I have not done
altogether wrong in introducing it; therefore, if you agree
with me in this idea, I will at future periods in my lectures
return to other phases of the same and similar arts. It will
now be a pleasure to me to read to you some more of the
tragedy of " Œdipus, King of Thebes."

I left off, upon the previous occasion, where Tiresias
quits the stage. Œdipus is still present, and Creon entering,
he addresses him as follows :—

" Darest thou come hither ?   In thy insolence
" Art thou so harden'd, as again to tread
" My courts, detected in thy base design
" To murder me, and from my brows to rend
" The regal crown ?   Now tell me, by the gods,
" Hast thou mark'd in me aught of cowardice
" Or folly, that encouraged thee to form
" Such daring thoughts ?   Or deem'st thou that the deed,
" Creeping with dark insidious step, mine eye
" Would not observe ; or if observed, my hand '
" Would not chastise ?   How frantic thy attempt,
" Nor friends nor forces thine, at sovereign pow'r,
" By multitudes and treasures gain'd, to aim ?
" If thou canst think no vengeance will pursue

" Injustice to a friend, thou art not wise.

" Was it not thy suggestion, thy advice,

" That I should send to this all-honour'd Seer ?

" What time hath pass'd since Laius by the hands

" Of ruffians fell ?

          " And was this prophet then

" Famed for his skill ?

            " At that time

" Made he of me no mention ?

              " Made you then no search

" To trace this bloody deed ?

              " Why did not then this Seer

" Declare these things ?

" Were he not basely leagued with thee, he ne'er

" Had said that Laius by my hand was slain.

            " I never shall be found

" A blood-stain'd murderer.

" CREON.

        " Is my Sister thine,

" By nuptial ties united ?

            " Dost thou not share

" With her the sovereign pow'r ?

              " Is not my seat

" The highest, next your throne ?

" ŒDIPUS.

        " And for that cause

" Dost thou appear a base and faithless friend.

" CREON.

" Not so ; wou'dst thou, like me, with temperate thought

" Ponder things well. For first reflect, what man

" Would chuse to be a king, with all the fears

" On royalty awaiting, might he sleep

" Secure of fear, yet kingly pow'r possess ?

" It is not in my nature, nor in his

" Who knows what wisdom is, to form a wish

" To be a monarch, rather than to use
" A monarch's potency. All things from thee
" I now obtain, nor feel the pangs of fear.
" Were I a king, I should do many things
" Against my will : can then the regal state
" Be sweeter to me than my princely rank,
" And pow'r that knows not care ? Nor is my mind
" By falsehood so beguiled, that it aspires
" To honours which no real good procure.
" Now all things give me pleasure ; all men now
" Greet me with courtesy ; now all, who want
" Favours from thee, address me, for their suits
" Through me they all obtain. And shall I quit
" These solid pleasures for the empty pomp
" Of royalty ? A mind to wisdom train'd
" Can not be so depraved : I never loved
" To form such measures, nor in such would deign
" To share with others. Dost thou want a proof ?
" Go to the Pythian shrine, and there enquire
" If faithfully the answer of the god
" I have reported : if thou find me leagued
" In counsils with the Seer, put me to death,
" And in the sentence shall my voice assent
" With thine : but on suspicion void of proof
" Condemn me not : the just not lightly deem
" The base man honest, or the honest base.
" For he, that throws a faithful friend away,
" Doth himself equal wrong as if he threw
" His life away, which is most dear to him.
" This thou wilt know in time ; for time alone
" Shows a just man ; the base a day unveils.
" What wou'dst thou then ? My exile from this land ?

" ŒDIPUS.

" No : not thy exile would I, but thy death.

" CREON.

" When thou hast shown me guilty of some crime.

G

" ŒDIPUS.

" Thou speak'st as one refusing to obey.

" CREON.

" Because I see thee not by wisdom ruled.

" ŒDIPUS.

" For mine own welfare wisely I provide.

" CREON.

" Mine claims an equal care.

" ŒDIPUS.

" But thou art base.

" CREON.

" What, though no crime thou know'st ?

" ŒDIPUS.

" I will be king.

" CREON.

" Thou shou'dst not be a tyrant.
" Thebes is not thine alone : some share is mine.

" *Enter* JOCASTA.

" Why, indiscreetly why this strife of words,
" Unhappy princes, have you raised, nor blush,
" Your country with afflictions thus oppress'd,
" To stir up private contest ?   Wilt not thou
" Enter these gates ?   Thou Creon, hence depart,
" Nor add a causeless grief to weighty woes ?

" CREON.

" Alas, my sister, with injurious rage
" A dreadful sentence Œdipus decrees,
" Exile or death, against me to inforce.

" ŒDIPUS.

" I own it : for I found him with base arts
" Against my person plotting base designs.

" CREON.

" If I have done this, of this heinous charge
" If I am guilty, let me not enjoy
" Th' light of heav'n, but fall a wretch accurs'd.

" JOCASTA.

" Believe him, I conjure thee by the gods,
" In this believe him, Œdipus ; regard
" His sacred oath, and me, and these thy friends.

" ŒDIPUS.

" What wou'dst thou I should yield ?
" Know'st thou what thou wou'dst ask ?
" Now be assured that, seeking this, thou seek'st
" My ruin, or my exile from this land.
" Then let him go, e'en though I needs must die,
" Or from this country with disgrace be driven.
" Thy mournful plea, not his, my pity moves ;
" Him shall my hate, where'er he goes, pursue.
" Then leave me to myself : begone.

" CREON.

" I go,
" To thee perchance not known ; but still by these,
" Just to my innocence, in honour held.

[*Exit* CREON.

" JOCASTA.

" Now, by the gods, inform me whence this rage,
" That with such fury flames, O king, arose.

" ŒDIPUS.

" I will inform thee (for than these more high
" I reverence thee) of Creon's base designs.
" He saith I murder'd Laius.

" JOCASTA.

" Said he this
" On his own knowledge, or from others heard

" ŒDIPUS.

" The prophet prompt to mischief he suborn'd,
" Whose rude licentious tongue knows no restraint.

" JOCASTA.

" Think of thyself, respecting this, no more.
" Hear me, and be assured no mortal man
" Knows by prophetic art events to come ;
" Of this I give thee a decisive proof.
" To Laius once an oracle announced
" (I will not say that from the god it came,
" But from his ministers) that time should bring
" On him this fate, to fall beneath a son
" That should his birth from him and me derive.
" Yet foreign ruffians him, as fame reports,
" Murder'd where three ways meet.   A son was born ;
" Not three days pass'd, the infant's feet he bound,
" Piercing the nerves, and by another's hand
" Upon a desert mountain cast him forth.
" The consummation then, that he should slay
" His father, or that Laius by his son
" Should fall, a fate so dreadful to his thoughts,
" Phœbus atchieved not ; yet th' oracular voice
" Decreed these things : regard them not : the god,
" What from his hallow'd shrine he gave command
" To trace, to your enquiries will disclose.

" ŒDIPUS.

" What wild amazement, lady, at thy words
" Seizes my troubled thoughts, and shakes my soul.

" JOCASTA.

" What perturbation moves thee thus to speak ?

"ŒDIPUS.

" Methought I heard thee say that Laius fell,
" Murder'd by ruffian force, where three ways meet.

" JOCASTA.

" Such was the rumour then : it still prevails.

" ŒDIPUS.

" Where ? In what land befell this dire event ?

" JOCASTA.

" Phocis the realm is call'd ; the separate roads
" From Delphi and from Daulia there unite.

" ŒDIPUS.

" What length of time, since this was done hath pass'd ?

" JOCASTA.

" Short time before the regal crown of Thebes
" Shone on thy brows, these tidings reach'd the state.

" ŒDIPUS.

" To me, O Jove, what hast thou decreed ?

" JOCASTA.

" Why hath a thought like this possess'd* thy soul ?

" ŒDIPUS.

" No questions now ; but tell me what the form
" Of Laius, what his stature, and his age.

" JOCASTA.

" Tall, and of manly port, his locks just tinged
" With gray ; his form not unlike thine.

---

* Possess'd here means disturbed.

" ŒDIPUS.

" O wretched me ! Unweeting* on myself
" What dreadful curses have I here denounced !

" JOCASTA.

" Why this ? I tremble as I look on thee.

" ŒDIPUS.

" Greatly I fear the prophet sees too well.
" Yet one thing more : That will give clearer light.

" JOCASTA.

" I tremble ; yet whate'er I know will speak.

" ŒDIPUS.

" Went he with few ; or, as became a King,
" With many guards attendant on his state ?

" JOCASTA.

" Without more train than five, an herald one
" Of these ; a single chariot bore the King.

" ŒDIPUS.

" Ah wretched me ! All now is clear indeed.
" What man was he who this relation† brought ?

" JOCASTA.

" A menial servant, who alone escaped.

" ŒDIPUS.

" Is he now here attending in the house ?

" JOCASTA.

" No : for returning thence when thee he saw
" Holding the sovereign power, and Laius dead,

---

* Unweeting means unwittingly, or incautiously.
† Relation here means information.

" Touching my hand me suppliant he implored
" Some rural charge among the pastured herds
" To give him, that within the walls of Thebes
" He seldom might be seen : I sent him : this,
" And greater grace he, though a slave, deserved.

" ŒDIPUS.

" Let him with swiftest speed then be recall'd.

" JOCASTA.

" He shall.   But why to see him this desire ?

" ŒDIPUS.

" I for myself have fears : much hath been said,
" Which prompts my eager wish to see this man.

" JOCASTA.

" He soon will come.   But am not I, O King ?
" Worthy what thus distracts thy thoughts to know ?

" ŒDIPUS.

" My expectation to such height is raised,
" That I will tell thee : for in whom more dear
" Can I, thus struggling with my fate, confide ?
" My father was the royal Polybus
" Of Corinth ; Merope,* who boasts her birth
" From Dorian Chiefs, my mother ; in that state
" I was esteem'd the greatest, till there chanced
" A circumstance, which might my wonder claim,
" But nought of anxious care : amidst a feast
" One fill'd with wine reviled me as not born
" The son of Corinth's King : ill brook'd I this,
" And scarce that day restrain'd myself ; the next
" My father and my mother I address'd,

---

* This must be a mistake either of the poet Sophocles, Dr. Potter, or the printer.   I am afraid the mistake is in the translation.   Œdipus's reputed mother (the wife of Polybus) was named Periboea.

" Earnest to trace the truth : the insult raised
" Their high resentment, though from heat of wine
" It sprung ; with their affection I was pleased ;
" Yet still this stung my heart, so deeply there
" It rankled.   Anxious to the Pythian shrine,
" My purpose not disclosed, I take my way ;
" To this enquiry no reply was deign'd,
" And me unhonour'd Phœbus sent away ;
" But show'd, the fates foretelling, other ills
" With woe, with horror pregnant : he declared
" That with my mother I was doom'd to mix
" Embraces, and to light produce a race
" By men to be abhorr'd ; nay, doom'd to be
" The murderer of my father.   When these words
" Reach'd my affrighted ear, from Corinth wide,
" My course thenceforth directing by the stars,
" I fled, where I might ne'er behold the shame,
" The infamy of these dire oracles
" Fulfill'd.   My way pursuing, to the place
" I came, where thou hast said this monarch fell.
" Yes, I will tell thee all the truth : as near
" This place, where three ways meet, I held my course,
" An herald, and exalted on a car
" One of such form as thy description mark'd,
" Met me : with force the leader of the way,
" And the old Chief himself against me rush'd,
" And drove me back ; the leader, who aside
" Had turn'd me, in my rage I strike : the chief,
" Soon as he saw me passing near the car,
" Smote me, against my head he aim'd the blow,
" He smote me twice ; but from this hand received
" Unequal recompence ; beneath my staff
" At once he sunk, and from his chariot roll'd.
" I slew them all.   Now should these kindred deeds
" Prove like relation 'twixt this stranger slain
" And Laius, lives there such a wretch as I ?
" Lives there a man so hateful to the gods ?
" Nor citizen nor stranger may henceforth

" Beneath their roof receive me, none with me
" Hold converse, from their houses all constrain'd
" To thrust me ; yet none other, but myself,
" Denounced these curses on me. I pollute
" The bed of him, who perished by these hands,
" These blood-stain'd hands ? and am I not most vile ?
" Am I not all defiled ? If I must fly,
" And exiled never, never see those friends
" That are most dear to me, and never tread
" My country's soil again ; if I must mount
" My mother's bed, in fated nuptials join'd ;
" If I must kill my father Polybus,
" From whom my life, my nurture I received ;
" Who would not judge, who would not say with truth
" That some remorseless dæmon wrought these woes ?
" But never, never, O ye holy pow'rs
" Of the just gods, may I behold that day !
" No : from the sight of mortals let me sink,
" Ere see a stain like this pollute my life.

" CHORUS.

" These things, O King, our consternation raise :
" Yet see this herdsman, hear him : meanwhile hope.

" ŒDIPUS.

" With eager expectation I await
" His presence : hope till his arrival lives.

" JOCASTA.

" What doth thy thought, when he appears, intend ?

" ŒDIPUS.

" I will inform thee : if his words be found
" With thine according, I escape these woes ?

" JOCASTA.

" What of high import heard'st thou in my words ?

" ŒDIPUS.

" From his report thou said'st that Laius fell
" By ruffians slain : that number if he still
" Assert, I slew him not ; it can not be
" That one be many ; by a single arm
" If he declares the monarch fell, on me
" The dreadful deed with all its guilt will fall.

" JOCASTA.

" Of his relation be assured ; his words
" He cannot now retract ; not I alone,
" But all Thebes heard them : with his former tale
" Be his tongue now at variance, yet, O King,
" Not of the death of Laius will he speak
" As by the god foretold, that he must fall
" Slain by my son : him my unhappy child
" Slew not, but perish'd, ere his death, himself.
" What then the faith of oracles?   Not that
" To thee denounced, nor this will I regard.

" ŒDIPUS.

" Thy sentiments are just : yet send with speed
" To bring this herdsman back ; omit not that.

" JOCASTA.

" This I will haste to do : but go we in.
" Whate'er to thee is pleasing I would do."

Having been compelled, for want of time, to break off in
my previous lecture, without explaining the scene between
Œdipus and Tiresias, I will do so now, and continue my
explanation of this I have just been reading to you.   After
the chorus concludes singing, Œdipus says :

" Well are thy vows address'd ;"

which means, you have pray'd well.

" Nor vain those vows,
" But of much force, and lenient of our ills."

Nor will your prayers be vain, but have great effect with the gods, for you have been moderate in your complaints. Now attend to me, regard my words. I am a stranger to the murder of Laius, and all circumstances connected with the deed. I speak to you because, as I know nothing of the circumstances myself, I seek your assistance to guide me in my search. I am not a Theban myself by birth; but being enrolled one, I charge you all, if the murderer of Laius be amongst you, I command him to come forth, and relate the circumstance. He need not fear confessing, for no harsher doom awaits him than banishment; he shall not be otherwise hurt. Or, if there be any one amongst you knowing that any of any other country did the deed, unfold him and your recompense shall be ample; I will both reward and thank you for your information. But, take this warning, if my words be disregarded, my solemn command shall be that no one shall receive him who knows of the murder, nor the murderer himself within his house. You shall not converse with him nor pray with him, you shall not make offerings with him to the gods, nor even bathe where he bathes, but chase him out of the land as a pollution; this is the command to me from the Pythian Oracle. I therefore (by the god's assistance) avow that I will join with you in pursuing the course I point out to you, as being the duty we have to perform; for, wherever the wretch may be who did the deed, I imprecate this curse upon him: May his days be wretched! may he be cut off from all social enjoyment of this life and wear out in misery! If I protect him in my house may all these curses fall on myself! I therefore charge you all swear to follow my example in this respect; it is a duty you owe to

Phœbus; it is a duty you owe your country and me your
King. Let us conjointly make it our duty to do this
although we have no direct orders from the divine powers—

" 'Tis plain by the line,
" Nor ought we, though no voice divine "—

that it is not intended to convey the impression that the
oracle supplying the prognostication is of divine origin. The
sacred part of the prophecy was made by the god Apollo,
before the birth of Œdipus took place. I am King, says
Œdipus, and it has become my fate to trace out this man's
assassins. It is my duty to do this, for I am not only King in
his place, but I have his wife, my wife now; even the children
I am blessed with might have been his children had he lived
(this is the most unphilosophical sentence in the whole play);
his fate has been disastrous, and I will be unswayed in my
search until I find the man who slew him. I will do this,
just as if I were acting for my own father's sake; and I
hope that you who do not do as I do in this respect may
find your lands fruitless, and yourselves childless. May you
waste with the plague that is now oppressing us—even severer
than this may your fates be! But to those sons of Thebes
who approve my plans, and assist me in accomplishing them,
may they meet with their just reward and may the gods be
propitious to them! In you, sage Tiresias, are our hopes
fixed, for though you are blind you are a prophet, and can
see into the future. It is not unknown to you the baleful
pestilence that is raging around us, and to relieve ourselves
from it we must all assist with all our might. It may be
you are not aware what mandate has been sent us from the
shrine of Phœbus. I will tell you: it is that the ravages of
our country shall cease soon as we discover the slayer of Laius,
and avenge his murder, either by the death or banishment

of the perpetrator. Therefore, do not you refuse to assist us with your prophetic arts, for your services are required to save the city; our hopes rest in you to put the pollution from this land. It is a glorious task doing good. Why are you thus sad* at what I say? it is not just nor friendly to with-hold your advice. Alas, says Tiresias, the knowledge I possess is fatal to your peace. Had I known 'twas for this you sent for me I would not have come. Dismiss me, let me go back home. Your granting me this favour will allow of a longer time elapsing ere your ills come to light. I can tell you of no good boding to yourself, and I am anxious not to be the harbinger of ill to you. You are unwise in pressing me to speak, and I will not disclose the ills I know of. Œdipus says: If you refuse to say what you know, you are not acting friendly nor justly to your country, therefore I implore you suppress not your knowledge, for if you do, it will be treachery to me, and ruin to the realm. I cannot help it, says Tiresias; I cannot destroy your peace of mind, nor my own happiness, therefore urge me no further, you shall not know anything from me. You'll know all too soon, though I say nothing; more I will not say; so, if you choose to be displeased with me, I cannot help it. Thou vilest of the vile, exclaims Œdipus, will you be so unfeeling as not to speak. You are casting dishonour and injury on the state. You should disclose what you know, although it bodes ill to me; but, as this is your determination, my suspicions are that, though you are blind, and did not do the deed yourself, it was you who instigated it. Nay, then, says Tiresias, as you taunt me thus vilely, hear the truth. Stand by the charge you have given your countrymen, and to that

---

* Sad here means silent.

which you have yourself sworn.   From this day forth neither
converse with these people nor with me; for thou thyself art
the accursed polluter of this land.   How dare you, exclaims
Œdipus, address me thus; have you any hope of escape from
my vengeance for your assurance ? By whom have you been
taught this ? surely not by the divine arts you profess. You
cannot hurt me, says Tiresias; I have already escaped injury
at your hands, by the mere assertion of the truth which I
have just uttered. You force me to speak. Well, says
Œdipus, speak it again, so that I may clearly understand
you; not that I believe you know what you say, for they are
merely words you utter.   Again I tell you, says Tiresias,
you yourself murdered the King. Shall I tell you more to
enrage you more ? Ha ! say what you will, remarks Œdipus,
it will not be believed. You shall not triumph in thus
taunting me a second time. Do you think my vengeance
does not await you for your insolence ?   I tell you, says
Tiresias, your intercourse is flagitious; you are not aware of
it, nor do you see the ills in which you are involved.   I have
no fear of you if there be any power in truth. It is unhappy
for you to heap these reproaches on me, for they will soon
recoil upon yourself. It is not my fate to fall by your power;
I am a devoted priest to Phœbus, and he has ample authority
over me without you.   Truth has power, says Œdipus, but
there's none in you; your soul and ears are as deaf to truth
as are your eyes to the light of day.   It is upon your
blindness you presume to taunt me, imagining that will
protect you.   Is what you have said to me the fiction of
Creon or of your own invention ? I see it is envy of my
greatness; no doubt it is Creon's working; he was faithful
once, and appeared my friend; he gave me the royal power
unsought by myself; but now, with secret malice, he is trying to work my ruin, and he has suborn'd you, thou cunning

wretch—thou, who art nothing but a sorcerer, and getting your living by deception; all you care about is to get money and delude the people; you know nothing of the science you profess. Where have you ever displayed a prophet's skill? You could not solve the enigma concerning the Sphinx; it required no common mind to accomplish that; that required a prophet's skill, but you showed no knowledge in the matter, neither from birds nor gods attained. But, I, a mere know-nothing, came and solved the mystery; I found out its dark device and subdued the monster; I judged by reason, not by the assistance of birds; yet you are calculating upon dethroning me, and upon having your seat next Creon when he takes his seat in my place; but you shall both of you feel my power; it is only your age that protects you for the present. 'Tis true, says Tiresias, you are the King, but at least I've a right to reply to your accusations. Creon never wrought you ill. Phœbus is my master not you, nor do I intend looking to Creon for support; therefore, since you taunt me with being blind, I tell you you cannot see with your own eyes what ills surround you; you cannot tell with whom you are living, nor from whom you gained your birth. You are the enemy of all connected with you by blood, and you don't know it, nor can you help it. You will shortly be banished from this land; and, although you now have your eyes, you'll then be blind. You have got married where you cannot hold your right, besides which, there are numerous ills surrounding you which you do not see, and they will descend to your sons. Now go revile Creon and the truths I have told you; yet for all this there's not a mortal on earth more vile than thyself. I would not have come here to have subjected myself to your revilings had you not sent for me. I would not have sent for you, says Œdipus, had I known you were so void of sense. You may deem me void of sense, replies

Tiresias, but they who gave thee birth did not think so. This very day will not only show who it was, but it will discover the other horrors of thy fate. To whom do I owe my birth? It seems you would wish to turn all my glory into reproach. Alas, says Tiresias, that glory was your ruin. Never mind that, retorts Œdipus, I have this realm, so I care not. Tiresias says, I now depart. Boy lead me home. I go, but, before I leave, I tell you I do not dread your frowns; for your vengeance cannot reach me. I repeat to you what I said before, the murderer you have been seeking is yourself. You are thought here a foreigner by birth, but 'twill soon appear that you were born in Thebes. You'll not remain in your present position long, for you'll sink to beggary, and, with loss of vision, you'll direct your steps to a foreign land. To the world you'll appear a brother to your own sons, a husband to your own mother, and the murderer of your father; therefore, go thou in and muse on what I have told you; then, if you find I have not related facts, you will be justified in saying I am not a skilful prophet.

The next scene between Œdipus and Creon is explained as follows:—Œdipus says, are you so hardened in guilt, being detected in your base design against me, as to brazen out your treachery by coming into my presence? Have you found me such a fool and coward, so to presume upon my credulity; or did you think by stealth to take me off my guard? What an insane idea on your part—you, who have no friends, nor forces, nor funds to pay them to assist you to the sovereign power. If you think I will not punish you for your injustice towards me, you are not wise. Was it not by your advice that I sent for Tiresias? Come now, tell me how long is it since Laius was murdered? Was this prophet of yours—this Tiresias—at that period famed for his skill? Did he then make any mention of me, or did you make any search to discover the perpetrators of the deed? How is it that this prophet of yours did not find them out? Were he not in league with you, he would not have dared to accuse me of the crime; but you cannot prove that I am a blood-stained murderer. Creon replies: Are you not my sister's husband? Does she not share with you the sovereign power of this realm? And is not my position the next highest to your own? Were you like me to think temperately of these facts, and to reflect, you would not think that I by choice would be the king, to subject myself to the dangerous position of royalty, even if my safety was secure; it is not my nature to covet that position,* nor would any wise man wish to be a monarch whilst he could do as I do—exercise all the privileges of a king without being liable to kingly responsibility. I hold all these privileges from you, yet I am not subject to the risks and dangers of your position. If I were king I might probably do many things against my inclination, to support my regal authority, that now I need not resort to. Can then the regal state have greater charms for me than the rank I hold as prince? As I am, I have not the care of the state on my shoulders. I am not so silly as to aspire to these honours from which I could gain no good. As I am, I gain pleasure from all things, all men are courteous to me, and those who require favours at my hands gain their object, if I think fit, through the influence I have with you. Is it likely then that I would wish to give up these secure pleasures for the empty pomp of royalty? My mind being with wisdom stored is not so disposed. I never cared for the position, nor would I even accept a share of the

---

* There could not have been a more consistent remark than this, for Creon has already in one instance given over the power and regal state of Thebes to Œdipus.

responsibility. If you doubt my report, and want proof of my mission from the gods, go yourself to the Pythian shrine, and get from them their answer, if I have reported to you correctly what I there learnt or no. Then, if you find that I am leagued in any conspiracy with Tiresias against you, put me to death, and I will admit the justice of your sentence. But do not condemn me upon mere suspicion; just men do not thus lightly deem bad men honest, nor honest men false, without proof; and he who throws a faithful friend away, wrongs himself as much as he does the man whom he condemns. You'll know this in time; for time alone proves who are just, and discovers who are false. Wherefore then, would'st thou wish to exile me from this land? No, says Œdipus, I do not wish to exile you, I desire your death, for you speak as if you refused to obey me. I refuse to obey you, says Creon, because I see you are not wise in your resolve. Wait till you prove me guilty of crime. Œdipus says: I provide by caution mine own safety. And does not my safety, says Creon, claim an equal care on mine own part? Yes, says Œdipus, but you are false to me. What! replies Creon, do you still persist in such an accusation, although you do not prove me guilty of any crime? Never mind that, says Œdipus, I am king, and I will exercise my authority. That's right enough, replies Creon, but you ought not act the tyrant. Thebes is not all yours, some part of it belongs to me.

Enter JOCASTA.

Unhappy princes why this dissension—why do you act so indiscreetly? You should blush to stir up private contention in face of the affliction with which your country is oppressed. Come, Œdipus, go in with me, enter your house, and you, Creon, depart. Do not add grief to his weighty woes. Creon addresses Jocasta, and says, Alas! my sister, Œdipus, with injurious rage, decrees the dreadful sentence of exile or death against me. Œdipus says, I admit it, for I have found him plotting against my person with base designs. If I have done as he says, interposes Creon, if I am guilty of the heinous charge he makes against me, may I not enjoy the light of heaven, but fall a wretch accursed. O believe him, says Jocasta, put faith in what he says, believe his sacred oath. Well, says Œdipus, do you know what you ask, do you wish me to yield? Be it so; but be assured in asking this of me you are forwarding my ruin, probably my exile from this country; let him go! for your sake, not for his, I yield. Even though I be driven from this country, or die, I'll risk it in mournful pity for your sake, but my hate shall pursue him wherever he goes. Creon, begone and leave my presence. Creon says, I will obey you by going where you will not know I am. Yet, by my sister and the people here I shall be held justly innocent and in honour.

[*Exit* CREON.]

Creon being now gone, Jocasta addresses Œdipus thus: Now tell me king why you are thus enraged; from what cause arose this furious passion? I will tell you, says Œdipus, for I revere you more than all the rest. He accused me of murdering Laius. Did he say this, answers Jocasta, from his own knowledge, or did he merely report to you what he has heard from other people? Not of his own knowledge has he accused me, says Œdipus, but he has suborned that mischievous prophet Tiresias, whose rude licentious tongue knows no restraint, to make the accusation. Then, if that be the case, replies Jocasta, think no more of it; attend to what I say. Rest satisfied, it is not in the power of mortal man by prophetic arts to foretel events. I will give you decisive proofs of what I say: An oracle once

told Laius (it was the priest's own prognostication, not
derived from divine authority) that he would fall by the
hand of his own son, who should derive his birth from me ;
but he fell by the hands of ruffians, being murdered by
foreigners where three ways meet. We had a son, but, before
the infant was three days old, his feet were bound, the nerves
being pierced by a servant's hand, and he was left upon a
desert mountain, so that the priest's prognostication could not
have been consummated. This dreadful fate thought of by
Phœbus could not have been achieved, therefore do not you
fear what the oracle has told Creon. What wild amazement, exclaims Œdipus, seizes my troubled thoughts. Lady,
thy words shake my very soul. Did I hear thee say that
Laius was murdered by ruffians, where three ways meet ?
Tell me where this was ; in what country did it take place ?
Jocasta tells him it was in the kingdom of Phocis, at a spot
where the roads from Delphi and Daulia unite. It took
place shortly before you ascended the throne of Thebes.
Œdipus now sees the probability of himself being connected
with the crime, and in horror exclaims, " O Jove, what fate
hast thou decreed ?" Why, what does this mean, says Jocasta,
what thought unnerves thee ? Ask me no questions now,
replies Œdipus, but describe to me what sort of man was
Laius, what was his height, and what was his age. He was
not unlike thee, says Jocasta, he was tall and of manly
figure, and his hair was just tinged with grey. The figure
of Laius flashes across Œdipus's mind, and he exclaims :
O wretched me ! Then remembering the imprecations he has
called down upon the head of him who assassinated Laius, he
says : What dreadful curses I have unwittingly called down
upon myself. I now begin to fear there is some truth in
what the prophet hath said. Tell me one thing more. Did
Laius go forth with few attendants or with a kingly train of

followers? Jocasta says, what can all this agitation mean?
I tremble looking at thee, but I will tell thee all I know.
His attendants consisted only of five people, and a single
chariot bore them; one of them was his herald; they were
all slain excepting a menial, who escaped. Where is he? in
horror ejaculates the king; is he now here attending in the
house? Ah, wretched me, all now is clear indeed; I see
it all too plainly. The man is not here, says Jocasta, for
when he saw you ascend the throne, he supplicated me to
give him some rural employment. I sent him to attend the
pastured herds; he was a faithful slave, and well deserved
the grace I granted him. Let him be swiftly sent for, says
Œdipus. I fear much that has been said prompts me eagerly
to see this man. My fears are raised to such a height that
I will relate to thee what transpired in my early life, for
there is no one in whom I can more fittingly confide, or
who is to me more dear than thyself. If I can but hold up
under my present woes I will tell thee all. My father I
believed to be the royal Polybus, King of Corinth, my
mother was Merope (there is no reason assigned in
Sophocles' works why he introduces Merope here. The
lady who was wife of Polybus, and who adopted Œdipus,
was named Peribœa, and there is no connection with the
two names that I can trace); in Corinth I was esteemed the
greatest person after the King and Queen, but a circumstance transpired which excited my wonder, and caused me
much anxiety. It was this: When at a feast, one who
was there, being full of wine, insinuated that I was not the
born son of the king. I could scarcely control myself
throughout the day from this taunt, and on the day following I entreated the King and Queen earnestly to relate the
truth. They were highly incensed at the insult offered me,
and I was much pleased with the affection they evinced; yet

my pride was so stung, and I felt it so deeply, that with
the greatest anxiety I resolved upon visiting the Pythian
shrine.   I did not disclose my purpose to any one.   I went,
but to my inquiry I received no satisfactory reply.   Yet
Phœbus declared that the fates had foretold that " ills with
my woe were pregnant with horror."   'Twas foretold that
with my mother I was doomed to mix embraces, and produce a race of children to be shunned by mankind ; furthermore, that I was doomed to be the murderer of my own
father.   These things alarmed me, and I fled in a direction
from Corinth, with a view of avoiding such dire events.
On the way, I came to the spot where you have told me
that Laius fell.   I kept my course.   A herald (which I
take to mean here an outrider) met me, followed by a car,
in which exalted high sat one whose description answers to
that marked out by thee as Laius.   The leader rushed at
me and turned me aside.   I, being enraged, struck him;
upon which, as I passed near the car, the chief himself
smote me.   He struck me a second time, when I raised my
staff with great force, under which he sank at once, and
rolled from his chariot.   I slew them all.   Now, if this
prove to be Laius, lives there such another miserable wretch
as I am? for, according to my own decree, no one henceforth may receive me into his house, none dare hold converse with me, and I pollute the bed of him who perished
by my hands; my hands are stained with blood, and I am
most vilely defiled. (Here the poet makes Œdipus call
Polybus his father, which is most inconsistent after the
conviction upon his mind being portrayed that Laius was
his parent.) Now, considering all these things, does not
our judgment lead us to suppose that some demon wrought
these ills upon me? With eager expectation I wait the
arrival of the herdsman you spoke of. Till then the only

hope I have is in his report, in which thou sayest he stated
that Laius fell, slain by ruffians. If he still asserts this, it
could not have been I who slew him, for one cannot be
many; but if he says that the monarch fell by a single
arm, the dreadful deed, with all its guilt, must be mine.
Jocasta, still anxious to buoy her husband up with hope,
says: Be assured he related as I have told you—that it
was by a band of ruffians they fell; it was not I alone who
heard him, but all Thebes listened to his tale; he cannot
now vary his statement; therefore, O King, it cannot
be said that Laius fell by the hand of his son, as was
foretold by the gods—my unhappy child slew him not, but
perished himself before the death of Laius; therefore I do
not regard the assertion of the oracle. Your reasoning,
replies Œdipus, is most consistent; but let me see this
herdsman. I will send for him hastily, says Jocasta, therefore let us retire.

The time drawing close for me to conclude this lecture,
I will explain to you that a messenger arrives at Thebes
from Corinth, and informs Œdipus that Polybus, King of
Corinth, is dead, and that the Corinthians have chosen him
(Œdipus) to be their king. This information gives Jocasta
pleasure, and she still consoles her husband that he need
not now fear the oracle's decree being fulfilled, as it is
impossible he can be the murderer of his own father (she of
course still believing that Œdipus is the son of Polybus).
But the herdsman, whom she has sent for by her husband's
instructions, arrives, and being recognised by the messenger
from Corinth as the man from whom he received the child
on Mount Cithæron, an explanation ensues, which opens
(by their description of facts) the horrors of Œdipus and
Jocasta's position. At first, the truth of the oracle's prognostications appears to Jocasta, from the statements of the

two herdsmen. She then endeavours to urge Œdipus not to seek further information; but he being determined to pursue his inquiries, the whole history is related of what transpired; upon which, Jocasta exclaims :—

> " Oh, by the gods enquire not, if thy life
> " Be dear to thee ! Enough that I am wretched.
> " Yet let my prayers prevail ; this search forbear.
> " I have strong cause : I warn thee for thy peace.
> " Never, oh never may'st thou know thy birth !
> " Alas, ill-fated man ! for by that name
> " Alone, ah me ! can I address thee now,
> " And by none other ever from this hour."

On this, Jocasta rushes from the stage, and destroys herself. Œdipus says :—

> " Is there a wretch like me ? My dreadful fate
> " Is now unveil'd. O light, thy beams no more
> " Let me behold, for I derive my birth
> " From these, to whom my birth I should not owe ;
> " My dearest commerce I have held with those,
> " Whose commerce nature starts at ; I have slain
> " Those, from whose blood the foulest stain I draw.
> " Woe, woe, woe, woe ! O miserable me !
> " Wretch that I am, ah, whither am I borne ?
> " Whose ears do now my cries of anguish reach ?
> " To what are thy decrees, O fortune, changed !
> " Ah me, this cloud of darkness thick'ning round,
> " Hateful, beyond expression, beyond cure,
> " And beyond hope ! Ah me, how keen the sting
> " Of frenzy, and the memory of my ills !
> " This was the work of Phœbus : O my friends,
> " Phœbus accomplish'd all my ills, my woes .
> " With his own hands no man e'er rent his eyes,
> " But I unhappy. Why should I have sight,
> " Since, had I eyes, nought pleasant could I see
> " What now is left me to be seen, or loved,

" Address'd, or heard with pleasure?   O my friends.
" Drive hence, my friends, quick from your country drive
" This pestilent destroyer, most accursed,
" Of mortal men, most hateful to the gods.
" Perish the man, who in the rural dale
" Unbound my feet, and from destruction snatch'd
" (To me no kindness) saved the helpless child :
" For had I perish'd then, this had not been,
" This misery to myself, and to my friends.
" Hither I had not come this guilty wretch,
" The murderer of my father, nor been call'd
" Husband to those who gave me birth. But now,
" Sprung from unhallow'd parents, giving sons
" To those whose son I am, what woes are mine !
" And if 'midst ills there be an heavier ill,
" With all its weight it falls on Œdipus."

This finishes my fourth lecture, and entirely consummates
the decree of the oracle.   My next will be on the tragedy of
"Œdipus at Colonus," where he is in banishment, led by his
daughter, Antigone, he being blind, having by his own
hands torn out his eyes in despair.   His daughter Ismene
is also introduced in my next lecture, she being with her
father as well as Antigone at his death.

PLAN OF A GREEK THEATRE.

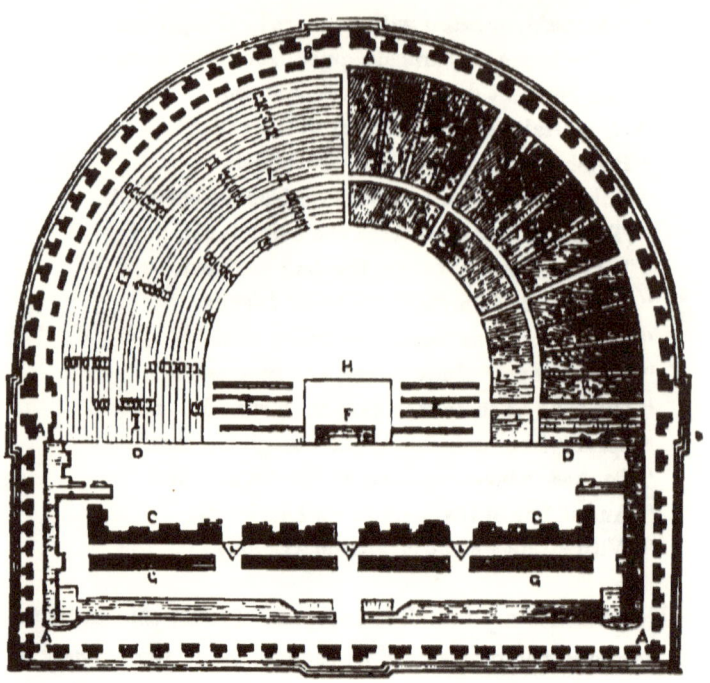

A. Lower Portico.	F. The Thymele.
B. Upper or Third Portico.	G. The Parascenium.
C. The Scenery.	H. The Orchestra.
D. The Proscenium.	I. The Seats.
E. The Hyposcenium.	K. The Staircases.

L. Triangular Machines for the Scenery.

LECTURE V.

My course being to diversify my lectures as much as I possibly can, consistently with the work I have in hand; and as I consider it necessary to afford you as much information as lies in my power, not only of my own knowledge from research, but such as I deem essential to furnish you with from the opinions of other authors more enlightened upon particular points than myself; therefore, in this instance, in which I am about describing to you the construction of the ancient Greek Theatre, I will deviate from my usual course, and, instead of offering you my own judgment upon the point, I will give you Franklin's description as I read it, appended to his edition of Æschylus's works.

I have two reasons why I determine upon this course; the first being that I am desirous not to lay myself open to a charge of plagiarism, and the other is that I believe it to be out of the power of any one living to afford a more accurate description than the author I have just named to you has so ably written. By adopting this course I afford you the best information upon record, without assuming to myself the credit of writing the article. I could not do it more accurately than he has, therefore let the credit add one more point to his fame. I am but a young author myself, and up to this point all I have written is my own; besides which, I have plenty more in store to supply you with, without committing piracy upon others' works. Yet I have reason to know that this has been done by some people to a considerable extent, for I have come across whole passages taken from some authors and inserted in new books, verbatim from the originals, and sent out to the world as new matter, without even a sentence altered. This I consider a bold invasion of honest rights; and rather than resort to such meanness myself, I'll stop short in the middle of my work, or openly avow the original author of such passages, sentences, or chapters I may deem essential to quote. Of course, by thus expressing my determination to you, I do not mean that I gain no other knowledge from previous authors, for how else could I get the ground-work of the subjects I am dilating upon. What I mean is simply this, I will not put forth to the world actual matter produced by other hands and call it my own,—no ; rather let one in a hundred say, ah, I knew this before, for I have read it in Franklin's works. I say one in a hundred, because I think I am considerably within compass, that not more than this proportion (if so much) of the public are acquainted with the subject I have taken in hand, and my object is to induce as many of the large majority as I possibly can to refer to old works I quote, by giving them a light and an amusing index to what I treat upon.

I know for certain that thousands of people never take an ancient book in hand to read, for the reason that they consider the matter therein contained too dry for their patience; and so they remain in ignorance altogether upon the point. Now, if I can induce some into a taste for ancient literature, by giving them light readings to begin with, who knows but I may myself shortly receive benefits from their more enlarged ideas upon the very subjects I introduce to them; there being yet abundant literary food as well as all other good things remaining in the " horn of plenty."

Let me now read to you a few lines I have recently culled therefrom :—

Ye hills on Hesperian Horn,
  Ye tract of Nysas land,
Where fair Amalthea was born,
  Where Hammon sought her hand.
He was the King of Lybia,
  And she a maiden fair ;
O never was in Lybia
  Found a more loving pair.
She fed him with the milk of goats,
  And for her kindly care,
We learn (at least, so hist'ry quotes,)
  In Heav'n he placed her there—
A constellation ever bright,
  He made her for her pains—
Where now she shines on starry nights,
  To light our roads and lanes.
Her Father was Melissus named,
  The King of Crete was he,
For bounty was Amalthea fam'd,
  A constellation she.
'Twas by her light god Bacchus found,
  When on wild Afric's plain,
As stretch'd with thirst upon the ground,
  No water could he gain.
Amalthea now guided him,
  O'er hills and o'er mountains,
Until he found, full to the brim,
  Crystal flowing fountains.
'Twas here the god allay'd his thirst,
  He drank the fountain empty,
This was the place I named at first,
  Call'd the Horn of plenty.

"The Ancient Theatre, in its highest state of perfection, was a most noble and magnificent structure, built with the most solid and durable materials, and capable, we are told, of holding thirty thousand spectators. To give my readers a proper idea of its form, I shall divide it into three principal departments; one for the actors, which they called the scene; another for the spectators, under the general denomination of the theatre; and a third, called the orchestra, allotted to the music, mimes, and dancers. To determine the situation of these three parts, and consequently the disposition of the whole, it is necessary to observe that the plan (here annexed) consists on one side of two semicircles, drawn from the same centre, but of different diameters; and on the other, of a square of the same length, but less by one half; the space between the two semicircles was allotted for the spectators; the square at the end, to the actors; and the intervening area in the middle, to the orchestra. Thus we see, the theatre was circular on one side, and square on the other. Round the whole were ranges of porticos (see letters A and B), more or less, according to the number of stories, the most magnificent theatres always having three, one raised above another. To these porticos, which might properly be said to form the body of the edifice, the women were admitted, being the only places covered from rain and heat; the rest were entirely open above, and all the representations in the daytime.

"The seats for the spectators (letter I) extended from the upper] portico down quite to the orchestra (letter H), differing in their width and number with the size of the theatre, and were always so formed, that a line drawn from the top to the bottom would touch the extremities of every one of them. Between each story was a wide passage leading to the seats, every one of which, for the better

accommodation of the audience, was at such a distance from
the seat placed over it, that the feet of the persons above
could not touch those who were below. The magistrates
were separated from the populace by a place appropriated
to them called Βελευτιχος; the Εφηθιχος, or seat of the
youths, was assigned to the young men of quality and distinction. There were also some προεδριαι, or first seats,
allotted to persons of extraordinary merit, where all those
were placed who had distinguished themselves by any signal
services to the commonwealth ; such in process of time became hereditary, and were appointed for particular families ;
all these were very near to, or sometimes in the orchestra,
and as close as the structure of the theatre would admit to
the scene, or place of representation.

"The orchestra, being between the two parts of the building, one of which was circular and the other square, partook
of the shape of both, varying in its size according to that of
the theatre, though its width was always double its length,
and that width always the semi-diameter of the whole edifice. To this they entered by passages under the seats of
the spectators, the whole being entirely on a level with the
ground ; this led also to the staircases (letter K), by which
they ascended to the different stories of the theatre, some
leading to the seats, others to the portico—of course turned
different ways, but all equally wide, disengaged from each
other, and so commodious as to give sufficient room for the
spectators to go in and out, without the least crowding or
inconvenience.

" Between the orchestra and the stage was the υποσχηνιον,
hyposcenium (letter E), so called because it was close to
the scene, or place of representation ; here, it is most probable, were placed the instruments that accompanied the
actors throughout the drama.

" Beyond this was the large and vacant space called προ-σκηνιον, proscenium, or λογειον (Letter D), representing the scene of action, which was always some public place, as a road, a grove, a court-yard, adjoining to some temple or palace. The length and breadth of this area or stage varied according to the size of the theatre, but was always of the same height, and in the Greek theatre never more or less than ten feet.

" At the extremity of the whole building was the παρα-σκηνιον, post-scenium (Letter I), that place behind the scenes where the actors dressed themselves, and prepared the habits, scenes, machines, and everything necessary to the representation. At the back of the stage (Letter L) were the triangular machines for the scenery, called by the Greeks περιακτοι, which as they turned on their own axis, might be shifted on any occasion, and exhibited three different views or changes of scenes; these were not made use of in tragedy, which required but one scene throughout, but most probably at the end of it, to prepare the exhibition of the comedy or mime, which in the ancient theatre frequently succeeded each other, perhaps two or three times on the same day.

" Among the many peculiarities of the Greek theatre, with regard to its construction, there is not perhaps anything so remarkable, and which we can so difficultly form any idea of, as the echæa, or brazen vessels, which, according to Vitruvius, were made use of by the Greeks, to render the articulation distinct, and give a more extensive power to the voice, an expedient doubtless extremely necessary in so large a theatre; for this purpose, we are told, that they had recourse to several round concave plates of brass, placed under the seats of the spectators, so disposed and contrived by the most exact geometrical and harmonic proportions as to reverberate the voice, and carry the words of the actor to the farthest part of the building. The manner in which this was performed is, I must confess, to me utterly incomprehensible. Certain it is that no idea can be formed of it without a thorough knowledge of ancient music, and ancient architecture. I shall not, therefore, trouble my readers with an explication of what few, I believe, would be able to comprehend; but, if any of them are desirous of a more intimate acquaintance with these brazen echoes, I must refer them to the sixth book of the learned Vitruvius, and Monsieur Burette's 'Treatise on Ancient Music.'"

To carry out the prediction of the oracle, Œdipus is banished from Thebes to Colonus, which now brings me to Sophocles' tragedy of

ŒDIPUS AT COLONUS.

Œdipus not only acquiesces in his banishment, but urges it himself. The two Scenes concluding the tragedy of "Œdipus, King of Thebes," I have omitted introducing in my previous lecture, because I could not refer to them without loss of time, and they are of little importance. I will therefore now just allude to them, to explain to you the context, and then proceed with him in banishment; the action of this play lies at Colonus.

The herdsman, into whose hands Œdipus was placed when an infant, and by him given to the shepherd of Corinth, is brought in. But first let me tell you that there is a slight disparity at this particular juncture. The history states that the child was hung up to the bough of a tree by his heels, and found by a shepherd of Polybus, King of Corinth; and, although the writings of Sophocles confirm this statement in some parts, the poet makes it appear elsewhere that the man into whose hands the infant was entrusted consigned him to the other shepherd. The

I

only way we can reconcile this difference is by supposing that the one man came up at the moment when the other was in the act of suspending the infant, after having bored the holes through its heels; or he must have stood by, watching it after he had hung it up, until the man of Corinth came and found it. The latter seems the most probable conclusion to arrive at.

One of the scenes I allude to is between the two herdsmen and the King. By the two men's statements corroborating, Œdipus is convinced beyond all doubt that he himself was the infant. The other scene is between Œdipus and Creon. The former acknowledges indirectly that his suspicions of infidelity on Creon's part are without foundation; and the latter shows no resentment, but commiserates with Œdipus in his distresses. This confirms my former remark, that the character of Œdipus exhibits meanness in urging the charge against Creon and Tiresias upon mere suspicion. I would willingly have read these two scenes to you; but having devoted nearly two lectures to the one tragedy, and having pledged myself that I would not run any play into a third, I could not consistently introduce them.

We must now suppose that Œdipus is at Colonus in banishment. He is here represented as being old, blind, and in poverty, led by his daughter Antigone, whose amiability of disposition induces her to abide by her afflicted parent to the last. Ismene is also introduced; but she does not appear to be quite so constant in her attentions as her sister, the noble-souled Antigone. We must not, however, accuse her of unkindness, or undutifulness; for she does not appear to be so strong-minded as Antigone; therefore, although it is probable her devotion to her parent is meant to be equally as intense, her resolutions are not so firm. This is apparent also in Sophocles' tragedy of "Antigone," in which Antigone resolves to bury the body of her brother Polynices, in face of the threatened death that awaits her, but Ismene has not the courage to aid her sister.

There is one more point I wish to comment upon before I read to you the opening speech of Œdipus. I think the poet has gone to too great an extreme in representing the great King of Thebes begging

" A slender pittance,"

merely for a day's sustenance. His fate was quite hard enough in being doomed the victim of the oracle, without adding this extreme penury to sum up the whole to so intolerable a climax. The characters represented in this tragedy are as follow:—Œdipus, Creon, Polynices, Antigone, Ismene, Theseus King of Athens, a Coloniate, and the Chorus, which consists of the magistrates. The scene represents the blind King of Thebes in his wanderings, led by his daughter Antigone. Œdipus says:—

" Tell me, thou daughter of a blind old man,
" Antigone, to what land are we come,
" Or to what city ? Who th' inhabitants ?
" Who with a slender pittance will relieve,
" E'en for the day, the wandering Œdipus ?
" I ask indeed but little ; and receive
" Less than that little ; yet for me e'en that
" Suffices my afflictions, the long course
" Of years so pass'd, and fortitude of soul
" Teach me with cheerfulness to bear my ills.
" But, O my daughter, some one if thou seest
" Or in the sacred groves, or on the seats

" Not hallow'd, lead me thither, place me there,
" That in what land we are we may enquire ;
" For of the natives, strangers as we are,
" We come to learn, and as instructed act."

Antigone answers him: My woe-enduring father, I see
the towers of some strongly fortified city rising in the distance. The spot we are now on seems to me to be sacred,
for here are laurels, vines, and olive-branches enwoven, and
amongst them I hear the nightingale's sweet notes. Rest you
here awhile, my father, on this rough unhewn stone, for you
must be weary. I know well we are upon Athenian ground,
but I am not acquainted with this particular spot. Go thou
in here and rest whilst I inquire. I need not go from you
for this purpose, for here comes a man. Now, my father,
he is here, close at hand; speak what thou hast to say, and
he will hear you.

" *Enter* COLONIATE.

. " ŒDIPUS.

" Stranger, I hear from her who sees for me
" And for her self, that thou in happy hour
" Art come to teach us what we wish to know.

" COLONIATE.

" Ere thou speak more, come from that seat ; the place
" That holds thee now, is hallow'd from thy tread. ·
" Nor touch, nor habitation dares profane
" That place ; for there the dreadful goddesses,
" Daughters of Earth and Night, have their abode.
" This people call them the Eumenides,
" The all-beholding pow'rs : in other realms
" By other honour'd names they are revered.

" ŒDIPUS.

" Their supplicant propitious may these pow'rs
" Receive ; that never from their seat here fix'd
" I may henceforth depart !
" It is the sign which ratifies my fate.
" Now by the gods disdain not to inform
" E'en such a wanderer what I wish to ask.
" What is this place, which now our feet hath reach'd ?

" COLONIATE.

" Whate'er I know, attend, and thou shalt hear.
" Sacred is all this place, for Neptune here
" Is lord revered ; and he, who bears the fire,
" Prometheus the Titanian : but the ground
" Beneath thy feet is call'd the brazen way,
" Which forms the firm base of th' Athenian tow'rs.
" The fields adjoining glory in their Chief,
" Colonus the Equestrian ; and from him
" All bear their common name.   I tell thee things,
" O stranger, not by fame alone renown'd,
" But by consent of ages honour'd more.
                              " This place
" Is govern'd by the king, whose royal seat
" Is in the city.
                    " The noble Theseus, son
" Of Ægeus late our king.
" Stranger, I would not thou shou'dst err : but since
" Noble is thy appearance, save the wrongs
" Of fortune, where I saw thee first, remain,
" Till I seek those who have their dwelling here,
" Not in the city, and relate these things.
" For they will judge, if here thou may'st remain,
" Or from this place behoves thee to depart."

The character designated the Coloniate means an inhabitant of Colonus.   When Œdipus first addresses him,
he stops him short, and says, Ere I enter into any con-

versation with you, come from that place, for it is hallowed
from the touch of any human being; not even the inhabitants of this country dare profane it, for it is the shrine of
the dreadful goddesses of Earth and Night; here they are
known by the name of the Eumenides, the powers that see
everything; in other countries they are known by different
names, equally honoured and revered.   Œdipus replies:—
Then may these propitious powers receive my supplications,
so that I may never have occasion to depart from the seat I
am now in, for it is the very sign that ratifies my fate; therefore I charge thee by the faith you put in the gods, do not
disdain to inform me, as I am a wanderer, what I ask. What
country is this which now we have reached? The Coloniate
says: What I know I will tell thee. This place is sacred to
Neptune and to Prometheus, for they are revered here. The
ground beneath this spot is called the brazen way, it is the
foundation of our city. In the fields adjoining we hold our
sacred festive rites to Colonus, the equestrian; and from
him this city bears its name. What I am telling thee, stranger,
is not a mere report, but a fact admitted by consent of all
people, of all ages, therefore honoured the more; it is presided over by a king, the noble Theseus, who holds his royal
establishment within the city. I am anxious thou should'st
not err, as I see by your appearance you are of noble birth;
therefore, remain where you are until I seek the opinions of
those dwelling outside the gates of the city, whether you
may stay or depart.

The Coloniate leaves, and shortly reappears with the
chorus, who, addressing Œdipus, tells him that he is on
hallowed ground, and that he must come off at once. They
inquire of him, who he is, and when they obtain his reply,
they desire him to quit the country. Through the pleadings
of Œdipus, however, joined by those of Antigone, the magis-

trates yield them hospitality, telling Œdipus that King Theseus will shortly arrive. The man to whom he first spoke having gone with speed to the palace, they are certain of this, as there has been much talk recently in Athens of Œdipus; therefore, they make sure that Theseus will soon attend to see him. Antigone now announces to her father, that she sees a woman advancing on a fleet courser of the Sicilian breed; that her head is shaded from the sun by a broad Thessalian bonnet. Then, expressing doubts, she hesitates; but, on the nearer approach of the horsewoman, she exclaims, " 'Tis she, 'tis she herself: Her eyes look cheerfully on me," which "assures me it is she; It is my dear Ismene, and none else." O! my father, I see thy daughter, thou shalt soon hear her voice, by which thou shalt learn that she has come to thee.

" *Enter* Ismene.

" Ismene.

" My father, and my sister, with what joy
" Do I once more address you! I with pain
" Have found you, and with pain I look on you.

Œdipus.

" My child, embrace me.
" Why art thou here ?"

She replies—I am here

" Through care of thee."

I have come hither with only one attendant, and the tidings I bring are of weighty import. I have suffered much in seeking thy place of abode; but I will forbear relating my own hardships, not wishing to add new griefs to your suffer-

ings by recounting my own. I come to tell thee of the
present ills existing between your two unfortunate sons. At
first they consulted whether they should yield the throne
to Creon, and so not pollute the city with the curse that
attends our family reigning there; but soon a contest sprang
up between them, as to which should seize the sceptre,
and the regal power. Polynices, the elder, has by force
been driven from his country, and rumour informs us that
he is in exile at Argos, there forming new alliances, and
arming his friends, who are organising a confederation to
avenge his cause, and they have determined to subdue the
realms of Thebes. These are not mere rumours I am relating,
but dreadful facts. Alas, I know not, my father, when the
gods will take pity on thy distresses, yet from recent oracles
I have some hope, for they have pronounced a decree that—

" The time will come, when thee
" Living and dead the Thebans shall require
" For their protection.
                              " It is declared
" Their pow'r depends on thee.
                       " The gods, whose pow'r
" Once sunk thee, raise thee now.
" Yet be assured that Creon for this cause
" Will come to thee : expect him here with speed."

They anticipate protection to Thebes, through your presence ;
they contemplate getting you into their power, and to locate
you somewhere near to the Theban State, but not to permit
you to pass its border. Œdipus asks her what succour
they anticipate by keeping him near their gates, and she
answers that the oracle has decreed that, if his tomb be
raised elsewhere, it will be fatal to Thebes. This, I am informed " By men who brought responses from the Delphic
shrine ;" both your sons heard it, and both of them know

it well. To me, 'twas grievous to hear, but I could not prevent it.

" ŒDIPUS.

" Could they hear this, vile wretches, and contemn
" Their father, whilst they grasp at regal pow'r ?
" The flames of this contention may the gods
" Never extinguish ; but to me be giv'n
" The issue of this fated war, which now
" They wage, with mutual fury lifting each
" The hostile spear against the other's breast :
" So should not he, the sceptre and the crown
" Who now possesses, hold them long ; nor he,
" Who flying left his country, e'er return ;
" For they their father, with disgrace thrust forth,
" Sustaiu'd not, nor protected ; but by them
" In this ill plight driv'n out I was proclaim'd
" An exile. Thou wilt say, at my request
" This, as a grace, the state then granted. No :
" It was not so : for at the time when grief
" Enflamed my soul to madness, when to die
" Had been most welcome to me, and with stones
" To have been crush'd, then not a man came forth
" To gratify my wish : but when my grief
" Was soften'd by the lenient hand of time,
" And I discern'd that my new ebbing rage
" Had punish'd more than my offence deserved,
" Then, after this long interval, the state
" Drove me by force an outcast from the land ;
" And these my sons, who then had pow'r to aid
" Their father, will'd not to exert that pow'r ;
" But e'en a little word not deign'd, by them
" Compell'd I wander thus, and beg my bread.
" But from these virgins, far as nature gives
" Their sex the pow'r to aid me, I receive
" Food that sustains my life, upon the earth
" Rest without fear, and all the dear supports
" Children can yield a parent. But my sons,
" Of filial piety regardless, grasp

" At sceptres, thrones, and sovereign rule o'er Thebes.
" But me they shall not win to league with them ;
" Nor shall th' imperial pow'r on them devolve
" What may advantage them ; this well I know,
" Hearing the oracles she now relates,
" And pondering the responses which the god
" Of old announced to me. Let them then send
" Creon to seek me here, or in their state
" Who else is potent, me they shall not move.
" If you, O strangers, with these aweful pow'rs
" Residing here, with your protection deign
" To shield me, to your state you will procure
" Much succour, and confusion to my foes."

This is a long passage, and somewhat abstruse. I will therefore explain it to you. When Ismene tells Œdipus of the new prophecy regarding him, and of the dissension between his sons, he says: Could these vile wretches listen to the decree of the oracle, and, in the face of it, condemn their father into banishment, whilst they grasped his regal authority? O! may the gods fan this fiery contention between them, so that I may gain my rights through their disagreements!—This is not a fatherly wish, but we must not lose sight of the provocation he has received, by his sons too readily availing themselves of a pretence to gain the regal power into their own hands. True it is, that Œdipus himself urged his own banishment, to fulfil the oracular prognostication; but this was at the time when he was in a state of great mental affliction, believing that he was existing under the ban of fate, and that nothing but his being driven from his country would save the people from the scourges they were labouring under; but now, having endured vicissitudes and deprivations, the natural desire of self-preservation returns to him. This is induced, in a great measure, by his comparing his daughters' piety

with his sons' undutifulness.   He says : I am glad my sons'
fury is mutual against each other, for it shall wrest the
sceptre and crown from him now possessing them, and prevent the other returning who fled from his country.—We
have here, another burst of vindictiveness displayed in the
character of Œdipus ; and his desire to return to his former
state, disregarding the sequel of the oracle, goes far to
show that, if such a people did really exist, they were
guided more by priestcraft than anything else, and soon
as these influences worked to their disadvantage, their natural
desires returned to throw them off. Men of this class when
in despair sometimes seek to become martyrs, but, when
they return to their sober reflections, they long for their
former state, and will mostly avail themselves of a tangible
plea to regain it.   Œdipus says : I am their father, and they
have thrust me forth in disgrace, neither affording me protection, nor the means of sustenance. My being driven out an
exile may perhaps be said to have been at my own request,
and that the state countenanced it as a grace to me. No, it
was not so, for at that time my soul was inflamed by grief to
madness, and it would have been a relief to die. I asked for
death at my country's hands, but this they did not grant
me ; and now time has afforded reflection, I see that my
punishment has been greater than my offence deserved.
When the state thrust me forth, my sons had the power to
save me, but they had not the will to do so ; therefore, am I
compelled to wander thus, and beg my bread. Now, they
themselves have brought the state into disorder, and gaining
information from the new oracle that has been propounded
respecting myself, they each seek me in league with them,
which I will refuse ; they may send Creon here, but they
shall not move me.   If the Athenian people here will but

deign to shield and protect me, I will remain where I am, and be a succour to Athens for their hospitality.

" *Enter* THESEUS.

" THESEUS.

" Hearing reported of in days long past
" The bloody deed that quench'd thy orbs of sight,
" I know thee, son of Laius ;"

I am confirmed that thou art he, by the information I have just received.

" Unhappy Œdipus, I pity thee."

I now ask you what request of me you have to make, that you have come hither; what can I do to serve thee and this hapless virgin attending thy steps, let me know—

                                    " Be it a task
" Of toil or danger, fear not a repulse ;"

for I have learnt by experience how to study a stranger's woes. I have myself experienced many toils and dangers in a foreign land, I therefore will not turn from thee, but I will yield thee protection; for by your misfortunes, it is an example to me, to know we cannot tell what may occur to-morrow, or what our own fate may be.

" ŒDIPUS.

" Thy generous spirit, Theseus, in few words
" Shines forth ; behoves me then a brief reply :
" For who I am, and of what father born,
" And from what country come, thou hast declared.
" Nothing for me remains then, but to show
" What at thy friendly hands I would request.

" I come this wretched body to bestow
" On thee ; a gift not to the sight indeed
" Alluring, but th' advantages it brings
" Are of more value than a beauteous form.
" Time, not the present hour will show thee this,
" When I am dead, and thou shalt bury me.
" O Theseus, I have suffer'd dreadful ills
" Added to illa."

O my friend! all (excepting the gods) by the powerful hand of time crumbles to dust ; e'en the earth as the body wastes away, and what is now grateful at some future period becomes detested, then delights again. So may it be that, although Thebes and Athens are now at peace, times may change, and some trivial cause may occasion discord. Then if

" Phœbus, son of Jove, declares the truth,"

my corse, when cold and beneath the earth,

" Shall drink their warm blood ;"

but in that it behoves me to be silent ; therefore permit me to proceed in this. Keep you but faith with me, and you shall never have to say that it was useless your affording me a habitation within your realm. Theseus replies : 'Tis but common hospitality towards those who come as suppliants within our power to make recompense by courtesy, which I will never refuse ; they shall always dwell secure in this land if they wish to abide here.—Then turning to his people, Theseus adds : I charge thee guard this man. Now, Œdipus, if it be your will to go with me, with thee my will assents. Now how do you decide ; will you accompany me into Athens ? Œdipus replies : I would

were it fated that I should do so, but it is decreed that I
remain here—

> " Here will I vanquish those, who drove me forth
> " An outcast,"

if you but be firm in faith, and prove true to your promise.
Theseus says :—

> " Confide in me ; I never will betray thee.
> " My word is pledged : there is no surer tie
> " I know that no man to my will opposed
> " Shall force thee hence.   I know that many threats,
> " Many vain words in rage are vaunted loud ;
> " But when cool reason reassumes the sway,
> " These manaces sink forceless.   So, though now
> " Perchance these threaten high, they soon shall find
> " Th' attempt to drag thee hence is but to dare
> " A wide rough sea, on which their bark will sink.
> " Nay, I exhort thee, e'en without my care
> " Be confident, if Phœbus be thy guide.
> " Though I may hence be distant, yet I know
> " My name shall guard thee from th' assault of ill."

This means, I am well sure no one here will oppose my
will by forcing thee hence, therefore, rest assured, you are
perfectly safe.   These enemies of thine may threaten you by
loud vaunting rage, but you need not fear, for when they
cool a little they will find they have no power here to act,
and their threats will sink valueless.   Be satisfied, I implore
you, and have confidence, for you are safe with my people,
though I be not present.   The knowledge that I am your
guardian will protect you throughout the realm.*

---

* Oh ! never spurn the weaker side,
  If fault lies with the stronger ;

In the scene following are introduced Creon, Œdipus, Antigone, and the chorus representing, as usual, the Athenians.

" CREON.

" Illustrious habitants of this fair land,
" I see, your eyes declare it, that surprise
" Hath on my coming seized you, mix'd with fear.
" But fear me not ; nor let your speech be harsh.
" No deed of outrage wish I to attempt,
" For I am old, and know that to a state,
" Potent as any Greece can boast I come.
" But I am sent on this man to prevail,
" Thus worn with age, t' attend me to the realms
" Of Thebes : this charge received I not from one,
" But all the citizens ; since most to me,
" Through near affinity of blood, belongs
" To mourn and pity his calamities.
" Then hear me, thou afflicted Œdipus,
" Return with me ; for all the sons of Thebes
" Recall thee, with just cause, I more than all,
" As more than others (else of all mankind
" I were the vilest) for thy sufferings griev'd,
" Beholding thee thus old oppress'd with woes,
" Ever 'mongst strangers wandering, destitute
" Of food, thy steps by one attendant led :
" Her, hapless virgin, never had I thought
" To see thus fall'n, sunk to this wretched state,
" To thee for ever minist'ring, for thee
" Begging the scanty meal, and at this age

Oppression may succeed at first,
  But justice triumphs longer :
For truth is truth, and right is right,
  Though wrong may rule a season ;
Whate'er opinion ye may hold,
  It must give way to reason.

J. E. CARPENTER.

" Of nuptual rites bereft, and still exposed
" To ruffian violence. With base reproach
" Have I then wrong'd my self, and thee, and all
" Our race ? Am I that wretch ? It is not so ;
" And things well known in vain would we conceal.
" Be then advised : by thy paternal gods
" I now conjure thee, Œdipus comply
" At my persuasion, willingly return
" To Thebes thy native city, and thy house,
" Seat of thy fathers ; to these regions bid
" A 'friendly farewell, they deserve it of thee :
" But justice to thy country, since thy youth
" Was nurtured there, an higher reverence claims.

" ŒDIPUS.

" O thou audacious in whate'er is base,
" And prompt from all just words to draw a train
" Of deep insidious ills, why this attempt ?
" Why seek again t' ensnare me, where I most
" Should grieve to be ensnared ? In days long past
" When with domestic miseries o'erwhelm'd
" My sickening soul in exile would have joy'd,
" Then to my wish this grace didst thou deny.
" But when my soul was glutted with its grief,
" And in my house it had been sweet to rest,
" For ebbing then I found my former rage,
" Then didst thou drive me forth an outcast thence,
" Nor was this near affinity of blood
" Dear to thee. Now again, when thou didst see
" This state benevolent to me, and all
" Its race, dost thou assay to drag me hence,
" Filing thy tongue to smooth thy harsh attempt.
" Why this delight to show thy courtesy
" When most it is unwelcome ? If to thee,
" What thy wants crave requesting to obtain,
" One should give nothing, nor e'en show a will
" To grant thee a supply ; but, when thy soul
" Enjoys its wish e'en to the full, would give,

" When the slow favour all its grace hath lost,
" Wou'dst thou this worthless pleasure wish to gain ?
" Such is to me thy offer'd grace, in words
" Pretending good, but baleful in effect.
" Nay, I will tell it these, that I may show
" Thy baseness : hence to draw me thou art come,
" Not with leave granted to possess my house,
" But to be stabled on your confines ; thus
" Your country should be guarded from the ills
" Fear'd from these realms. This never shall be thine ;
" But thine shall be those ills ; for in that land
" My vengeful spirit always shall reside.
" Nor of my kingdom shall my sons share more,
" Than to die in it. Seem I not to know
" Better than thou the destined state of Thebes ?
" Much better, as by more unerring guides
" Instructed, Phœbus and his father Jove.
" Yet hither hast thou brought that treacherous front
" Harden'd 'gainst shame : but that fine-filed tongue
" Shall work thee woe, not safety ; be assured
" With me thou never shalt prevail : begone,
" Let us live here ; not ill we here should live
" E'en as we are, could we delight in life.
" Greatly shall I rejoice if neither me,
" Nor these here present thou hast pow'r to move.
" Pow'rful art thou in speech ; but I ne'er knew
" A man revering justice, who could smooth
" His tongue to gloze all arguments alike.
" Though brief, yet well adapted are those words.
" Begone, for I will speak for these ; nor take
" Thy station watching where behoves me dwell.

" CREON.

" From these apart thou shalt have cause of grief.
" Of thy two daughters one I lately seized,
" And sent away : this soon I hence will lead.
" Thou soon shalt have more cause to sigh.
" Pass a few moments this too I will seize.

"" Now is your time ; seize her, and lead her hence,
"" If wayward she refuse to go, by force.
                    "" Him I shall not touch :
"" The virgin's mine. I lead away mine own.
"" On these two props no more shalt thou support
"" Thy wandering steps ; but since thou wilt o'ercome
"" Thy country and thy friends, at whose command
"" I, though their Sovereign, do this ; have thy will,
"" O'ercome : yet thou wilt know in time, I ween,
"" That neither what thou now hast done avails
"" To thee for good, nor what thou didst of old ;
"" The counsils of thy friends thy pride disdain'd,
"" And rage indulged hath always work'd thee woes.
"" I charge thee be thou silent.

                "" ŒDIPUS.

                    "" Silent ! no ;
"" May not these aweful pow'rs restrain my tongue
"" From one curse more, this curse on thee, vile man,
"" Who from my sightless steps hast drawn by force
"" My tender guide ! For this may yon bright god,
"" Th' all-seeing sun, give thee and all thy race
"" To close your lives with an old age like mine !
"" Ah me, unhappy me !""

To explain this long scene to you which I have just read
Creon enters, and addressing the Athenians, he says :—

"" Illustrious inhabitants of this fair land,"

I see by your looks you are alarmed and surprised ; but do
not fear me, nor let us use harsh words. I mean no outrage,
as I know this to be as potent a state as any in Greece. I
am sent here merely to prevail upon this man to return to
Thebes ; this mission I receive not from one only but from
all the Theban people ; they have sent me because I am
nearly allied to him by relationship, therefore my duty is to

mourn with him, and pity his calamities. Hear me, Œdipus, return with me to Thebes, for all thy people recall thee, and I most. We grieve for thy sufferings, thy woes, and destitute state, also for the hapless virgin attendant on thee. All things that have passed we wish to conceal; let bygones be bygones. Be advised, Œdipus, return with me willingly to thy house, the seat of thy fathers; bid these friends farewell, they deserve thy thanks, but thy country claims thy reverence.—Œdipus (having been informed by his daughter Ismene of the true purport of Creon's visit) replies to him: Audacious, base man—plausible in words but deceitful in purpose art thou—your attempts to ensnare me will fail. When, in former times, my griefs demanded your sympathy you gave it not, but drove me forth an outcast, and now you see the people of this state treating me benevolently, you wish to drag me from amongst them. The false courtesy of thy deceptive tongue to me is most unwelcome; your words are apparently full of grace, but your intentions are hateful. I know your purpose; you wish to draw me hence, not to put me in possession of my house, but to keep me a prisoner in the suburbs of the Theban state; this is your design, to guard your country from the ills that await her through my absence; but, as you have banished me, you shall endure the consequences,—my vengeance shall rest with you, and my sons shall receive no more benefit from my kingdom than to die in it. You see I know the destiny that awaits you all much better than you thought I did. I receive my instructions from Jove and Phœbus; by them I am guided. Your shameless treachery is apparent; but your deceptive tongue shall work your own sorrows. With me you shall never prevail, therefore begone, and leave us to live here in peace, and I shall rejoice to know that here you have no power over me, nor influence with these people. I know well the plausibility of your speech; but your arguments are not honest; begone, remain not here a spy over me.—Creon, seeing that Œdipus is aware of his base intentions, turns to brow-beat him, tells him that he has one of his daughters in his power, and that he will shortly have the other. Then, beckoning to his attendants, he exclaims:

"Now is your time; seize her, and lead her hence;"

if she prove wayward take her by force. You shall not have these two maidens with you any longer to support you, since you will not support your country. I am their sovereign, and I do this to overcome your present determination. You shall know in time that what you are doing will avail you not, and your indulging in rage will only bring you more woes. Now be silent.—Œdipus replies: I will not be silent, if I am not restrained by the powers here; and I will hurl one more curse upon thee, thou vile man, for dragging from me my tender guides. O! may the bright all-seeing gods inflict on thee and all thy race the curse to end your lives in afflictions like mine!*—During this contest between Œdipus and Creon, the Athenian people endeavour to restrain Creon's lawless acts, but failing in their efforts, they call their country to arms; upon which, Theseus enters and says:

"What means this cry? What outrage raised your fears,
"That at the alter while the victim bleeds
"An offering to the monarch of the sea,
"The god o'er this Colonus who presides,
"You call me? Speak, inform me what the cause
"That urged me hither with uneasy speed?

* By this it would seem that the law affording hospitality to belligerents or rebels takes its origin from a much earlier period than has been generally comprehended.

" ŒDIPUS.

" My generous friend, for well I know thy voice,
" Dreadful my recent sufferings from this man.
" This Creon, whom thou seest, has forced from me •
" My daughters, the sole comfort of my woes."

Theseus says : What is the meaning of this outrage, to dis-
turb me and my people from their devotions, who were in
the act of offering our sacrifices to the god who presides
over this state ?   Tell me what has compelled my presence so
inconveniently ?   Œdipus replies : I know thy voice, thou
generous friend.   The sufferings I have recently endured at
this man's hands are most dreadful ; he has forced my
daughters from me, who were my sole comfort in my afflictions.   Go swiftly, one of you, says Theseus, bear this my
charge to all the people assembled at the altars, and tell
them to leave their sacred rites ; and call out my troops, both
horse and foot ; let them invest all the passes that unite the
roads, e'er these virgins are conducted through them. Were
I to shrink from this my duty, I would deserve to be scorned
after pledging my faith.   " Go, as I command, and use thy
utmost speed."   As regards Creon, were I to yield to
anger, as his actions prompt, I ought not to let him go un-
punished ; but I will treat him in conformity with the laws
that govern his own state—he shall not leave this country
until he causes the virgins (who were placed under my protection) to be brought back to my charge. You, Creon, have
done that which casts dishonour on the state which I
govern, and which you have entered.   Here we revere the
voice of justice, and no deed like this shall violate my laws.
You have infringed upon their sacred rights, by depriving
me of my prerogative, in using force, by bearing hence those
who had placed themselves under my protection.   You have
done this, probably imagining that I was not prepared for

your onslaught; thinking I would submit through fear, and without spirit. According to the laws of your own state, you are not justified in this wanton proceeding. We admire not these unjust actions, nor will we sanction them. The state shall not submit to be plundered, by permitting those suppliants of the gods to be seized by force, who have placed themselves under our rule. I would not act so, however just my claims might be, without first gaining the sanction of the sovereign who governed the land; knowing how unlawful it is for a stranger to use force, or to demean himself by such disgraceful proceedings. It seems that thy age has not confirmed wisdom in thee.

" But I tell thee now, what I before declared,"

lose no time, but send quickly, and let the virgins be brought safely back. If you do not, I decree that you shall be detained here against your will; I tell you this plainly, for such is my determination. I am resolved, in accordance with the words I have expressed. Creon replies: I have not acted as I have, disdaining your power and judgment; but, believing by former assurance you would not detain here any one of my race, without my consent—this is my excuse. Besides which, this man is unholy, his hands are stained with his father's blood, he has polluted his race by wedding his own mother: I felt sure your wisdom and honour would not permit such an outcast to reside amongst you. Confiding in this belief, I have attempted to seize the wretch. I would not have persevered in pursuing this course, had he not imprecated curses on me, and my race. You now have my statement; act as your judgment inclines you. I am here, comparatively alone; my attendants are few, but my cause is just; therefore, as you treat me in the matter, so will I reciprocate.

Œdipus interposes thus:

" Unblushing insolence !"

Do you call these reproaches on my head, or your own? You know the crimes you are referring to were committed by me unconsciously. The gods were pleased to inflict the punishments, to avenge some offence committed against them by my ancestors. You know you are not justified in charging the sins you have alluded to, as premeditated acts on my part; if the fates decreed that my father should be slain by his son, I could not subvert them, and I became an unconscious instrument in their hands; and it is not just to revile me for these deeds—it was my fate, and was foretold before my birth. When I slew my father, it was done in self-defence, and I knew him not—I cannot be blamed for doing what I did unknowingly,—and you ought to blush to allude to my misfortunes with my mother, she being your sister.—After further explanation on the part of Œdipus, Theseus says: We have heard enough of this, for while we stand inactively thus, those who have seized the maidens are hastening with their spoil from these dominions, and we are thereby enduring a wrong done to ourselves; therefore, go you on, lead the way, and guide us to where they are. You must direct us to the place. Your doing so will not alter circumstances, for there are people in pursuit who will swiftly overtake them. Now, lead the way, and learn from me that you may consider yourself my prisoner; for having seized those who had placed themselves under my protection, I seize thee. 'Tis clear to my mind, that you anticipated assistance, or you would not have made this rude attempt, being furnished only with the small force you have commenced with ; this demands my particular attention.   Are my words understood by you, or are they vain like the attempt you have made ?   Creon replies : There is nothing you have said I quarrel with now ; but when I return to Thebes, your words will demand my attention.   Theseus remarks : You may threaten hereafter, but now go on, lead the way.   You, Œdipus, rest quietly here ; be assured I will not be satisfied until I restore your daughters to you.

Here I end my fifth lecture ; my next will finish this subject and carry me into part of Euripides' Tragedy of the "Phœnician Virgins."

LECTURE VI.

WE learn that Sophocles continued writing tragedies until he advanced to extreme old age, and it was considered by his family that he neglected them, applying himself almost wholly to his dramatic compositions. His sons, in consequence, instituted a suit against him in a court of judicature, suggesting that his understanding was impaired, and that he was incapable of managing his estate. An inquiry took place, and Sophocles, defending himself, asked permission to read a play which he had recently finished. It was the manuscript of the tragedy I am about finishing in this lecture—" Œdipus at Colonus." He had it with him in court, and his request being granted, after the recital of it, appealing to the judges, he asked them if they discovered by his writings any symptoms of insanity about him. The result was a decision in favour of his mental soundness. This tradition is related in Melmoth's translation of Tully's " Essay on Old Age."

I left off in my former lecture where Theseus goes in pursuit of the abductors of Œdipus's two daughters, Antigone and Ismene. During his absence, the chorus sings the following verses—but, before I commence them, permit me to read to you a short composition of my own, which I was solicited to write in commemoration of the death of the good Queen Adelaide, wife of William IV., she being the patroness of a charitable institution in which I then took some interest. The subject was given me as being applicable to the principles of the charity in question, and I think not inappropriate to Œdipus's present position. It was set to music by the late talented composer N. J. Sporle, and was the last effort of his pen. It was sung at the London Tavern by Mr. Jolly, of Brunswick-square.

THE PENITENT.

In this sad heart—this heart of mine,
This heart so full of woe,
There is no hope, no peaceful time;
Oh! whither shall I go?
I am a lost and lonely one,
No happiness I know,
My cares are great, I have no home;
Oh! whither shall I go?

My parents dead; my friends all gone,
Ah! sad for me to know
I am forlorn and all alone;
Oh! whither shall I go?
I am forlorn, I am betray'd,
Oh treachery, to know!
Ah! would that I were lowly laid;
But whither should I go?

Yes, yes, there is a haven there,
Tho' life may ebb and flow,
For which my soul I will prepare,
And thither may I go.
Oh! Heaven grant me this I pray,
And teach my heart to know
There is above a judgment day
To which we all must go.

Although I have introduced to you this humble effort of

my earlier days, I do not presume to think it anything
compared to what I am now about reading to you, emanating
from the much more potent author—the Grecian Sophocles.

" CHORUS.

" Were I where the dauntless train
" Swells the battle's brazen roar ;
" On the hallow'd Pythian plain ;
" Or the torch-illumined shore,
" Where for men their holy flame
" O'er the sacred Mysteries wakes,
" And 'mongst Priests of honour'd name
" Where his station Silence takes,
" Wont his golden key to bear
" In his firm tongue-locking hand !
" There the warrior Theseus, there
" Join'd the virgin sisters stand ;
" There they shall soon the conflict share,
" And pour the torrent rage of war.
" Westward haply on the plain,
" Where the white and rocky steep
" Tow'rs o'er Oia's rich domain,
" May th' ensanguin'd battle sweep:
" Where impetuous in their speed,
" Glowing with the flames of war,
" Warriors spur the foaming steed,
" Other warriors roll the car.
" Brave the youths who here reside,
" Brave th' Athenian troops in fight ;
" Shine their reins with martial pride,
" All their trappings glitter bright ;
" These honours in their rich array
" To Pallas all and Neptune pay.
" Is the dreadful work begun ?
" Or does ought their force delay ?
" O let me give the glad presages way
" Soon shall yon bright ætherial sun
" Behold him, vaunting now no more,

" Compell'd th' afflicted virgin to restore,
" Afflicted through her father's woes.
" Each day some deed effected shows,
" The ruling hand of righteous Jove.
" I am the prophet of a prosperous fight.
" Had I the pennons of a dove
" High o'er the clouds to whirl my flight,
" Then should my raptured eyes behold
" The victory my thoughts foretold.
" Thou in heav'n's high throne ador'd,
" Sovereign of the gods above,
" Give strength, O pow'rful all-beholding Jove,
" Give conquest to my country's lord ;
" With glory mark his purple way,
" And make the ambush'd foe an easy prey !
" Pallas, propitious hear my pray'r,
" And show that Athens is thy care !
" Thee, Hunter Phœbus, skill'd to trace
" The sylvan savage in his rapid flight ;
" Thee, whom the pleasures in the chace
" Of the fleet, spotted hind delight,
" Thee I implore, chaste Hunter Maid,
" Aid her brave sons, our country aid !

" *Enter* THESEUS, ANTIGONE, *and* ISMENE.

" ANTIGONE.

" My father, O my father, would some god
" Give thee to see this best of men, who thus
" Hath brought us back to thee !

" ŒDIPUS.

                              " My children here !
" Are you both here, my children ?
" Come near, my children ; and, what ne'er again
" We could e'en hope, support me with your arms.
" O my dear blossoms !
" Ye tender props of my old age !

" What is most dear to me I hold ; and now
" Were I to die whilst you thus near me stand,
" I should not be quite wretched : but support,
" On each side prop me, growing to the trunk
" From which you sprung ; to an afflicted wretch
" Outcast, and late abandon'd, give some rest.
" What hath been done now tell me but in brief,
" A short relation will from you suffice.

" ANTIGONE.

" Theseus is here, who saved us ; it is meet
" Thou learn from him : so shall my words be brief.

" ŒDIPUS.

" My daughters thus beyond my hopes restored,
" Marvel not, generous Theseus, if my words
" Exceed due measure.   Well I know from thee,
" And thee alone, this dear delight, in them
" Which I receive, is giv'n me ; for thy hand,
" And thine alone, preserved them.   May the gods
" On thee and on thy state their blessings pour
" Ample as my warm wishes ; for 'mongst you
" Only of all mankind have I discern'd
" A reverence for the gods, a fix'd regard
" For justice, and a manly love of truth.
" The worth, which I have proved, my words extoll,
" For what I have, I have from thee alone.
" Disdain not then, O king, to stretch thy hand
" That I may touch it, and, with leave obtain'd,
" Kiss thee.   What have I said ?   How then can I,
" Born wretched, wish to touch a man, whom stain
" Of ill hath ne'er approach'd ?   It shall not be :
" Such grace must be refused.   Of all mankind
" Those only, who have suffer'd ills, can feel
" A touch of pity for my ills.   I now
" Bid thee henceforth farewell ; and let thy care,
" Thus far extended to a wretch like me,
" Through what of life is left me, yet extend.

" THESEUS.

" I marvel not that many are thy words
" Through pleasure that thy daughters are restored ;
" Nor that, ere mine, thou joy'dst in their address.
" I have no care ought splendid in my life
" To show in words, but honourable deeds ;
" And let these speak : I pledged to thee my faith ;
" In nothing I deceived thee, but have brought
" These virgins back alive, and from his threats
" Uninjured : how this contest was atchieved
" Why should I vaunt ? in private thou may'st learn
" From them.   To an incident which late
" Occurr'd, as hither I return'd, attend.
" Things of small semblance oft with import high
" Are pregnant : prudence slights no circumstance.
" A man, they say, no habitant of Thebes,
" But to thy blood allied, a suppliant sits
" At Neptune's altar, where the victim slain
" I offer'd when I hasten'd at your cries.

" ŒDIPUS.

" Whence is he ?   In this hallow'd seat why placed !

" THESEUS.

" I know but this, short conference he requests
" With thee, in nothing to molest thee more.

" ŒDIPUS.

" Why this ?   No trivial cause hath placed him there.

" THESEUS.

" With thee he wishes to converse, and asks
" Permission thence in safety to return.
" At Argos is there none to thee allied,
" Who may with ardour wish this grace from thee ?

" ŒDIPUS.

" My honour'd friend, forbear.

" No more entreat———

" What I have heard shows who the suppliant is.

" It is my hated son : of all mankind

" Him with most pain should I endure to hear.

" His voice, O king, is to a father's ear

" Most hateful : urge me not perforce to yield."

Now, ere I proceed any further, let me explain to you what I have been reading. After the few lines of my own, I commence in this lecture with the second intermede ; the characters composing which have already contemplated a war ensuing between the Athenians and the Thebans, through Theseus protecting Œdipus. The meaning of the lines is as follows : If I were one of the soldiers helping to increase the battle's roar on the hallowed Pythian plain, or the torch-illumined shore, from whose light the priests see to go through the sacred mysteries ; amongst them our King Theseus seated takes his place ; by his side shall the virgin sisters stand, and by their presence share in the conflict of war—by their presence they will incite and influence the Athenian army to espouse Œdipus's cause with enthusiasm. " The torch-illumin'd shore " alludes to the Eleusinian rites, in which the goddess Ceres was worshipped for having assisted in the search after Proserpine. The ceremonies took place by torchlight, in which none but the pure and good were permitted to share. The chorus classifies their King Theseus one of this character, concluding he will be present amongst the priests to go through the worship. This part of the tragedy is recited during the absence of Theseus, who has gone with his followers in search of Œdipus's daughters, Antigone and Ismene, to rescue them from Creon. All that transpires through the chorus is consequently mere surmise, of course consistent with the position of affairs, but not related as things having actually occurred—'tis all conjecture. Thus far, I have explained the first part of Strophe. Now, Antistrophe says: The fight may probably take place to the west of where we now are, perhaps on the plains of Marathon, or in the Eleusinian country; or it may occur amongst the tribe of Oia, in the rocky, mountainous district. Our Athenian soldiers are brave in battle, they fight valiantly, and their horses' trappings are ornamented in rich array, in honour of Neptune and Pallas. Respecting Neptune, the compliment is made, because he was supposed to have created that noble animal the horse, and as regards Pallas, it alludes to the richness of the armour the men wore, she being always represented attired in a full suit of mail. Pallas is a man's name, but it applies to Minerva, she having assumed it; a full explanation why she did so I have given in another part of my lectures. Strophe's second recitation means, I here presage that, ere this sun goes down, we shall behold that Creon's vauntings were unavailable, for he shall be compelled to restore the virgins to their afflicted father. I prophecy this act of justice shall fall out through the ruling hand of righteous Jove. The second part of Antistrophe is so clear, that it requires little further explanation than to tell you that "Hunter Phœbus" means Apollo, and the "chaste Huntress Maid" means Diana. I have already prepared a short explanation of the latter, which I will relate to you in due course, and ere I finish, I hope to enlighten you upon the brilliant characteristics of the former.

On his return with Antigone and Ismene, Theseus tells Œdipus that, on his way, as he was passing the altar devoted to Neptune, he beheld a man supplicating there.

He says he is not an inhabitant of Thebes, yet he is connected with Œdipus by consanguinity. I saw him, says Theseus, sitting on the very stone on which you were seated when I first visited you at your request,—in the very place where I made sacrifice to the god in your presence. The man desires a conference with you; and he promises not to molest you. Have you no relatives at Argos likely, through anxiety for your welfare, to seek an interview with you? At first, Œdipus is in doubt who it can be; but, immediately Theseus suggests the possibility of its being some relative from Argos, Œdipus concludes it is his son Polynices. At first he refuses to see him, but, through Antigone's entreaties, at last yields. Here is her pathetic appeal :—

" ANTIGONE.

" Hear me, my father, nor despise my youth.
" Indulge this man, assenting to his wish
" And to the god, in what his soul desires.
" Refuse us not, but let my brother come.
" His words, though ill accorded to thy state,
" Thee from thy stedfast purpose will not draw
    By force : what ill from hearing words can rise ?
" The honourable purpose of the heart
" Is signified by words. Nay, weigh this well,
" Thou art his father : though his deeds to thee
" Be of the vilest, the most impious, right
" Wills not that thou repay him like ill deeds ;
" His own will bring their vengeance. Impious sons
" Have injured other parents, and have raised
" Anger as fierce ; but by th' advice of friends
" This harshness hath been charm'd e'en to assume
" A milder nature. On th' afflicting ills
" Thy soul has suffer'd for thy parents' sake
" Reflect not now ; dismiss them from thy thoughts,
" Adverting only to the dire effects

L

" Of raging anger ; those thou soon may'st know ;
" For violent the proofs of this thou bearest,
" Thy orbs of sight extinguish'd.   Yield thee then ;
" Ill it becomes thee that a just request
" Repeatedly be urged, or that a grace
" Received with grace thou know'st not to repay.

" ŒDIPUS.

" Your painful pleasure thus declared, my child,
" You overcome me : be it as you will.
" Only if hither he must come, my friend,
" Protect me, o'er my life let none have pow'r.

" THESEUS.

" Of this enough : it is not mine to boast.
" Me if the gods protect, be thou assured
" Old man, in my protection thou art safe.

" *Enter* POLYNICES.

" POLYNICES.

" Alas, my sisters, 'midst these various ills
" My own misfortunes shall I first bewail,
" Or those which on my father's hoary head
" I see have fall'n, whom, in a foreign land,
" Exiled, by you attended I have found ?
" But how attired ! his mean and squalid garb,
" Worn bare by length of time, his aged limbs
" Contaminates ; and on his eyeless head
" His matted locks by each rude gale are waved ;
" And to his garb akin his wretched food
" But ill supports him.   Late, too late I know
" The ruin I have caused.   I call the gods
" To witness, vile, flagitious as I am,
" I come with wholesome food to cherish thee,
" And lighten thy accumulated woes.
" E'en by the side of Jove and on his throne
" Sits Moderation tempering every act :

" Nigh thee, my father, let her stand. Offence,
" Though not to be extinguish'd, may be heal'd.
" Why art thou silent ? O my father speak,
" Speak something to me ; turn not from me thus.
" Wilt thou not answer me, not e'en a word,
" But send me thus with mute contempt away,
" Nor why thy anger burns declare ? But you,
" Ye daughters of this man, my sisters, speak,
" Plead with my father for me, try to move
" His unrelenting heart ; nor let him send
" The suppliant of the god dishonour'd hence,
" A word to me disdaining to reply.

" ANTIGONE.

" Speak, my unhappy brother, speak thy self
" What sad occasion brought thee hither.   Oft
" Words as they flow delighting, or perchance
" Offending, or to pity soothing mild,
" Have giv'n a voice e'en to a speechless tongue.

" POLYNICES.

" Then I will speak, for well hast thou advised,
" Imploring first this god, that he would deign
" To be my guardian, at whose altar placed
" The sovereign of this country raising me
" Gave me to come, to hold free converse here,
" And back in safety to return.   And this
" Of you, O strangers, of my sisters this,
" This of my father wish I to obtain.
" To thee, my father, I would now unfold
" Why I am here.   From my paternal realms
" I am driv'n forth an exile, on thy throne
" Because I aim'd in regal state to sit,
" My birth-right ; but Eteocles, to years
" By nature less indebted, thrust me out,
" Not his just right triumphant, nor his claim
" Brought to the proof of arms, or noble deeds,
" But winning with insidious arts the state.

" Of this I know, and from the Seers have heard,
" That the chief cause was thy infuriate curse.
" In Doric Argos I sought refuge ; there
" The daughter of Adrastus made my bride,
" Associates in my cause I raised the Chiefs,
" Lords of the Apian land, and honour'd high
" For martial deeds ; that I 'gainst Thebes might lead
" Seven bands commanded by seven valiant Chiefs,
" And bravely die, or from my country chase
" Those who have wrong'd me.   But of this enough.
" What sanction, hither coming, claim I then ?
" To thee, my father, supplicating pray'rs
" For me, and my compeers in arms, I bring,
" Who with seven bands beneath seven spears arranged,
" Are now encamp'd o'er all the plain of Thebes.
" In martial prowess first, and first in skill
" To mark the flight of birds, Amphiaraus ;
" Ætolian Tydeus marches next, the son
" Of Oeneus ; and next him of Argive race
" Eteoclus ; there tow'rs Hippomedon
" Sent by his father Taläus ; in arms
" Advances Capaneus with menace high
" Instant to rend the rampires to the ground.
" Parthenopæus, an Arcadian, fierce
" Advances, from his mother's virgin state
" His name deriving, the undoubted son
" Of Atalanta.   I these chiefs among,
" Thy son, or if not thine, at least the son
" Of unpropitious Fortune, yet call'd thine,
" Lead against Thebes th' intrepid Argive troops.
" By these thy daughters, by thy life, we all
" Suppliant entreat thee, O my father, yield,
" Remit thy anger, raging 'gainst this wretch
" Now roused in arms t'avenge the wrongs sustain'd
" From a base brother, who hath driv'n me out,
" And robb'd me of my kingdom.   But the fates,
" If there be faith in oracles, declare
" That where thou art, there Victory attends.

" Now by our country's fountains, by her gods,
" Let, I implore thee, my entreaties touch
" Thy heart ; be thou appeased ; for I, like thee,
" Am poor, and wander in a foreign land ;
" One fate to us assign'd, to thee and me,
" Submissive to another's will we live.
" He lives in royal state, unhappy me !
" And 'midst luxurious pleasures laughs alike
" At thee and me.   But if thy fav'ring mind
" Accord with mine, him with no mighty toil,
" No arduous effort, will I put to flight,
" And lead thee back, replace thee in thy house,
" Replace myself, and drive him out by force.
" This boast, if thou assent, I will atchieve;
" But without thee my efforts have no pow'r.

" ŒDIPUS.

" But that the sovereign of this land, my friends,
" Had sent him to me, and esteems it just
" That I should answer him, he had not heard
" My voice : that grace now deigned, let him begone ;
" Nor will he find a joy in what he hears.
" For thou, vile wretch, the sceptre and the throne
" Holding, which now thy brother holds at Thebes,
" Didst drive thy father out, by thee constrain'd
" An exile from my country far to rove,
" And wear these loathsome weeds ; the sight of which
" Draws tears from thee, by fortune now reduced
" To suffer want and wretchedness like mine.
" These things I must not weep, but I must bear ;
" And always keep alive, whilst I shall live,
" The memory of thy impious deed ; for thou
" Hast made me long familiar with these toils,
" Thou hast to exile driv'n me, and by thee
" I wander thus, from strangers day by day
" Begging a poor subsistence.   Were not these
" My daughters, had they not with tender care
" Supported me, long since (to thee no thanks)

" My life had been no more: but these preserve,
" These cherish me, in bearing toils with me
" These take, beyond their sex, a manly part.
" But you, my sons——Away, you are not mine.
" For this cause fortune looks upon thee now
" Not as she soon will look, when thou shalt lead
" These troops to Thebes : it is not in thy fate
" To rend her rampires down, but there to fall
" Welt'ring in blood ; such too thy brother's fate.
" These curses on you I before denounced,
" And now as my associates call them down,
" That to a parent you may learn to show
" Due reverence, nor disdain a father more
" Though blind.   My daughters have not been thus base ;
" Therefore thy seat, thy throne shall they possess ;
" Since Justice long renown'd, by laws of old
" Establish'd, shares th' imperial throne of Jove.
" But get thee hence, thou hast no father here,
" Detested wretch, thou vilest of the vile,
" And take these curses with thee, on thy head
" Which I call down : by arms thy native land
" Never may'st thou recover, nor again
" Visit the vales of Argos ; may'st thou die
" Slain by thy brother's hand, and may thy hand
" Slay him, by whom thou art to exile driv'n.
" These curses I call on thee, and invoke
" The parent gloom of Erebus abhorr'd
" To give thee in his dark Tartarean realms
" A mansion : I invoke these awful pow'rs,
" And the stern god of war, who 'twixt you raised
" This horrid hate.   Thou hast my answer ; go,
" Tell all the Thebans, tell all thy faithful friends
" Confederate in thy cause, that Œdipus
" Confers this meed of merit on his sons.

" POLYNICES.

" Much for my journey hither I lament,
" Much for my ill success ; but for my friends

" I feel a deeper anguish.   Wretched me !
" Is this then the event that waits our march
" In arms from Argos, never to return !
" This to no friend, not one, shall I make known,
" That must not be, but silent meet my fate.
" But, O my sisters, since the dreadful curse
" Of my relentless father you have heard,
" Do not, should all his cruel menace find
" Like terrible effect, and should you e'er
" Return to Thebes, ah ! do not, by the gods,
" Leave me unhonour'd, but with funeral rites
" Lay my dead body in the tomb.   The praise,
" Which for a father your unwearied toils
" Have won you now, will equal glory win,
" If you perform these offices for me."

When Polynices enters, he finds his father demure, austere, and evidently incensed with him ; he, therefore, despairs of success, and cannot sum up courage enough to speak to him.   He addresses himself instead to his sisters, Antigone and Ismene, who through generous affection receive him kindly.   He says: Alas! my dear sisters, I scarcely know which to bewail most, my own misfortunes, or those which I have been partly instrumental in bringing on my unfortunate father, whom I see here exiled in a foreign country.   By you he is worthily attended; but, alas ! in what a plight do I find him—attired in threadbare garments, which by their squalid state contaminate his aged limbs. Too late now I see the ruin I have caused; yet, though my conduct has been vile in the extreme, I call the gods to witness I repent.   Then turning to his father, he says : I come now to make amends and lighten thy woes.   And, with a view to soothing Œdipus, he reminds him that even Jove himself uses moderation towards repentant sinners. Therefore, says he, O my father, be thou temperate towards

me for the offence I have committed; for, though I do not
expect you to forget the wrongs I have done you, let me by
a sincere repentance sooth thy sorrows. Œdipus being still
silent, Polynices says: Wilt thou not answer me, but treat
me thus in contempt?   O then, my sisters, sue you for me,
cause my father to relent, and let me not supplicate him in
vain.   I have sued to the god to be my guardian, at whose
altar the king of this realm found me, and gave me permission to attend here; therefore, to you, my father, I
address myself, and, if you will permit me, I will state why
I have sought you.   I have been driven from my native land
by my younger brother, who, by insidious arts, has wrested
the State of Thebes from my hands.   I was, therefore,
compelled to seek refuge in Argos, where I married the
daughter of the King Adrastus.   Six chiefs sojourning at
his court have associated themselves in my cause, who,
with their followers, undertake to redress my wrongs. They
are now encamped in martial throng on the plain near
Thebes.   I, with them, lead the troops against my brother
Eteocles, who has basely wronged me, driven me out, and
robbed me of my kingdom.   But the oracles have decreed
that whichever side you espouse, victory will follow. I, therefore, implore you, let my entreaties reach your heart, and
be appeased; for I am a wanderer like yourself, our fates
are similar, we are both subject to the will of him who has
assumed the power in Thebes, where he luxuriates and
laughs at us.   If you will accord me your favour, I will
not deem it a toil, nor find the effort arduous, to put him
to flight, and replace you in your former state; but without
your concurrence my efforts will be fruitless.   Œdipus
replies: But that Theseus, the king of this land, who is my
friend, expressed a desire that I should answer you, you
should not have heard my voice. Now, however, that I give

utterance to words, I say, begone, for you shall find no joy in what you hear from me, for you are a vile wretch. Conjointly with your brother you drove me out of Thebes, to wander an exile in a foreign land. I must bear this; but as long as I live, I will remember the impious deed. Had it not been for the tender care of these, my daughters, my life had been exhausted long since. They have supported me; but to you I owe no thanks; therefore, away, begone, I disown you, you are no more my son, nor is it fated that you shall succeed in breaking the barrier of the Theban walls; but under them you shall fall vanquished, weltering in your blood. This also shall be your brother's fate—this curse I pronounce on you both. My daughters, who have not been base like you, shall inherit the Theban throne. Get thee hence, for I am no more thy father. May'st thou die by thy brother's hand, and he by thine. Thou hast my answer; go! Polynices says: I now repent my journey, and my ill-success, more particularly for sake of my friends. O! my sisters, since you have heard my father's relentless curse, do not, when you return to Thebes, leave my body unhonoured, but see it entombed with funeral rites. By performing these offices you will gain equal glory to that you have earned by your duty to my father. Antigone says: Let my prayer prevail, lead your troops back to Argos, and do not destroy both your country and yourself. You have heard my father denounce death to both you and your brother—that you shall slay each other—you have heard his prophetic voice. To which Polynices replies: This must not be ; for if I show fear, how can I hope to raise such forces again should I require them. A brave chief speaks to raise courage not despair. This warlike march demands my care; though ruin, woe, and death are the results of my father's curse. Adieu! Take my last farewell, for living you will never see me more.

Lament me not: If it be my fate, I will die; for honour demands that I persevere in the course I have adopted. Farewell my sisters: I pray the gods that ills may never reach you, and that you may never feel affliction.

[*Exit* POLYNICES.

A storm now ensues, and Œdipus hearing the thunder, feels a presentiment that his end is drawing near. He says this is the fated day that ends his life. He tells his daughters to send for Theseus. Here the King enters, to whom Œdipus speaks: To my wish, O King, art thou come; my life draws towards its end, let me now do thee some good.

" ŒDIPUS.

" Now, son of Ægeus, I will show thee things
" Glorious to thee and to thy State, which time
" Shall never darken.   To the fated place
" Where I must die I now will lead the way,
" Not led, nor guided : but to mortal man
" Never disclose the secret spot, nor where
" It lies ; it shall be then thy strong defence
" For ever, more than close-compacted shields
" And spears of neighbouring States to thee allied.
" But things mysterious, not as yet by words
" Unfolded, thou shalt learn when thither come
" Alone : to none of all thy citizens,
" Nor to my daughters to my soul though dear,
" Would I reveal them : lock them in thy breast :
" But when thy life approaches to its end,
" Declare them only to the Chief that stands
" In highest honour ; to his successor
" Let him disclose them.   Thus thy royal seat
" Shall in this city stand impregnable
" To all the inroads of the dragon-race.
" For oft we see that States, though founded well
" On righteous laws, are prone t' abuse their force
" To insolent oppression : but the gods

" Exact, though late, observe when one disdains
" Their holy mandates, and to madness turns.
" That, son of Ægeus, that be far from thee.
" But I instruct a mind in all the parts
" Of virtue skill'd. Now go we to the place
" (For the strong impulse of the god I feel
" Urging me on), nor fear lest we profane
" The sanctity we reverence. Follow me
" This way, my daughters ; I am now become
" A guide to you, as to your father long
" You have been guides. Go then, but touch me not ;
" Let me unguided find the sacred tomb,
" Where these old limbs are destined to repose
" Beneath the earth. Go this way, this way go ;
" For this way Hermes, who conducts the dead,
" Leads me, and she o'er the dark realms who reigns.
" O light, thy beams though I no more behold,
" (Once I beheld them) now these aged limbs
" Feel thy last touch ; with feeble steps I go
" To close my last of life in death's dark shades.
" But be thou blest, my noble, honour'd friend,
" Thou, and thy country, and thy faithful train :
" Yet 'midst success, 'midst glories always yours,
" Think on the dead, remember Œdipus."

[*Exeunt* THESEUS, ANTIGONE, ISMENE, *and the* COLONIATE
led by ŒDIPUS.

During their absence, the chorus sing some verses,
at the conclusion of which, the Coloniate returns and
informs them that Œdipus is dead. He says : You know
how he parted hence, leading the way; though blind,
he led us to the craggy rock's verge,—to the brazen
way; and when we arrived at the mouth of the yawning
gulf he paused, and seating himself on a stone, he threw
off his squalid garments, and desired his daughters to bring
him water and a clean robe, which they did; and after, he

went through his libations, bathed, and re-robed himself as for funeral rites. Then embracing the virgins he said : My daughters, on this fated day you will become fatherless. And handing them over to the care of our good king Theseus, after again embracing them, he bade them adieu, when suddenly we were all horror-stricken, for we heard a god call "Œdipus! Why, Œdipus, delay we to depart?" Soon as he heard this, he bade Theseus approach him, and taking his hand, he called him his honoured friend; then turning again to his daughters he once more embraced them, and bade them depart; for, said he, the fates decree that it must be so, for none but Theseus may remain to witness the event that will transpire. Then mournfully we departed; but ere we had gone far, we turned and Œdipus was nowhere to be seen. The king was there alone with his face covered by his hands, as if struck with terror; so he stood for some time; then falling on his knees in prayer, the matter ended. Œdipus was borne by the god away, for not the fire nor the earth consumed him, and his fate is known but to Theseus alone.

Ere I proceed any further in these lectures, it is necessary to explain to you as I proceed from whose translations of the original tragedies I take my extracts. Up to this time I have used Potter's translations; therefore, if any of my hearers are desirous to compare notes, it will be necessary for them to provide themselves with the same work, otherwise they will be confused; for it will be found that the language used by the several translators differs widely, although the sense be similar. This is to be attributed to the various modes of conveying the same meaning in the English language. It is remarkably apparent in comparing Sophocles' works as translated by Potter and by Franklin.

I will now proceed to name to you the different editions of Sophocles' tragedies that have been published; in doing so I will not detain you long, because my remarks in this respect may to some be uninteresting, and perhaps appear rather dry; but, as I profess to provide something useful for all parties, I think the information I am about giving will be found serviceable, at all events, to the student.

The editions of the Greek tragic poets most in use are those translated by Thomas Franklin and Doctor Potter; after these, Michael Wodhulls's translation, and the edition in Greek by Richard Porson. The other editions of Sophocles' works I am acquainted with (and I think I know them all) are as follow :—

ALDUS. Venet., 8vo. Published in 1502.

FRANCINI. Florent., 4to., 1522. Cum Scholiis.

JUNTÆ. Florent., 4to. Cum Schol. The first edition of this work was published in 1522, and the second, with corrections, in 1547. The two plays I have last lectured upon were much improved in the edition of 1547.

The COLINÆUS edition, 12mo., Sine Scholiis, was published in Paris, in 1528, and is very scarce.

TURNEBUS. Paris, 4to., 1553. Cum Schol. As regards this edition, I learn from a statement by the Rev. Ths. Frognall Dibdin, F.S.A., that it was much revered, and for many years was considered the best authority. At first a manuscript of this edition was written by Demetrius Triclinius, which he copied and revised from the more original manuscript by Æmarius Ranconetus. A very singular coincidence occurs in this work : on the title page the date 1553 is printed, and at the end of the book 1552. This caused Harwood to make a mistake, in stating to the world that two editions were printed. I think it is more than probable that the printer made a mistake also, by inserting the dates in the wrong places. The intention of the author, doubtless, was to show that the publishing of the work was commenced in 1552 and finished in 1553.

H. STEPHANUS. Paris, 4to., 1568. A most valuable edition. But there were others of minor importance; for instance, CAMERARII. Hagenoæ, 8vo., 1534. Cum Schol. BRUBACHIUS. Francof, two editions; one, 4to., published in 1544—55. Cum Schol.

IDEM. 8vo., 1550, 1555, and 1567. Sine Schol.; also one published in Rome in 1518.

Then we have an edition by CANTER, published at Antwerp, in 1579, 12mo. Sine Schol. At the end of this volume occurs the date 1580; which evidently means that it was commenced in 1579, and finished in 1580. Probably it was brought out in parts, and the same might have been the case with Turner's edition. Stephens's edition was reprinted in 1603, by Paul Stephens, at Geneva, both in the Latin and Greek languages. JOHNSON's Oxford edition appeared in 1705, in two volumes, and was reprinted, and published in London in the year 1746, in three volumes, both in the Greek and Latin languages.

EJUSD. Glasgow, 8vo., 1745. In two forms, one edition in a single volume, the other in two volumes. This work was again published in London in two volumes, in the year 1758, also in the same form at Eton in the year 1775. The best of these editions is considered that which was published at Eton, and edited by J. T. Tweedie, who was a Scotchman.

CAPPERONNERII. Paris, 4to., 1781. This edition was began by Capperonnier and finished by VAUVILLIERS.

The play of Œdipus Tyrannus has been published in 8vo. by Brunck. There has also been an Eton edition, published in 1786.

BRUNCKII. Argent, 4to. In two volumes.

EJUSDEM—Ibid. 8vo., 1786-9. Gr. et Lat. 3 vols.

Two more editions were published by Brunck, in the years 1786 and 1788; also another in 1789, which is an octavo edition. Then again, I believe, there were two editions published at Strasburg, but I have not the dates of these. At Oxford, another edition was published in the year 1800, in three volumes, which is estimated as being one of the very best extant. There have been some other editions printed in the present century; the first was in 1806, both in Greek and Latin, two volumes, by BOTHE, Lipsiæ, 8vo., sine Scholiis; and I believe the last work upon Sophocles has been brought out by Bohn, the publisher. It is a prose translation, but I cannot speak of its merits, as I have not seen it, nor have I made search for others that may have been published in the present century. I have now kept you long enough upon this dry theme, therefore, I will postpone my catalogue of the editions published of Æschylus and Euripides for a future occasion. By thus dividing the information, I am in hopes I shall neither tire your patience nor say too little.

It is only about four centuries since the taste for Greek literature appears to have taken root in this and continental countries; that is to say, about one hundred years prior to the birth of our own Shakspeare. Many writers have attributed to him a total want of knowledge of the classics—a most uncharitable opinion to form, considering that the revival of ancient literature at the period of his manhood was comparatively in its infancy. Yet, for all this, to my humble thinking, Shakspeare appears to have had a tolerable notion of classic literature. At all events, supposing he knew but little concerning the subject, we cannot consistently deny him the credit of making good use of the knowledge he possessed—the more credit due to him ;—for he does not appear to have fallen into the bigoted error that existed about the period of his life. It was then the practice of many deeply learned in the classics to sneer at everything written in the way of dramatic literature that did not treat upon the ancient poets. I am free to admit that through this pride then existing many gems of poetical genius were brought to light, which have happily been handed down to us, and adorn our age. Had it not been for this somewhat bigoted notion then extant, you, my good friends, might never have been enlightened upon the subject, and my poor humble notions might not now exist. Of course, you will clearly understand I do not mean by these remarks that I am in any way improving upon the ideas propounded by others, perhaps possessed of much greater talent than I aspire to; and I trust that what I am stating may be received in a spirit acquitting me of all selfishness, bigotry, or egotism. My simple object is to illustrate the truth, and to afford credit to all and every class of writers that have produced works worthy of our consideration and esteem. In thus expressing myself, I trust I am delineating a righteous sensibility of rendering unto genius that which to genius is due. Criticisms such as I have alluded to have been more or less erroneous; for there can be no view of matters more narrowed than those which are founded on a determination to appreciate productions wholly by the standard of one's own ideas, exclusively based upon models set up by individuals. To be a true critic, we should never fetter ourselves with conventional notions; but always make due allowance for the education and habits of life connected with the period. The authors we peruse were influenced by, and existed under, the bigotry I complain of; which, I am afraid, sometimes assumed the form of a national delusion, for, from circumstances like these, slight as they may seem to the casual observer, whole nations have often become estranged from neighbouring countries, particularly in politics. But happily politics is a subject not pertaining to my present theme; I will, therefore, confine myself as much as possible to the work I have in hand—namely, the fine arts, or what some people designate polite literature. I will not quarrel with this term; but I fear upon investigation it will be found not universally applicable; many men being esteemed for their acquirements, but often censured for a total want of politeness, and even condemned for rudeness and incivility. I fear that those individuals are mostly found amongst that class we ought least expect to see them in—I mean those placed in the position to administer public justice. I am free to confess that amongst our superior judges a most wise selection has been made; and the higher courts are presided over by as good a set of men as might be found. I wish, sincerely, I could say the same of some of those designated the inferiors,—a term often most applicable. I could point out several, were it my province to do so here, whose peculiarities, if related, would make you giddy with laughter; but I am pleased to remark my theme is of a far more edifying character. I will, therefore, return to it, lest I be chided for digressing from my avowed course; but,

> Can I forget, poor Mary Bone?
>   What sights there have I seen!
> Where was a Judge's wisdom shown
>   On cabbages so green.

THE PLAINT.

A COW IN A CABBAGE GARDEN.

The sapient Judge in rage exclaim'd :
  " In a cabbage garden !—
" I know I'm right—I'll never yield ;
  " You shan't get one farden !
" How dare you, Sir, your cabbage field
  " Designate a garden ?
" It must have been a cabbage field,
  " Not a cabbage garden !"
Poor Hodge exclaim'd : " My Lord, I mean
  " A market-garden field;"
But Judge would have the man was green,
  And so he'd "never yield."
I don't pretend, good folks, you know,
  To say much on the point ;
But don't you think by such a show
  " The time was out of joint"?
I might relate more unto you
  Were I so here inclined ;
But I must leave the stupid noo——
  Who is not right in mind ;
Or who, if right he is in mind,
  In heart he's queer, I ween ;
His judgments are of strangest kind,
  His face most ugly seen.
So now no more of Doleful grim,
  No more of Mary Bone ;
I sing no more of this poor thing,
  And him I let alone.

I will here make a few remarks regarding the different opinions that have been expressed respecting the ancient tragedies being divided into acts. Franklin differs from both Barnes and Vossius. He says that nothing of the kind existed, and that, " so far from dividing them into acts, the old editions of the Greek tragedies do not so much as make the least separation of the scenes; even the names of the persons are not properly affixed to the speeches : no notice is taken of the entrances and exits of the actors ; the asides are never marked, nor any of the gestures or actions which frequently occur pointed out to us in the margin ; defects which, however inconsiderable, may mislead the young and injudicious reader, and which ought therefore to be carefully supplied by the critic or translator." Franklin is right to some extent in these remarks ; but in using the word "injudicious," in the general sense, he is rather injudicious himself; and he is decidedly wrong in stating that gestures and actions "frequently" occur; for the ancients studiously avoided action of the limbs, and very rarely made gestures of any description. What he means by "the names of the persons" not being affixed, I suppose, alludes to the description of character, not the names of the people who enacted them. This is a misnomer on his part; for most people reading the extract I have just quoted would be led into the belief that the old editions of these plays contain the names of the actors indiscriminately placed, or partly obliterated. Such is not the case, for I know of no instance where the actors' names are stated at all. I will now conclude this lecture by thanking you for your polite attention, and bidding you farewell.

LECTURE VII.

—·—

In undertaking to give my young friends present a little advice respecting books, let me recommend them to select such, the perusal of which may afford them information, instead of wasting their time (as I am afraid too many do) over a variety of trashy romances and novels. It is by perusing good books, that I am now enabled to relate to you particulars concerning a variety of historical facts. It may be that there are some persons present who know much more than I do myself upon the subjects I advance; but I am afraid there are also some whom it is necessary to admonish, entreating them to leave romance alone, and enlighten themselves upon facts, so that they may become acquainted with, at all events, the little knowledge which I myself have gained.

Perhaps, if I were to tell you that one year has not yet transpired since I first took this subject in hand, you would be surprised; but it is a fact; therefore, it is quite in your power to acquire as much as I have myself, if you will but select the proper materials to cultivate your mind with. My simple advice is: read good books, and amongst them pay particular attention to a work called the "Antiquities of Greece," by one of England's greatest scholars, John Potter, D.D., formerly Archbishop of Canterbury. I purpose by-and-bye relating to you something concerning this learned individual. In the mean time, my friends, I say to you, read his works, old or young, neglect not my advice! Ye aged of threescore and ten put on your spectacles and search through Potter's works, for one more pleasurable reminiscence of the past, ere you close your eyes for ever to the graces yet extant upon this sublunary orb! Ye lisping children, listen to the feeble voices of your grandsires, whilst they repeat to you once more a short and potent lesson from the pages of the great John Potter! Ye lads and lasses of tender years, pay attention to my injunctions; remember well the advice I am now proffering you; neglect it not! Let the first book you hoard up your pocket money to purchase, be " Potter's Antiquities of Greece." Now, to you young men and women who more immediately require to acquaint yourselves with the contents of Potter's works, get the book, I say; for therein you will find authenticated matter, pertaining so far back as the period when the great patriarch Jacob was living. In Potter's works you will discover the fundamental principles of good laws propounded, moral precepts laid down, and the rules of righteousness and social order described so that you cannot fail to be enlightened and edified. In Potter's works you will find principles inculcated which have, to this very hour, laid the basis of much of the consistency there is existing in the codes of laws by which we ourselves are governed. Ye who are destined to the practice of these laws, lay well to heart my suggestions; read Potter's works; reflect well upon the good therein described, such as was practised by that just arbitrator Theseus, King of Athens—may his example lead you to act with justice and truth to all parties.

To you, my gallant friends, who have become devotees of Mars and Minerva, read the work I have alluded to, from which you will learn that it is not the mere trappings

on your body that make the soldier ; it must be in your
hearts to show your courage, in your heads to direct you to
discipline and obedience, and in your general demeanour to
entitle you to that respect to which a gallant man aspires. Let
not the mere thirst for blood be your guiding influence, for
that is a propensity savage as it is inhuman. Let not the
vain glory of pomp and pride lead you into the ranks for
mere show and fascination, but prove the utility for which
Providence has created you by entering sincerely into the
common cause to defend your native country from invasion
or pollution of a foreign foe. If you take my advice, and
select such works to peruse as the one I have recommended,
you will improve your minds, and perhaps enable yourselves to be of some benefit to your fellow-man. If, however,
you waste your time on romance and fiction, you will under-
mine your understanding, and make your mind as superficial
as the trash you peruse. I will just relate to you a little circumstance that transpired a few days since, and then proceed
with Euripides' Tragedy of the " Phœnician Virgins." Pray
understand me, that what I am about relating is not
stated from any motive of egotism, but simply to illustrate
what a man may do by assiduously applying himself to the
work he takes in hand, and the difference between reading
good books and romance and fiction.

I was at the house of an old acquaintance, who is about
the same age as myself. When reading the first number of
my lectures, he exclaimed, " Where the D—— do you get so
many ideas from ? Here are allusions to persons and things
I never heard of in my life, yet I went to the same
school, and think when we left I knew quite as much
as you. I suppose you read the ancient authors, and devote
your time to history, rather than to the rubbish that is so
much perused by most people. I dare say now you select

a bit here, and a bit there, first from one author then from another, and so you make out the 'Hundred Lectures,' which you are going to astonish the world with." " That's just it, my dear fellow," said I. "How else do you imagine I will be able to accomplish my task ?   I do not profess to have been born with a Greek lexicon in my head, nor a Murray's grammar at my fingers' ends.   Of course, I gain my knowledge from reading good and useful books.   I am sorry to hear you say you know so little of them ; but it is not too late to learn. Read good books ; put aside that enchanted castle, with its turreted towers, and rambling ghost story ; read my lectures, my friend, and don't forget Bishop Potter's works : you will then know quite as much as I do."

Now, ere I proceed further, let me relate to you something from history, relative to one of the characters so ably and honourably treated by the poet Sophocles, in the tragedy I last lectured upon.   It is plain by the writings of the ancients themselves, that they venerated the memories of their ancestors quite as much, or perhaps more, than we of the present generation do ; for 'tis clear they took as much pleasure in relating the histories of righteous individuals, as we in listening to or reading them.

Theseus was the son of Ægeus, who was one of the four sons of Pandion the Second, eighth King of Athens. Ægeus's cousins, who were the sons of Metion, deprived his father Pandion of his regal power ; and they in their turn were dispossessed of their authority by Pandion's four sons, whose names were Ægeus, Lycus, Pallas, and Nisus. Pandion was reinstated ; and at his death he divided his kingdom into four parts amongst his sons, so that they might be equivalently rewarded for their fidelity, and mutually reciprocate each other's welfare.   But an unfortunate obstacle ensued through the sovereignty of Athens falling to Ægeus's share. His brothers were the more envious of him because (as is stated by Plutarch) he was only the adopted son of Pandion ; others assert that he was an illegitimate son. Apollodorus tells us that Pandion was not reinstated on the throne at all; and that when his four sons displaced their cousins, who had usurped the power from their father, they divided the kingdom equally between themselves. Ægeus was married to Æthra, daughter of Pittheus, King of Trœzene, whose parents were Pelops and Hippodamia. Pittheus was a great scholar ; and though he was a king, he did not deem it beneath him to teach in the public school of the country he governed. On this head I will have more to say anon; when I will show you the different motives that influenced kings of the period I am writing upon, to those that guide many monarchs of the present age.

Amongst the various good things that Pittheus did, he undertook himself the education of his grandson Theseus. For this purpose, when Ægeus ascended the throne of Athens, he left his wife Æthra and his son Theseus at Trœzene, from which place he instructed his wife not to send his son, until he attained the age of manhood; and then to do so as secretly as possible, for he feared Theseus's safety, through the rebellions which were constantly breaking out around the dominions which he governed. Through the instrumentality of his fifty nephews, the sons of his brother Pallas, this confederacy was denominated the Pallantidæ ; the appellation originating with their father's name Pallas. When Theseus left Trœzene to attend his father at Athens, he resolved to distinguish himself on his way : therefore, instead of going direct by sea, he made his way across the country, and on his journey he performed the following services to the people whose provinces he passed through. Of course it must not be considered that he did all these things I am about relating to you single-handed; for, he being the son of a king, the grandson of a king, and a king in embryo himself, he doubtless travelled with a tolerable retinue of attendants and servants.   Amongst the many wondrous feats attributed to him, was that of destroying the wild sow of Cromyon.   Some authors tell us that this animal was neither more nor less than an abandoned woman, who seduced strangers, then murdered and robbed them. Theseus also captured and killed the following notorious robbers, who infested the districts he passed through:— Procrustes,* Synnis,† Sciron,‡ and Corynetes;§ and he subdued Cercyones,‖ King of Eleusis, and killed him.

---

* Procrustes is described by different authors variously ; by some he was called Polypemon, by others Damostes. It has been stated that he committed the following cruelty upon his victims :—He had them bound upon a bed; those who were shorter than the instrument of torture he used, he had stretched to its full length, and those who were longer he had so much of their feet or legs cut off as to bring them to the exact length he willed they should be, and so he left them to die.

† Synnis.—This name is sometimes spelt Scinis. The way this monster used to torture his victims, after waylaying and robbing them, was, he caused two trees to be strained towards each other, and confined so by ropes ; then suspending his victims by their limbs, an arm and leg to each tree, the ropes were suddenly cut, the trees sprang to their natural positions, and instantaneously tore the limbs from the body of the individual practised upon.

‡ Sciron was son of Æacus, and was married to a daughter of Cychreus, who was King of Salamis. He was the chief of a band of robbers who infested the state of Attica. His practice was, after robbing his victims, to despatch them by throwing them down a steep rock into the sea. Ovid relates that at Sciron's death the earth and sea both refused to receive his body, and that, after his flesh decayed, his bones remained suspended in the air, and that they were ultimately changed into rocks which were called "Scironia Saxa," located between Megara and Corinth.

§ Corynetes, sometimes spelt Coryneta, was a son of Vulcan, the chief of a band of robbers called after his name.

‖ Cercyones was son of Neptune (by some he is described as a son of Vulcan); he was King of Eleusis and was a great wrestler. He challenged Theseus, who conquered and slew him.

During the period I am now alluding to, Medea, wife of Jason and daughter of Ætes, King of Colchis, being neglected by her husband, flew to Athens, and put herself under Ægeus's protection. She was an enchantress, and many wonderful acts and cruel murders are attributed to her (a description of this lady you will find in one of my future lectures, which will be published in due course) here at Athens. On Theseus's arrival she was living illicitly with his father, the king, over whom she had much influence, and fearing her powers would be lessened by Theseus's presence, she resolved to destroy him. Her scheme was so cunningly devised as to determine that the cup of poison she destined to effect her purpose, should be given him by the hands of Ægeus his own father. You must please to understand that, although Medea through her magical contrivances knew of Theseus's arrival at Athens, Ægeus, the king, was kept in ignorance of it until Theseus presented a sword, which had been given him by his mother to produce to his father. One statement of this circumstance is, that Ægeus saw the sword hanging by his son's side and recognised it. Amongst the many extraordinary feats attributed to Theseus, was one of killing his fifty cousins (the Pallantides), who all set upon him to murder him. He destroyed the famous Bull of Marathon; and he went to Crete, where he subdued the celebrated Minotaur, which was a monster, half-man and half-bull, who used annually to devour seven Athenian youths, who were sent to Crete as a tribute. Another statement is, that the tribute consisted of seven maidens as well, and that they were all given to the Minotaur to be devoured; but Theseus delivered them and killed the monster. The way he accomplished this is described in another of my lectures, under the head of Theseus and Ariadne, who was daughter of Minos, King of Crete. She fell in love with Theseus, and

assisted him in saving his country people.   I am sorry to
say that the blot (the only one I know of) in Theseus's
character, was his act of abandoning this maiden, leaving
her after seducing her.   The particulars of this circumstance
are also related in the same lecture I have before alluded
to, under the head of Theseus and Ariadne.   On his return
to Athens he immediately ascended the throne, 1235 years
before the birth of Christ.

There is much more to describe of this great man's character; but I must break off here lest I become prosy by
occupying your attention too long upon one subject; yet you
must not imagine I am going to neglect my duty by leaving
the subject only half explained.   It is my intention to re-
vert to it again on a future occasion, when you shall be
informed of all I know upon the point.

Euripides, one of the three great Greek tragic writers,
was son of Mnesarchus and Clito; he was born in the year
490, B.C., on the Island of Salamis, to which place his
parents had retired with many of the citizens of Greece, in
consequence of Xerxes invading their country.   They were
people occupying a high position in society; consequently,
able to give their son the best education attainable.   Amongst
his teachers was the refined Prodicus.   As Euripides grew
to manhood, he was much admired for his modest and ami-
able character.   His writings consisted of, according to some
statements, seventy-five, and others, ninety-two, tragedies;
we have eighteen of them perfect, and translated into English.
The general opinion of their merits is that they are somewhat unintelligible, from the fact of there being so many
disconnections and changes of characters in them.   Besides
these errors, the poet seems to have introduced a super-
fluous number of speakers.   Yet for all these defects he
stands in great estimation as a true delineator of the

natural passions, and for his appropriate groupings. He also displays considerable eloquence, and was held in high estimation by the orators Cicero and Demosthenes.

A proof of the value Cicero set upon this poet's works we gather from the following facts :—When Cicero, after having retired into Tusculum out of the way of his enemies, and after twice putting to sea to get further from their reach, was driven back by contrary winds, he secluded himself at his country house near Formiæ. Here, when discovered by his murderers, he was reading Euripides' tragedy, "Medea."

Euripides, when young, studied as a painter, but ultimately he became the great competitor of Sophocles in the tragic muse ; and, though they each of them gained prizes in their turn, one against the other, they, nevertheless, lived in the greatest cordiality and friendship. Sophocles was five years younger than his friend, and Æschylus, who had been a competitor of the other two, and now getting an old man, was twenty-nine years senior to Euripides, and thirty-four to Sophocles. It was during Euripides' early days that the great Anaxagoras of Clozomene came to Athens, and ventured to throw doubt upon the stupid doctrines then extant, in which the people attributed everything to fate and chance. Anaxagoras boldly declared his belief in an immortal, omnipotent, and eternal God, to whom he ascribed the creation of all things; he also declared his belief to be that the Omnipotent was indefinite and divine. Euripides was one of the first who was converted to this true belief, and he followed Anaxagoras's example, but was deterred from preaching in public, through fear of becoming a victim to the bigotry and superstition that surrounded him. About this period he became acquainted with Socrates, who also became a convert to the sublime truth of the existence of one great Deity. Euripides was a great favourite of Archelaus, King of Macedonia, who invited him to his country. The invitation being accepted, he left Athens and went to the court of Archelaus, at Pella; where he became acquainted with Agatha the poet, Tomotheus the musician, and Zeuxis the painter. They formed a friendship for each other, and were constant companions, until Euripides unfortunately came to an untimely end, by being torn to pieces by a pack of hounds. His death was mourned at Macedonia; and at Athens Archelaus raised a monument to his memory, on which were inscribed the following words :—

"Thy memory, O Euripides, will never perish."

Soon as his death was known at Athens, Sophocles showed his respect for his friend by appearing at the exhibition of a new tragedy he had produced, in deep mourning, and he caused the actors to play their parts with their heads uncovered, out of respect to his memory. Of the relative merits of the three great dramatists I have alluded to, Quintilian has remarked :—Æschylus the sublime and daring, Sophocles grave and majestic, Euripides flowing with a copious stream of eloquence throughout his works.

The Athenians applied to Archelaus to permit the removal of Euripides' body from Macedonia to Athens, which request was refused by Archelaus, and he had him buried amongst his own ancestors. In Athens a cenotaph was erected to Euripides' memory. The names of the tragedies he wrote are as follow :—"The Bacchæ," "Ion," "Alcestis," "Medea," "Hippolytus," "The Phœnician Virgins," "The Supplicants," "Hercules," "Heraclidæ," "Iphiginia in Aulis," "Rhesus," "The Trojan Dames," "Hecuba,"

"Electra," "Orestes," "Iphiginia in Tauris," and "Andromache."

The chorus of "The Phœnician Virgins" is composed of some females sacred to the shrine of Apollo. They are detained at Thebes, having been taken by the Thebans in a war against the Phœnicians. Thebes being now invaded by the Argives, these ladies form part of the plot of the tragedy, although they are not interested in the success of either party, they being a religious sisterhood protected by the rites of the Temple. The scene is laid at Thebes, in the court before the palace. Œdipus and Jocasta are both introduced into this tragedy; but it must be borne in mind that in Sophocles' tragedy of "Œdipus King of Thebes," which I have already lectured upon, they are described—Jocasta as having destroyed herself, and Œdipus being banished, the prerogative of power having been wrested from his hands by his sons Eteocles and Polynices, and now exercised by Eteocles only. In this tragedy, "The Phœnician Virgins," Jocasta has thrown off her robes and rich garments, assuming that of mourning. The other characters represented are Antigone, Phorbas, Creon, Tiresias, Menœceus, and a messenger. Some of the characters here represented must have been very old people; for Jocasta says to Polynices, speaking of Œdipus, "The poor old man still mourns with many a tear." Now, if Œdipus was old, Jocasta must have been quite an aged woman, as she was his mother, and the chorus address her as a "venerable dame:" she herself says that her steps are feeble which she has to "drag along with trembling age."

The play begins by Jocasta describing the history of it; but, as I have done this elsewhere, I will merely relate to you the foundation upon which it is based. Jocasta reflects with sorrow upon the ill-fated day that Cadmus left the

Phœnician shore and set his " ill-omened foot on the Theban land." The omen of ill alluded to by Jocasta applies to Cadmus as follows :—He was son of Agenor, King of Phœnicia. Cadmus was ordered by his father to follow Jupiter, who had abducted his half-sister Europa. His father gave him strict orders not to return without her. Finding his efforts to recover Europa fruitless, he settled in Bœotia, where he built a city by the assistance of five men, whom he raised from the earth by sowing the teeth of a dragon, which he first subdued and killed. Soon after this he married Hermione, who was a daughter of Mars and Venus. At their marriage, we are told, that all the gods and goddesses attended, with the exception of Juno, who was (as usual) in one of her sulky moods. Vulcan was so incensed at Venus's infidelity towards him, and having broken her marriage vow, that he resolved to be avenged upon her by afflicting the children she had by Mars with all sorts of crimes. In those days, as in ours, the sins of the parents descended to their children; so did Venus's crimes fall on Hermione and her offspring by Cadmus. Juno was also anxious to avenge herself upon this race, on account of Jupiter, her husband, falling in love with Venus, which he did before Vulcan married her. The children of Cadmus and Hermione were named as follows : Polydorus, Antonoe, Semele, Agane, and Ino. The various ills endured by this family so preyed upon the minds of Cadmus and Hermione that they prayed to die; but they were changed into serpents, some think for their impiety in not bearing their afflictions with fortitude and resignation. Polydorus, the son of these, was father of Labdacus. Labdacus's mother was Nycteis : she was daughter of Nycteus, who was King of Thebes; and Labdacus was father to Laius, who was Jocasta's first husband and father of

Œdipus. So far back as Cadmus Jocasta describes the ancestry of Œdipus; she also states Menœceus was her father; but as there is a character in this play of the same name, let me remind you that this is not the same Menœceus as alluded to by Jocasta. The one here represented is a son of Creon, the brother of Jocasta; consequently, he is her nephew. The parents of Labdacus died when he was quite a child, and he was left to the care of his grandsire Nycteus, who also died before Labdacus came of age. During the minority of Labdacus, Lycus, who was brother to Nycteus, acted as regent. Whilst Lycus was regent, Antiope suffered certain indignities; to avenge which, Amphion and Zethus drove Labdacus from the throne, soon as he arrived at the regal powers; but shortly after this, matters were reconciled, and Labdacus reascended the throne of Thebes.

Now to go back to Telephassa: she also went into Thrace in search of her daughter Europa, and died there of a broken heart; and to conclude this narrative, the father of Agenor was Neptune, who was, as no doubt you are aware, one of the very earliest gods, brother to Jupiter, and son of Saturn. The character Phorbas here introduced I take to be the same shepherd who found Œdipus when a child. Phorbas, as will be recollected, came to Thebes to inform Œdipus of the death of Polybus, King of Corinth. From that time till now, we may fairly suppose that Phorbas has remained a follower of Œdipus's family, and here in this tragedy is represented as an old man protecting his master's daughter, Antigone. He says, as he is leading her to the tower, to reconnoitre the enemy's position:

" Pride of thy father's house, sweet-breathing flower,
" Since, with leave granted, thou hast left th' apartments,

N

" Where virgin modesty retires to shun

" The gaze of men, and to this tow'r approachest

" Anxious to view the Argive troops beneath,

" Yet stay thy steps, Antigone ; mine eye

" Shall first explore the pass ; haply some Theban

" May be in sight, and with opprobrious taunts

" Revile me as a slave, nor spare e'en thee

" Of royal birth ; this caution had, my tongue

" Shall tell thee all, whate'er I saw, or heard

" From th' Argives, to thy brother when I bore

" The offer of a truce, and thence return'd.

" But nigh this house no Theban is in sight ;

" Come then, ascend this height, let thy foot tread

" These stairs of antient cedar ; thence survey

" The plains beneath ; see what an host of foes

" At Dirce's* fount encamp, and stretch along

" The valley where Ismenus† rolls his stream.

" Lean on my hand ; in lucky hour thou comest ;

" In motion is the wide Pelasgian‡ host,

" Each wheeling phalanx forming round its chief.

" Not tamely Polynices to this land

" Returns, but raging leads a numerous host,

" Horsemen, and deep'ning ranks of foot in arms.

---

* The second wife of Lycus. She was tied to the tail of a wild bull by Zethus and Amphion, the sons of Antiope, for persecuting their mother, and was thus dragged over the country, until the gods, pitying her distresses, changed her into a fountain and stood her near the river Ladon.

† The river Ladon, which passed through the plain on which the Argive host had gathered. It was afterwards called the Ismenus after the name of one of Apollo's sons, whose mother's name was Melia, one of the fifty daughters of Nereus and Doris ; she was one of the sea nympths, called the Nereides.

‡ This word is derived from the name of Pelasgus, who was one of the most ancient kings in the world. He first established himself at Argolis, which was situated in the Peloponnesian country ; and we are told that, close upon nineteen hundred years before the birth of Christ, this people went into Æmonia, and ultimately they divided themselves into small parties and migrated into Greece, Italy, and other places, some into Crete, some into Lesbos, and others into Epirus.

" Be confident ;
" Within the city is secure ; but view
" That chief, if thy desire to know excite thee."

Phorbas addresses Antigone as the pride of her
father's house, and calls her a sweet-breathing flower. He
says: Since leave has been granted you to approach the
tower, I will first explore the way to ascertain if all be
secure, so that you may reconnoitre in safety. When I have
taken this precaution, and you are in perfect security, I
will relate to you what I saw and heard in the Argive
camp, when I went there with the flag of truce. Your
approach here is most opportune, for the Pelasgian host is
now just in motion, going through military evolutions round
its chief. Your brother, Polynices, is leading a numerous
host of both horse and foot soldiers against this city ; but be
confident, for you need not fear, as within the city all is
secure, and you are safe. Antigone replies, by asking
Phorbas who is the chief she sees with a bright helmet
and white plume—he who is in the rear of the troops he
is marshalling. That warrior, says Phorbas, is a chief from
Mycenæ*, his ancestors and family are of this place, in the
district of Lerna.† He is called the King Hippomedon.‡
How haughtily he moves, replies Antigone; his towering
height makes him look an earth-born giant. Yonder is
another chief, whose arms are different. Who is he? He,

---

* Mycenæ was a city built by Perseus, and named after Mycene, a
lady of Laconia. It dates back nearly fourteen hundred years before
Christ. It flourished for eight hundred years, and was ultimately destroyed
by an invasion from Argos.

† District in Argolis where festivals were held called the Lernœ, in
honour of Proserpine in the spring of the year, Ceres in the summer, and
Bacchus in the Autumn.

‡ A note to this name appears in my next lecture.

says Phorbas, is the son of Œneus; his name is Tydeus.* Is
he the prince, asks Antigone, who is married to the sister
of my brother's wife?† How very different are the arms he
bears to the others. Yes, says Phorbas, in the fight he is
most fierce. These Ætolian ‡ warriors hurl with certain
aim the flying lance. The knowledge I am imparting to you
I gained when I was in the enemy's camp with a flag of
truce. I noted the impression upon each of their shields, by
which I now recognise the chiefs who carry them. What
chief is he, says Antigone, now passing by the tomb of
Zethus?§ His name, says Phorbas, is Parthenopœus;‖ he
is a son of Atalanta; he fights against us in the just cause
of your brother Polynices, who is standing there near the
tomb where Niobe¶ interred her seven slain virgin daughters.

---

* Ditto ditto.

† Antigone's brother Polynices was married to a daughter of
Adrastus, King of Argos, so also was Tydeus.

‡ Ætolian is from Ætolia in Greece; the founder of the place was
named Ætolus. These people were great warriors, and joined the Romans
in subduing several of the Grecian States.

§ Was the son of Antiope, by Jupiter. He reigned for a short time
in Thebes, conjointly with his brother Amphion. They killed Lycus, who
acted as regent to Labdacus; after which, when Labdacus became of age,
he subdued these brothers and terms were entered into, through which
Labdacus ascended the throne which was originally occupied by his
Polydorus.

‖ This name is also noted in my next lecture.

¶ Niobe was the daughter of Tantalus and Dione; her husband's name
was Amphion. There are several opinions respecting the number of their
children, but it is generally thought that they had seven daughters and
seven sons. They were all destroyed by Apollo, excepting one whose
name was Chloris, the wife of Neleus. Diana assisted Apollo in the
destruction of these children, and Niobe herself was changed into a stone;
so also were several of her friends, who attempted to bury the bodies of
her children. There is some disparity respecting Euripides' version of the
burial of Niobe's children; he says she buried them, but the mythology is
that they were buried by the gods on the tenth day after their bodies had
been exposed.

He and Adrastus are both in armour, standing there together. I see him, says Antigone, but not very distinctly. Oh! could I but fly through the air to him, my dear brother, who has been so long an exile, I would embrace him. Look, observe him, thou good old man, see how gracefully he stands in his golden armour, which glitters like the bright orient sun. And who is he in that high-seated car, to which are attached those white horses? His name is Amphia-räus,* replies Phorbas; he is a prophet, and can foretell the fates of people. Yonder there stands Capaneus†; see how he scans the walls, how minutely he seems to be noting their height. Antigone replies :—

" O ye deep-roaring thunders
" Of Jove, ye livid lightnings' blasting flames,
" Vengeance, 'tis thine to quell his arrogance!
" Shall he to proud Mycenæ, and the fount
" Of Lerna‡ gushing from the Trident's‖ stroke,
" To Amymone's§ banks, Neptunian stream,
" In slavery lead th' unhappy dames of Thebes
" The captives of his spear ? Never, ah! never,
" Daughter of Jove, revered Diana, thou
" That braid'st with gold thy tresses, may I live
" To suffer slavery !

---

* Amphiaräus : this name is also noted in my next lecture.

† Capaneus, ditto, ditto.

‡ Lernos' fount was a lake situated, and partly concealed in a grove of laurels. Into this lake the forty-nine daughters of Danaus threw the heads of their husbands after they had murdered them. It was in this grove where Hercules had his contest with the Hydra, which was accounted one of his twelve labours.

‖ This alludes to Neptune's striking the rock with his trident, and turning Amymone into a fountain.

§ Amymone was one of the Danaides. Her husband, whom she murdered the first night of her marriage, was named Enceladus. The fountain which was raised by Neptune was to supply the City of Argos with water, in honour of Amymone, whom some consider he carried away, having fallen in love with her.

" Phorbas.

   " Go, my child, retire

" To thy apartments, there remain ; thine eyes

" Have been indulged with what they wish'd to see.

" For, as the storm of war rolls near the town,

" A troop of females to this royal house

" Advances ; and that sex hath nature form'd

" Prone to complain ; if once they take th' occasion,

" Small though it be, to give their words a vent,

" Another, and another still is added ;

" And 'tis their pleasure 'mongst themselves to speak

" Nothing* that owns the pow'r of moderation.

               " *Exeunt* Phorbas *and* Antigone."

I will now read you some poetry recited by the chorus. The lines are tolerably good ; but my principal reason for going through them is, that there are several words and names used by the poet, explanations of them may, I think, be interesting to you.

          " Chorus.

          " strophe i.

   " Bounding o'er the Tyrian† flood

    " From Phœnicia's‡ sea-girt isle,

---

* By this expression from Phorbas it would seem that ladies in those days were somewhat similar to what they are now—viz., rather prone to talking very fast. Phorbas evidently considers them chatterers.

† Tyrian flood alludes to the tide of the river Tyras, in Sarmatia. It is now called the Niester, and runs into the Euxine.

‡ Phœnicia is situate in Asia, near the Mediterranean Sea. Syria and Palestine are both in what was considered the Phœnician country. The sea-girt isle alluded to here applies to the Island of Aradus. The City of Sidon was situate in Phœnicia, in which place it has been conjectured the first system of writing was invented. The people inhabiting this place were of a very enterprising character and great navigators ; they migrated to many places on the Mediterranean, established colonies, and carried on their commerce from one to another. We are told that they originated Carthagenia and Utica. They were invaded by Alexander, and became tributaries to Macedonia. The name takes its rise from from Phœnix.

" Hallow'd to the Delphic* god,
" I come, the first-fruits of the spoil ;
" Destin'd to dwell, attendant at his shrine,
" Where cover'd with eternal snow
" Parnassus† lifts his forked brow :
" Our oars brush'd lightly o'er th' Ionian‡ brine,
" Along Cilicia's‖ wave-wash'd strand,
" A wide wild waste of barren sand ;
" Whilst the mild zephyr through the liquid skies
" Whispers pleasure as he flies.

.**" ANTISTROPHE I.**

" Cull'd from Tyre,§ its brightest grace,
" Worthy of the god, I came
" To Agenor's high-born race,
" Glorying, Cadmus, in thy name,
" To kindred tow'rs where sceptred Laius reign'd ;
" Nor will the god more precious hold
" The sculptur'd forms that breathe in gold.
" Yet thus far have these walls my zeal detain'd :

---

* Delphic God alludes to Delphi the son of Apollo.

† Parnassus lifts his forked brow. The mountain of Parnassus had two points to it, which were considered the highest in Europe ; the names given these pinnacles were Tithorea and Hyampea. The biceps muscles in the human body being two, take their names from these mountains. The mountain itself is called after Parnassus, who was a son of Neptune and Cleobula, the wife of Amyntor and the mother of Phœnix ; her parents were Boreas and Orythya. Cleobula also married Phineus who was a son of Argenior, from whom she was divorced ; by this marriage she had two sons named Pandion and Plexippus. At the temple of Apollo, which was erected on the top of the Hyampea pinnacle of the mountain, the oracles propounded were invariably recited in verse, and were considered sacred to the muses ; it is to this circumstance, that people who delight in poetry are supposed to be inspired by Parnassus.

‡ Ionian brine means the salt Ionian sea.

‖ Celicia's wave alludes to the sea on the coast of Cyprus, which is situate on the west of the Euphrates.

§ Tyre alludes to the river Tyra or Tyras in Sarmatia.

" As yet Castalia's* silver wave
" These flowing tresses waits to lave,
" Delicious stream, where bathes the virgin train,
" Serving at Apollo's fane.

" EPODE.

" Thou rock iradiate with the sacred flame,
" That blazing on thy awefull brow
" Seems double to the vale below !
" Thou kindred cliff,† on whose rude height
" To Bacchus swells the tow'ring shrine ;
" Whose crags among, a wond'rous sight,
" Glows the daily-ripening vine,
" And fills the goblet with its nectar'd stream !
" Ye caves, beneath whose horrid shade
" His bulk the Delphic Dragon‡ laid !
" Ye mountain watch-tow'rs of the gods,
" Whose steeps with snows eternal crown'd
" The virgin train encompass round,
" O take me to your bless'd abodes ;
" And far from Dirce's troubled waves
" Protect me, Phœbus, in thy hallow'd caves !

" STROPHE II.

" Now th' impetuous god of war‖
" " Shakes these walls with loud alarms ;
" And his squadrons leading near
" Fires their blood, and shouts to arms :

---

* Castalia's silver wave applies to the stream which ran by the town of Castalia in Greece.

† Thou kindred cliff, &c., alludes to the pinnacle on Mount Parnassus called Tithorea, where was situated an altar sacred to Bacchus.

‡ The Delphic Dragon means the serpent Python. This monster was raised from the mud, by Juno, which remained stagnated, from the deluge of Deucalion. It was killed by Apollo when quite a child for having tormented his mother Latona. It is from the circumstance of this victory that the Pythian games were first originated.

‖ Mars.

" Ah, be their fury 'gainst these bulwarks vain!
" For touch'd with pity's social glow
" Friend shares with friend the common woe ;
" And sad Phœnicia, should misfortune's train
" Around these seven-tow'r'd rampires spread,
" Would bow with friendly grief her head ;
" From Iö boasting their high descent,
" I the woes of each lament.

" ANTISTROPHE II.

" Now the thund'ring storm of war
" Rolls along these groaning fields ;
" Now with fierce terrific glare
" Blaze around the fiery shields,
" Portending carnage red with gushing gore ;
" And Mars in all his ruthless pride,
" With rage and horror at his side,
" Bids on this royal house the ruin roar.
" Pelasgian Argos, how I fear
" The fury of thy vengefull spear ;
" For the brave youth the sword of justice draws,
" And the gods assert his cause."

The flag of truce having been sent from the city by
Eteocles into the enemy's camp, Polynices, his brother, is
invited to enter the city of Thebes, for the purpose of ne-
gotiating terms to abstain from hostilities. The gates are
thrown open to him, and, as he enters, he says: They turn
easy on their hinges to admit my entrance. I may perhaps be caught in an ambush here. My return may probably be prevented by my being assassinated; I will therefore keep a cautious look out on every side, lest by
treachery I am destroyed. But if any attempt on my life
be made, I will brave the attack, and with this good sword
I will cut my way through mine enemies. He starts,
alarmed; but checking himself, he says, Being adventurous

to tread on hostile ground naturally creates fear. I have
risked this approach, confiding in my mother's assurance for
safety; yet, even in her I have my doubts. Then, as he
approaches near to the blazing altars, he says, Here at least
I am protected, therefore, I will sheathe my sword, and
question these people whom I see standing before the
palace. Then, addressing the ladies of the chorus, he says:

" Ye female strangers, tell me from what country,
" Advance you to the houses of our Greece ?

" CHORUS.

" Phœnicia is my country, gave me birth,
" And nurtured me, till captive by the spear,
" Selected from the virgin train, the sons
" Of Cadmus led me hither, to Apollo
" An hallow'd off'ring. Whilst th' illustrious house
" Of Œdipus prepared that I attend
" The awefull shrine, and altars of the god,
" Th' embattled Argives march'd against the city.
" Now tell me who thou art, that thou hast enter'd
" The seven-tow'r'd rampires of the Theban land.
" O thou, whose high blood to Agenor's sons,
" My lords that led me hither, is allied,
" Thus lowly at thy knees, O king, I fall,
" Holding my country's custom. Art thou come,
" After this length of absence art thou come
" To thy paternal land !—What, ho ! come forth,
" Thou venerable dame, open thy doors ;
" I call thee to thy son : dost thou not hear ?
" Why this delay to quit thy lofty mansion ?
" Haste, come, and in thy fond arms clasp thy son.

" *Enter* JOCASTA.

" JOCASTA.

" Hearing, ye virgins, your Phœnician voice
" Within the house, I hither drag my steps

" Feeble with trembling age.—My son, my son,
" After this length of time, this tedious absence
" Do I behold thy face ? Ah ! fold thine arms
" Around me, clasp me to thy bosom, lean
" Thy cheek 'gainst my fond cheek, and shade my breast
" With the dark ringlets of thy clust'ring hair.
" Can I believe I hold thee in my arms
" Unlook'd for thus, so much beyond my hopes ?
" What shall I say to thee ? How tell thee all ?
" To touch thee thus, to hear thy voice, is joy,
" Is transport ; and my throbbing heart once more
" Feels its old raptures. O my son, my son,
" Long hast thou left thy father's house forsaken,
" Forced into exile by the brother's fault.
" How have thy friends, and how hath Thebes wish'd for
        " thee !
" With many a mournfull cry my hoary locks
" For thee I clipt away, for thee threw off
" My splendid robes, and chang'd them for these weeds,
" This sable dress of grief. Within the house,
" His eyes extinct, the poor old man still mourns
" With many' a tear, with many' an ardent wish,
" The discord of the brothers ; and his grief
" Swelling to madness arm'd his hand to strike
" At his own life, bewailing his rash curses
" Utter'd against his sons, with sighs and groans
" In solitary darkness lies conceal'd.
" For thee, my son, the nuptial bed, I hear,
" Rais'd in a foreign house, gives thee the joys
" Of love, and fondly to a foreign stem
" Allies thee : to a mother grievous this,
" Grievous to high-born Laius, this disgrace
" To be allied to strangers : nor did I
" Light, as our country's rites require, the torch
" T' attend thy nuptials, office well beseeming
" An happy mother : his unconscious stream
" Ismenus roll'd, and his delicious wave
" Fill'd not the bridal bath : through silent Thebes
" No voice of joy hail'd, as she pass'd along,

" Thy ent'ring bride. Be these ill omens vain ;
" Whether the sword, or discord, or thy father
" Be the sad cause, or Ate in the house
" Of Œdipus her horrid orgies holds.
" On me with all their weight these sorrows fall.''

This speech of Jocasta is so clear, that it is unnecessary for me to give any explanation, further than to describe the meaning of Ismenus and Ate. Ismenus was a river, the source of which was in Bœotia, and emptied itself into the Euripus. Ate was the most mischievous goddess in heaven, constantly creating discord amongst the host there. Jupiter, who was her father, was so enraged with her, that he drove her from heaven, and it is thought that she it was who first created dissension amongst mortals. By some writers she is considered the same as Discordia.

" POLYNICES.

" With confidence, though mix'd with some distrust,
" I set my foot amongst my foes : such love
" Our country claims perforce : whoe'er suggests
" A different argument, may please himself
" With empty words, but his sad heart is there.
" Yet so far troubled thoughts arose, and fear
" Lest treachery from my brother should attempt
" My life, that as I pass'd I grasp'd my sword,
" And each way roll'd mine eye ; yet did the truce
" Assure me, and thy faith, which hath induced me
" To enter thus this fortress of my fathers.
" The tears gush forth as after this long absence
" I view these roofs, the altars of the gods,
" The circus where my active youth first learn'd
" Its martial exercise, and Dirce's stream ;
" From these unjustly exiled I seek refuge
" Midst strangers in a foreign state, whilst tears
" Incessant dew my cheeks. But to my griefs
" This grief is added, thus to see thy head

" Shorn of its honour'd locks, these sable weeds,
" The garb of mourning : ah, my miseries !
" When discord rages in the house of friends,
" How dreadfull, how implacable the strife !
" But of my father tell me, whose sad age
" Sits darkling in the house ; of my two sisters
" Tell me ; unhappy, mourn they yet my exile ?

" JOCASTA.

" Some vengefull god pours ruin on the race
" Of Œdipus, e'er since thy luckless birth,
" And my unholy nuptials with thy father,
" Who gave thee being. But of this no more :
" Whate'er the gods ordain, 'tis ours to bear.
" Much would I ask ; but how ? I fear t' offend
" The feelings of thy mind, for thou art come
" Indulging my fond wish."

Polynices's meaning is, that it is a pleasure to him to tread his native soil ; but he has a feeling of mistrust respecting his own safety, as he has no confidence in his brother. All people have a feeling of regard for their country, that which gives them birth, however some may say to the contrary, for their doing so is but for sake of argument, and merely empty words. They may say they care but little for their native country, and appear contented elsewhere ; but their hearts are nevertheless always yearning for home. Although I feared treachery from my brother, I felt assurance in the truce, and I put faith in your sincerity, my mother. I therefore have entered this fortress of my fathers ; my tears flow with sad remembrance of the past as I view the altars and things around me. From all these I loved most dear I have been exiled by my brother, and compelled to live amongst strangers. To all these miseries more are added in seeing thee, my mother, thus deploring our families' misfortunes, robed in mourning. But tell me some news respecting my father and my sisters. Do they mourn my exile? Jocasta answers him, reverting to her unfortunate connection with Œdipus; but checks herself and asks Polynices if he feels being exiled from his country a great ill to himself. Oh! says Polynices, the worst of ills, even more to feel than tongue can describe. It checks us in expressing our thoughts freely; we feel constrained to bear the follies of those in authority without murmuring; and, for sake of our own interest, we are compelled to act with deference, and to submit with slavish complacence. Even hope herself is slow, though her looks are gracious. One day she has the sweetest and most attractive charms for us, next day she forsakes us altogether. When we are prosperous, our friends flock around us; when in adversity, they vanish.

LECTURE VIII.

—◆—

RESPECTING Polynices's marriage with the daughter of
Adrastus, King of Argos, there is a legend existing, which I
will relate to you :—Adrastus, having consulted the oracle
of Phœbus, was told to marry his two daughters—one to
a boar, the other to a lion.   Now it so occurred that,
about the same period that Polynices sought refuge at Argos,
Tydeus, son of Œneus, King of Calydon, having committed a murder in his father's country, fled also to Argos
to do penance; it being the custom in those days, if a
man perpetrated a crime of this description, to banish himself from his native land for a year which thus absolved him
from the consequences.   A storm ensued, when Tydeus and
Polynices both sought shelter in the vestibule of the citadel
called Lariffa, where they disagreed, and a quarrel ensued between them, the noise occasioned by which brought the king
to ascertain the cause, and having quelled it he invited them
both to partake of his hospitality.   Then observing that Tydeus
had the skin of a boar over his shoulders, and Polynices that
of a lion, so slung as to form a cloak or cape, he concluded
that these appearances made out the oracle that had been
decreed, and he gave each of his guests one of his daughters
in marriage, making them swear everlasting fidelity

to each other, to which they both gladly acceded. Tydeus afterwards became one of the seven chiefs against Thebes, in support of his brother-in-law's cause. A full description of Tydeus I will relate by-and-bye, in conjunction with the other six chiefs. I now return to the scene where Polynices is at Thebes, in conversation with his mother, Jocasta. Eteocles entering, addresses Jocasta as follows :—

" ETEOCLES.

" Well, mother, I am here, this grace to thee
" Conceding ; what is to be done ? Some one
" Begin the conference : for the walls around
" My squadrons marshal'd and well harness'd cars,
" I check them, till from thee I learn the terms
" Of amity, for which thou hast receiv'd him
" Within these walls, with leave from me obtain'd.

" JOCASTA.

" Restrain thy heart : the hasty spirit errs
" From justice : slow-form'd counsils perfect wisdom.
" Repress that firey eye, and those fierce thoughts :
" 'Tis not the Gorgon's head thou here beholdest,
" It is thy brother that revisits us.
" And thou, my Polynices, turn thy face,
" Look on thy brother ; better wilt thou speak,
" Eye fix'd on eye, and better he receive
" Thy words. O that my voice might counsil you
" To gentler reason ! When a friend incens'd
" Against a friend met face to face holds parle,
" The end, for which they meet, should be regarded
" Solely, no mention made of grievance past.
" My Polynices, be thy words first heard,
" For thou art come, leading the troops of Argos,
" For injuries done thee : such thy plea : betwixt you
" Some god be umpire, and accord your strife.

" POLYNICES.

" The words of truth are simple ; justice needs not
" The circling train of wily argument,
" Clear in its proofs.   Injustice, in it self
" Unsound, requires this medicinal trick
" Of glozing sophistry.   For me, my care
" To save the honour of my father's house,
" My own, and his, my wish t'avert the curse
" Which Œdipus denounc'd against his sons,
" Led me to leave this land, a willing exile,
" And give him for one rolling year to rule
" His country ; then return to take my share
" Of regal pow'r ; not with discordant hate
" And slaughter to atchieve outrageous deeds,
" Or suffer them, though this hath been my fate.
" He gave assent, and with a sacred oath
" Call'd the just gods to witness : yet his faith
" In nothing kept, but holds perforce the pow'r,
" And my part of this regal feat.   Yet I,
" Receiving my just right, am not averse
" To send these pow'rs away, in mine own house
" To hold my state the stipulated time,
" Then peacefull yield it to his rule again.
" I have no wish to desolate my country,
" Nor fix the firm machines to mount these walls.
" My right refus'd, with arms will I assert
" My cause, and to the gods make my appeal.
" My faith hath been held sacred, but to me
" Foul wrong is done, and by unrighteous force
" Am I driv'n forth an exile from my country.
" This is my plea, without collected proof
" Of circumstance, but just and clear to all
" Wise or unwise : so seems it to my thoughts.

" ETEOCLES.

" Of honour and of wisdom if alike
" All judged, nor contest, nor debate would rise
" 'Mongst men : but 'tis not so : the names they use

O

" In common ; but each gives his sense to them.
" My sense of them I freely shall avow.
" For honour I would mount above the stars,
" Above the sun's high course, or sink beneath
" Earth's deepest center, might I so obtain
" This idol of my soul, this worship'd pow'r
" Of royalty ; and never to another
" Would I resign her, but my self enjoy
" The splendid dignity : to give up greatness,
" For low rank ill exchang'd, were base indeed.
" And shame forbids that he, who comes in arms
" Spreading o'er these rich realms the waste of war,
" Should his rude will enjoy : and Thebes would blush
" At my dishonour, should I shrink through dread
" Of th' Argive spear, and to his hand resign
" My sceptre.   Seeks he to be reconciled ?
" This arms effect not : friendly speech does all
" The hostile sword could do.   On other terms
" Would he inhabit here: it is allow'd him :
" This grace, though much unwilling, shall I grant.
" A kingdom in my grasp, shall I submit
" To live his vassal ?   No : come fire, come sword,
" Yoke thy proud steeds, fill all the fields with chariots,
" Thou never shalt extort my kingdom from me.
" If wrong must be, when empire is the prize
" The noble cause gives glory to the wrong :
" In all besides let justice hold her course.

" JOCASTA.

" Think not, Eteocles, my son, that age
" Inherits nought but ills : Experience waits it,
" To wisdom train'd beyond the reach of youth.
" Why dost thou court that banefull pest ambition ?
" Do not, my son : her pow'r is built on wrong.
" Where'er the Demon sets her foot, that house,
" That state sees all its high-rais'd glories vanish,
" And desolation enters : yet on her
" Art thou enamour'd.   Juster honours wait

" On moderation : she links friend to friend,
" And state to state in firm society :
" For on the mind of man her equal laws
" Hath Nature stamp'd : but wild ambition's flight
" Each rank below opposes, and at once
" Begins the war. Her equal laws first fix'd
" Equality of measure, poised the scale,
" And taught the nice array of marshal'd numbers.
" The dark-brow'd night, the radiance of the sun,
" In fair succession walk their annual round,
" Unenvious each of th'other's reign : hence night
" And the sun's ray are useffull to mankind.
" But thou wilt brook no equal, nor to him
" Allow his share of rule : where then is justice ?
" Why with unbounded heat dost thou pursue
" This flourishing injustice, royalty ?
" What are its honours which thou prizest thus ?
" To be conspicuous ? That's an empty glory.
" Or wou'dst thou labour much, whilst thy rich house
" Possesses much ? And what is this abundance ?
" 'Tis nothing but a name : the temperate mind,
" Its wants supply'd, checks each desire of more :
" And mortal man enjoys not as his own
" His treasur'd stores ; but holds them as the gift
" Of the high gods, who at their will resume them.
" Wealth then hath no stability, but fleets
" With each loose hour. Yet further let me ask,
" Is it thy wish to reign, or save thy country ?
" Say'st thou, to reign ? Should he be conqueror,
" Should thy troops fall beneath the spear of Argos,
" Then shall thine eyes behold this city vanquish'd,
" Then shall thine eyes behold its captive virgins
" Drag'd by the rude hands of th' insulting foes.
" So shall this love of empire, which inflames thee,
" Be ruinous to the Thebans : yet thou art
" Ambitious of its honours. This to thee.
" Now, Polynices, be to thee my words.
" Unwisely hath Adrastus to thy will

" Indulged this grace ; and foolishly hast thou
" Advanced in arms to desolate thy country.
" Shou'dst thou subdue this land, (may no such ill
" Await it !) by the gods, how wilt thou raise
" The trophies of thy spear ? How consecrate
" The hallow'd victim for thy country vanquish'd ?
" Or wilt thou on the banks of Inachus
" Engrave upon the spoils, "Thebes laid in ashes,
" The victor Polynices to the gods
" Fix'd here these shields."   Ah, never may that glory,
" Won by the arms of Greece, be thine, my son !
" Shou'dst thou be conquer'd ; should his arms prevail,
" How wilt thou, leaving thousands of her sons
" Here slain, revisit Argos ? Every tongue
" Will clamour, " In ill hour this fatal love
" Didst thou allow, Adrastus ; for one bride,
" And her unhappy nuptials, on our heads
" Hath ruin fallen."   With eager speed, my son,
" Thou runnest on double ill, to be bereav'd
" Of these thy friends, and fail in this attempt.
" Check then, my sons, O check your wild ambition ;
" Both are imprudent, and conflicting thus
" Bring on the greatest and most hatefull ills."

I need not explain this scene to you more than a few
sentences, for dull indeed must be the mind that conceiveth
it not.   One can well understand the anxiety of a mother's
mind who is endeavouring to make peace between her two
only sons, who are at war with each other; but hard is that
effort when each of them is obdurate, and determined to pursue
the bent of his own will.   It is evident that Jocasta's
thoughts are with Polynices's cause; but she is struggling
against the indomitable nature of her younger son, who has
grasped the sole authority; she therefore endeavours to
appeal to Polynices's sympathies, urging him not to fight
against the country of his ancestors.   Polynices seems to

feel his position acutely, and he says all that he asks of his brother is to act up to the compact entered into between them—that is, that they shall each reign a year alternately in Thebes. But Eteocles being in power, and backed by Creon's influence, declares he will not yield to live under his brother's rule, and he excuses his tyranny by a false declaration of honour; he nevertheless consents to withdraw the decree he made, banishing Polynices from Thebes; but this concession is made in such a bad spirit, that mean indeed would Polynices prove himself were he to succumb. Finding the inadequate terms offered by his brother, he repels them, and he is peremptorily ordered by Eteocles to leave the state, who threatens him to delay not on pain of death. Then, after a parley of more words, in which each threatens the other, Polynices says:—

> " Thou earth that nurturedst, and you, ye gods,
> " I call to witness, that dishonour'd, wrong'd,
> " Calamitous, I hence by force am driv'n,
> " Spurn'd as a slave, an alien to the blood
> " Of Œdipus. Should aught of ill hence fall
> " On thee, my country, charge the fault on him,
> " Not me: reluctant am I come, reluctant
> " Was I driv'n hence. And thou, imperial Phœbus,
> " Presiding o'er these streets, farewell : ye mansions,
> " That hold the loved companions of my youth,
> " Ye hallow'd statues of the gods, farewell.
> " For that again it may be mine t' address you
> " I cannot warrant : yet hope slumbers not,
> " Nor my firm trust that, with the gods, this hand
> " Shall kill him, and secure my reign o'er Thebes.
>
> [*Exit* POLYNICES.
>
> " CHORUS.
>
> " STROPHE.
>
> " When Cadmus from the Tyrian strand
> " Arriving trod this destin'd land,

" Heav'n-taught the Heifer* led the way,
" Till down to willing rest she lay,
        " Marking his future seat :
" By fate assign'd the furrow'd plain,
" Thick-waving with the golden grain ;
" Assign'd the verdure-vested meads,
" Through which the beauteous Dirce leads
        " Her crystal currents fleet.
" The pregnant mother† here of yore
" To Jove the blooming Bacchus bore ;
" And instant o'er the boy divine
" With wanton wreaths‡ the ivy twine
        " Entrail'd its pale-green shade :
" To Bacchus hence through festive groves
" The train of Theban matrons roves ;
" The virgins hence in frolic bands,
" Waving their ivy-twisted wands,
        " The dance fantastic lead.

" ANTISTROPHE.

" A dragon there in scales of gold
" Around his firey eyeballs roll'd,
" By Mars assign'd that humid shade,
" To guard the green extended glade,
        " And silver-streaming tide :
" Him, as with pious haste he came
" To draw the purifying stream,
" Dauntless the Tyrian chief represt,
" Dash'd with a rock his sanguine crest,
        " And crush'd his scaly pride.

---

* This alludes to the state established by Cadmus, called Bœotia, he having been directed to the spot by a heifer ; an oracle at the shrine of Apollo having told him to build a city in the meadow where he would behold such an animal stop to graze.

† Semele, daughter of Cadmus.

‡ Bacchus is generally represented with a wreath of ivy round his brow ; and at the feasts devoted to him, those maidens who danced, carried wands in their hands, with ivy twisted round them.

" Then at the martial maid's* command
" With his deep plough-share turns the land,
* " The dragon's teeth wide scattering round ;
" When sudden from the furrow'd ground
      " Embattled hosts arise :
" But slaughter's iron arm again
" Consigns them to their native plain,
" And their lov'd earth, that to the day
" Show'd them in heav'n's ætherial ray,
      " With streaming crimson dies.

        " EPODE.

" Thee, whom to thund'ring Jove of yore
" On Nile's moist margent Iö bore,
" Iö,† from whom this mighty race
" Their heav'n-descended lineage trace,
" Thee, Epaphus,‡ I call : my pray'r,
" Barbaric though my voice, O hear !
" Barbaric though my pray'r, attend,
" This race, this progeny, defend !
" Come, O come, and with thee join
" The double-named Proserpine,§
" And bounteous Ceres, smiling queen,
" That holds o'er all her golden reign ;
" For all things take from her their birth,
" Nurtured by the fertile earth :
" Bring these deities, whose sway
" The copious-rising fruits obey,
" This land to guard, once their abode :
" All things are easy to a god."

To explain the meaning of these verses, Palæphatus, who

---

* The martial maid alludes to Minerva, who assisted Cadmus to subdue the dragon.

† Iö was daughter of Inachus, transformed into a heifer by Jupiter.

‡ Epaphus was the son of Iö whose father was Jupiter.

§ Proserpine was sometimes called Proserpina ; but the double name
alluded to here is that which the Greeks usually called her by—Perse-
phone. She was daughter of Jupiter and Ceres.

was a Grecian philosopher, tells us that Draco, a son of Mars, was King of Thebes, and he was slain by Cadmus. Draco's sons continued an ineffectual war against Cadmus; and, being beaten in their retreat, seized some treasures belonging to Cadmus, amongst which there were some elephants' teeth.   They afterwards made frequent incursions in the country round Thebes, and occasioned considerable devastations in the suburbs, which caused the people to say that Cadmus brought the evils upon them by killing Draco. And relative to the dragon here alluded to by the chorus, which was that slain by Cadmus, Bryant tells us that all the poetical accounts of heroes engaging with dragons have arisen from a misconception about the Ophite Towers and Temples, which (he says) those persons either founded or took in war; or (he says), " If they were deities of whom the story is told, these buildings were erected to their honour."   Mr. R. Potter gives us a most philosophical version of this tradition. He says that the dragon which was slain by Cadmus was Draco, or a chief of an Ophite Tower, who opposed Cadmus making a settlement in Bœotia, and that the teeth of the dragon alludes to the forces which opposed Cadmus.   He says these sprang from the ground in arms, and that Minerva (which means here wisdom) sowed dissension amongst them, and that some of them espoused the cause of Cadmus, who then married a lady of the country, named Harmonia, or Hermione.   Palæphatus* says she was the sister of Draco, and that from this alliance Harmonia was called the daughter of Mars and Venus, through whom came the blessings of peace. These inferences are so entirely consistent with reason, that

---

* Palæphatus wrote a work in which he explains mythological facts by historical facts (as indeed they may by philosophical reasonings all more or less be traced to).

I have not the least hesitation in endorsing them; and, indeed, bearing in mind that Bryant is of a similar opinion, I think there cannot remain a reasonable doubt upon the point.

. Whilst Eteocles is gone to the walls to repel the enemy, the scene is taken up within the city by Creon, Tiresias, Menœceus, and Manto. But, ere I commence it, let me venture to read to you a little effort of my own, applicable to the fearful struggle now ensuing between the two brothers and their hosts.

'Tis thro' the truth that lights the mind
  That virtue only takes its place ;
Thro' virtue 'tis and truth combin'd
  We only meet the soul of grace.
For thro' our walks in social life
  We meet with guiles and with passions,
Man wars with man—wars to the knife—
  Just to carry out old fashions.
But O ! if love and truth did dwell
  In holy, sacred brotherhood,
How might our souls with pleasure swell,
  And worldly peace be understood !
How then like heav'n would be this earth ;
  No mournful tribute of our tears
Would tinge our paths, destroying mirth,
  And oft embitt'ring all our years.
For whilst our bark is on the surge,
  Being toss'd by tempest'ous wave,
Shall we create the fun'ral dirge,
  And thrust each other in the grave ?
No ; rather let us live in peace,
  Alleviating others' pain ;
By doing good we but increase
  Our chance in bliss to live again.

" TIRESIAS.

" A little onward lead me, be an eye
" To these dark steps, my daughter, as the star

" That guides the mariner ; o'er level ground
" Direct my slow feet, lest we tread unsafe :
" Feeble thy father.   In thy virgin hand
" Hold my oracular tablets, which I mark'd,
" Skill'd in each auspice of the flying wing,
" When in my consecrated seat my voice
" Prophetic of the fates foretells the future.
" My child Menœceus, son of Creon, tell me
" What of our way remains, that through the city
" Will bring me to thy father ; for my knee
" Fails me ; with pain I tread this length of way."

. Tiresias, being aged and blind, cautions his daughter to
lead him clear of obstructions ; and he speaks of his skill in
foretelling future events by the flight of birds (this was an
old superstition, doubtless as little reliable as were many
other myths of priestcraft then in existence, and perhaps
still extant in many parts of the world).   Then turning to
Menœceus, who is also attendant on him, he says, How
much further have I to wend my way ere I be in the presence
of your father.   On this, Creon being present says :—

" Be comforted : Tiresias, thou hast steer'd
" Nigh to thy friends thy foot.",

Which of course means I am here, my feet are near thine
own.   Well, says Tiresias, now I am here, what is the reason
of my being summon'd so hastily ?

" One night hath only pass'd since with much toil
" From Athens I came hither : there his spear
" Eumolphus rais'd in war, wherein I made
" The sons of Cecrops glorious conquerors ;
" And therefore wear this golden crown thou seest,
" Rent from the foe, an honourable meed."

The Eumolphus alluded to by Tiresias, was King of

Thrace, and son of Chione and Neptune, who was daughter of Dædalian, a son of Lucifer. He was at war with Erectheus the Sixth, King of Athens, who was son of Pandion the First, whose father was Erichthonius, the fourth King of Athens, said to be a son of the god Vulcan. The Cecrops alluded to by Tiresias was an Egyptian by birth. He invaded Atica about the middle of the sixteenth century, B.C., and is supposed to have been the founder of Athens. There was another of this name (Cecrops), great-grand-son of Erichthonius; he was the seventh King of Athens, and was married to a daughter of Dædalus; her name was Metiadusa; they were the parents of Pandion the Second, who was also King of Athens. Tiresias says that he has rendered this race his assistance, and for his services he has been rewarded with a golden crown, which he is now wearing. Creon replies :—

> " I hail the omen : that victorious crown
> " Portends to us like victory :"

This is merely a little flattery on Creon's part, for no meaning can be gathered from the remark. He is about asking Tiresias's advice, and like most sycophants he glozes the way with hypocrisy. He then says that the king, Eteocles, has commissioned him to learn from Tiresias what they are to do to save the city. As regards Eteocles, says Tiresias, I will not speak (this is said in contempt by the old man, as his advice has been disregarded by Eteocles in a former instance), but respecting yourself, if you are resolved to learn from me what the oracle decrees, I will tell you. Know then that to save the city thy son Menœceus must be sacrificed.

> " 'Tis fated thus, and thou perforce must do it."

Creon, upon hearing this, exclaims, Then let my country perish the rather; and, falling on his knees to Tiresias, he entreats him not to declare the decree; but the former tells him it is too late. You have demanded it, and now I am not permitted to be silent. Your son must be taken to the cave.

> " Where lay the earth-borne dragon,
> " Guardian of Dirce's fountains,"

and his life's blood must be poured on the earth, as a sacrifice to Mars, who is incensed against the race of Cadmus, for that he did slaughter an earth-borne dragon. It is quite evident that Euripides alludes to the dragon which inhabited the cave near to Dirce's fountain in Thebes; and it is somewhat difficult to comprehend how this can be the same animal which Cadmus slew in Bœotia. I have little doubt but that the term dragon alludes to a race of men, probably designated so from the device they bore on their shields. Mars demands human blood for blood, says Tiresias, and you with your two sons are the only three left that sprang from the teeth of the dragon which Cadmus sowed. It must not be your son Hæmon, as he is affianced in marriage to Antigone, the daughter of Œdipus; therefore Mencæceus must be the one sacrificed, so to appease the god of war, who will then espouse the cause of the Thebans, and assist them against Adrastus and his host.

There is an extraordinary enigma in this part of the play. Euripides makes Tiresias say that Mars is incensed against Cadmus and his race for having slaughtered the earth-borne dragon, and that he demands human blood for human blood; therefore you, Creon, and your two sons being the only ones left that sprang from the teeth of the dragon, one of you must be sacrificed. How can this possibly be appeasing the god for the sacrifice of the dragon—slaughtering the produce of one of its own teeth? Those teeth were not the seed of Cadmus; it is therefore somewhat puzzling what Euripides means by human blood for blood.

In the next scene Creon urges his son Menœcceus to quit Thebes before the chiefs hear of the oracle which has been decreed and related by Tiresias; for, says Creon, though I would willingly lay down my own life to save my country, I cannot consent to sacrifice you, my son. Go quickly far hence; wend thy steps through Delphi,* thence across the Ætolian† country to

" Dodona's hallow'd mount,"‡

---

* Delphi, situate in the valley of Parnassus. At this place the serpent Python, which was sent by Juno to worry poor Latona was destroyed. The town itself was named after Latonas, grandson of Delphus. Here the celebrated temple of his father Apollo was situate, at which shrine all who consulted the oracle had to make rich presents, and the town became so opulent in consequence that incursions were frequently made by the Phocians, who plundered the place regardless of religion, sanctity, or the god that was supposed to preside over it. Delphi (or, as it is now called, Castre) was in after ages also plundered by Nero and Constantine, each of them carrying off treasures of considerable value.

† This country was named after Ætolus who was a son of Endymion, he the son of Æthlius and Calyce. Ætolus is sometimes confounded with Æolus, son of Hippotas. The mother of Ætolus was named Iphianassa, who was a daughter of Prœtus, King of Argos, the son of Abas and Ocalea.

‡ The hallow'd mount alludes to the temple which was erected here to Jupiter. This land was discovered after the deluge in a somewhat similar manner to what Delphi was. Delphi was supposed to be about the centre of the earth: of course no notion then existed of the world being spherical. Two doves were believed to have been let loose from the extremities of the earth by Jupiter, and they alighted here both at one time. Dodona was discovered by a black dove, and Herodotus tells us that Ammon in Libya (where was situated the great temple of Jupi-

which is situate on the Thesprotian* coast. Menœceus apparently assents to his father's proposition; but inwardly resolves to sacrifice himself to save his country, and he does so.

In the next scene a messenger enters, and relates the circumstance in the following beautiful speech, in which he also describes to Jocasta the full particulars of what is transpiring before the Theban walls.

" MESSENGER.

" Soon as the son of Creon, on the tow'rs
" Conspicuous standing, drew his gloomy sword
" And plung'd it in his breast, with glorious zeal
" Dying to save his country, sev'n firms bands
" With their brave chiefs at the sev'n gates thy son
" Close-stationed, 'gainst the Argive foe a guard,
" Horse rang'd for fight 'gainst horse, and shield oppos'd
" To shield, a ready aid, whene'er our force
" Might on their rampires feel disorder.   Soon
" From our high tow'rs we view the Argive host,
" Their white shields glitt'ring to the sun, advanc'd

---

ter) was discovered in like manner. We read something very similar to this in the Bible attributable to the time of Noah.   Dodona was situate in Epirus. The temple here was one of the most ancient in Greece, it was founded by Cuthites, and was officiated over by females.   Pausanias tells us that the Peliades were prophetesses here; and he says that the first oracle they exhibited related to the establishment of Zeuth and the restoration of the earth to its pristine state. I think Pausanias means Zethus, or Zetus, a son of Jupiter and Antiope; or he may mean Zeus, which applies to Jupiter himself; this name the Greeks gave him, the meaning being the father of mankind, or the father of all living things. The Peliades were the four daughters of Pelias, their names were Alceote, Pisidice, Pelopea, and Hippothoe. Hyginus tells us there were five of them, the fifth he names Medusa, but the only Medusa I find alluded to by other authors is a daughter of Phorcys and Ceto.

* Thesprotia, situate on the south coast of Epirus. Through this land ran the rivers Cocytus and Acheron.

" From high Teumessus :* on with rapid march
" They moved, and in embattled phalanx reach'd
" The trenches nigh the town : the song of war
" They rais'd, and with the sounding trumpet gave
" Fierce sign of battle, from the walls return'd
" With notes as fierce.   Parthenopœus first,
" Sprung from th' Arcadian huntress, led his troop
" Horrent† with close-wedged bucklers 'gainst the gates
" Of Neis : on his massy shield pourtray'd
" Stands Atalanta grasping in her hand
" The distant-wounding bow, in act to wing
" The flying shaft against th' Ætolian boar,
" Domestic impress.   To the Prœtian gate
" The fate-foretelling chief Amphiaraus
" Advanc'd, the hallow'd victims load his car ;
" His shield no boastfull argument displays,
" No pageant marks his modest arms. · Before
" Th' Ogygian gate Hippomedon rear'd high
" His royal crest ; and on his shield he bore
" An Argus studded round with eyes ; of these
" Alternate some waked with the rising stars,
" Some with the setting closed ; this might we see
" When now the chief lay breathless on the ground.
" At th' Omolean gate his post in arms
" Held Tydeus, on his shield he bore impress'd
" A lion's shaggy spoils ; a Titan he,
" A bold Prometheus, in his right hand waved
" A blazing torch, as he wou'd fire the town.
" To the Crenean gate his armed force
" Thy Polynices led, and on his shield
" The Potnian mares‡ insculptur'd start and bound,

---

* A mountain in Bœotia.

† I take this passage to mean, a closely marshalled troop of tall men, well guarded by their bucklers, so carried forming a fair line of defence to their persons.   Bucklers were shields of an oblong shape, frequently used of such large dimensions as almost to cover two-thirds of the entire man.

‡ Potnian mares.   This alludes to a fountain of water, situate at

" Whirl'd by the well-form'd caveson* within,
" Around the boss, showing their firey rage.
" Not less than Mars to daring deeds enflamed
" Against th' Electran gate fierce Capaneus
" His phalanx led : his iron-sculptured shield
" An earth-born giant held impress'd, whose strength
" Bore on his shoulders a whole town, by force
" From its foundations rent with massy bars,
" Emblem of ruin menaced to this city.
" At the seventh gate Adrastus held his post,
" His left hand bore his shield, whose ample orb
" An Hydra with an hundred hissing heads,
" The boast of Argos, fill'd ; and from the walls
" Seiz'd in their viperous jaws the dragons bore
" The sons of Thebes. Each impress I observ'd,
" When to the chiefs I bore the word of war.
" First with our bows we fought, and missive spears,
" Far-wounding slings, and fragments rent from rocks :
" Their battle bleeding, Tydeus call'd aloud,
" Thy son soon join'd his voice, " Ye sons of Greece,
" Why, e'er these vollied weapons thin our ranks,
" Rush we not on embodied to the gates,
" Foot, horse, and rolling car ?" Soon as the word
" Was heard, with furious expedition on they roll'd :
" There many fell, their helms besmear'd with blood ;
" And many from the walls might'st thou behold
" Tumbled precipitate on the ground beneath
" Breathe out their lives, with streams of gushing blood
" Moist'ning the thirsty earth. Th' Arcadian then,
" No Argive he, the son of Atalanta,
" Impetuous as a whirlwind's stormy force
" Rush'd to the walls and cried, Flames here, a spade,
" As from their deep foundations he would heave

Potniæ in Bœotia, from which when horses drank, they went immediately mad. The description by the messenger is, that the horses are represented on the shields rampant mad.

 * Caveson (or cavesson), the nose-straps by which the horses were governed.

" The shaking ramparts ; but his headlong fury
" Neptunian Periclymenus repress'd ;
" Rent from the battlements a pond'rous stone
" His strong hand heav'd, and on his helm discharg'd ;
" Full on his head it fell, th' enormous mass,
" And crush'd the shatter'd bone ; his auburn locks
" And purple-blooming cheeks distain'd with blood ;
" Him on the heights of Mænalus* no more
" His beauteous-quiver'd mother shall receive
" In life's warm glow.   Soon as thy son beheld
" His arms successfull here, to other gates
" He hasted ; I attended ; Tydeus there
" I saw ; in close array his warriors stood
" Grasping their shields, and to the battlements
" Hurl'd their Ætolian spears ; the rampired heights
" Our flying troops abandon ; these thy son
" Like a bold hunter chear'd, and to the tow'rs
" Led back embattled : thence to other gates,
" The martial ardor here revived, we haste.
" But with what words can I express the rage
" Of Capaneus ?   He to his post advanced,
" A ladder in his hand of length to scale
" The walls, and in his pride vaunted aloud
" That not the awefull fire of thund'ring Jove
" Should check him mounting o'er the rampires' height
" To storm the town ; thus menacing, amidst
" A storm of hurtling stones he dared th' ascent,
" Beneath his shield collected, and had reach'd
" The battlements, when Jove with thunder smote him ;
" The earth rebellow'd to the roar, that all
" Trembled with dread ; and from the steps his limbs
" Asunder torn, as with an engine's force,
" Were scatter'd diverse ; tow'rds Olympus† flew

---

* A mountain named after Mænalus, who was a son of Lycaon, King
of Arcadia.

† There were two mountains bearing this name ; the one alluded to
here was in Arcadia, and was of minor import to the celebrated Mount

" His hair, his blood fell on the earth ; his hands,
" His feet roll'd whirling like Ixion's wheel,*
" And to the ground his flaming body fell.
" When now Adrastus to the Argive arms
" Saw Jove averse, back o'er the treuch he led
" His forces ; ours the fav'ring signal fill'd
" With added courage ; on their whirling cars
" They drove, mail-clad ; and through the deep array
" Of Argos in close fight their spears advanced.
" All now was rout ; some died ; some from their cars
" Fell headlong, o'er them roll'd the bounding wheels ;
" Axle with axle clash'd ; the dead on heaps
" Lay whelm'd beneath the dead. Thus have we stay'd
" Destruction from our tow'rs, this day at least ;
" The future, whether fortune to this land
" Assigns success, is heav'n's important care.

" Jocasta.

" Well have the gods appointed, fortune well :
" My sons are living, and my country stands
" Rescued from threat'ning danger. In my nuptials
" With Œdipus th' unhappy Creon seems
" Alone to suffer, of his son deprived,
" With glory to the public, to his soul
" A private grief. But say, resume thy tale,
" This past, what measures will my sons pursue ?

Olympus in Macedonia, which was supposed to be the residence of the Gods.

* The wheel in hell to which Ixion King of Thessaly was tied by order of Jupiter, for having seduced Juno, the Queen of Heaven. This office was performed by Mercury, Jove's messenger. Ixion's punishment was supposed to be eternal, as the wheel was believed to be continually on the whirl. An explanation of the names of the chiefs alluded to here by the messenger, together with the particulars of their lineage, and the devices they bore I intend to give in my lecture on the tragedy of the " Seven Chiefs against Thebes," by Æschylus, which is based upon the same subject as this I am now describing and will follow next after it.

" MESSENGER.

" Why wilt thou not, these joyfull tidings told,
" Dismiss me?   Why must I relate the ill?
" Thy sons are bent on most unseemly deeds
" Of dreadfull daring, from each host apart
" T' engage in single combat : to the sons
" Of Thebes alike and Argos have they spoken
" The word that ill becomes them.   From his station
" On the high tow'r Eteocles began,
" Silence to either army first proclaim'd,
" ' Warriors of Greece, that on these fields impress
" ' Your hostile steps, ye Argive chiefs, and you
" ' Embattled Thebans, sell not here your lives
" ' In Polynices' quarrel, nor in mine.
" ' I from that danger bid you cease ; alone
" ' I will engage my brother : if I slay him,
" ' Mine be the realm alone ; but should I fall,
" ' To him I yield the city ; you, no more
" ' In arms contending, shall return to Argos,
" ' Nor leave your sweet lives here ; of Thebes' high race
" ' Enough lie breathless on th' ensanguin'd ground.'
" He spoke, and Polynices from his ranks
" Rush'd forth, with joy assenting to his words :
" And all of Argos, all of Thebes, with shouts
" Applauded, deeming just the terms proposed.
" Soon to the space 'twixt host and host advanc'd
" The chiefs in truce, and ratified their faith
" On each side with the sanction of an oath.
" Now whilst in brazen mail the youthfull sons
" Of Œdipus invest their limbs, our chief
" With friendly zeal the Theban nobles arm :
" Their chief the Argive princes : radiant now
" They stood ; no sign of fear, none of remorse
" Obscured their brows ; but with infuriate rage
" Each grasp'd his spear advancing : as they pass'd,
" Their ardor with these words their friends enflamed,
" ' Now, Polynices, is it thine to raise
" ' To Jove the trophied image, now to give

" ' Glory to Argos.'   To Eteocles,
" ' Now dost thou fight thy country's champion, now
" ' Let conquest grace thy arms, the royal prize
" ' A kingdom waits thee.'   With such words their souls
" They kindle to the fight.   The sacred seers,
" The victims slain, attentive stand, and mark
" Th' increasing fires, the bursting gall, the flames
" Ascending, which a twofold omen bear,
" Portending conquest one, and one defeat.
" But hast thou aught of pow'r to sooth this rage,
" Or words with wisdom fraught, or charmed strain,
" Go, check thy sons, prevent this horrid fray ;
" For great the danger, as the prize is great ;
" And in the bitterness of grief thy tears
" Will flow, of both thy sons at once deprived.

" JOCASTA.

" Antigone, come forth ; come forth, my child :
" Not to the dance, nor to the virgin bow'r
" Th' appointment of the gods now leads thee forth.
" But it behoves thee, joining with thy mother,
" To stay the mighty chiefs, thy brothers, bent
" On death, from falling each by th' other's hand."

Here enters Antigone.   Jocasta continues :—

" Haste, daughter, haste.   If yet I may prevent
" My sons before their combat, heav'n's fair light
" Shall chear my life ; but if thou comest too late,
" 'Tis ruin all ; thou too art lost ; and I
" Will clasp my dying sons and die with them."

[*Exit* JOCASTA, *followed by* ANTIGONE.]

In the next and last scene Creon enters, lamenting the death of his son Menœceus, and he is not aware of the engagement of single combat that has taken place between Eteocles and Polynices ; nor is he aware of Jocasta's death (all of which have taken place) until the messenger describes these circumstances to him in the following language :—

" MESSENGER.

" Ah wretched me, what language shall I use,
" What words ?
" Ah wretched me ! for mighty are the ills
" I come to utter.
" No more thy sister's sons behold the light.
" With her two sons thy sister lies in death.
" 'Twixt host and host the rival chieftains stood,
" Ready to lift their spears in single fight :
" His eye tow'rds Argos Polynices roll'd,
" And utter'd thus his pray'r, Imperial Juno,
" Goddess revered, for thine I am, since join'd
" Iu marriage with the daughter of Adrastus,
" Thy land receiv'd me an inhabitant,
" Give me to kill my brother, and to stain
" With his warm life-blood this victorious hand
" In the fierce contest : an inglorious crown
" I ask, to kill a brother : tears gush'd forth
" From many, as their eyes each glanc'd on each,
" Pitying their fate.   But to the hallow'd dome
" Of Pallas glorious with her golden shield
" His eyes Eteocles turn'd, and thus address'd her,
" Daughter of Jove, give my victorious spear,
" Lanc'd by this hand, to pierce my brother's breast,
" And kill him, for he came to waste my country.
" But when the torch was hurl'd, which, as the sound
" Of the Tyrrhenian trumpet, gives the signal
" Of bloody battle, furiously they rush'd
" In dreadfull opposition ; as two boars
" Whetting their savage tusks, their jaws besmear'd
" With foam, they met impetuous with their spears.
" But each beneath his round shield lay at ward,
" That the steel glanc'd in vain : if either rais'd
" His eye above the verge, the other drove
" With eager haste full at his face the lance ;

" But to the grated openings that adorn

" The rim, his eye with caution each applies,

" And disappoints the spear.   With throbbing hearts,

" More than the combatants, their friends around

" Intent and anxious for their chieftain glow.

" It chanced against a stone Eteocles

" Impress'd his foot, thus turn'd without the verge

" Of his broad shield : this Polynices saw,

" And where the part was open to the blow

" Drove through the plated greave his Argive spear ;

" All the Pelasgian troops shouted aloud.

" His shoulder in the effort left exposed

" The wounded chief observ'd, and aim'd his lance

" With well-directed force against the breast

" Of Polynices, to the sons of Thebes

" Requiting joy ; but faithless to his hand

" The steel point broke : now in the heedless truncheon

" No more confiding quick a backward step

" He moved, then seiz'd and whirl'd a rugged stone :

" Full on the spear the pond'rous marble fell,

" And crash'd it in the midst : the combat now

" Was equal, of the spear each chief depriv'd.

" Their falchions then they grasp'd, and furious rush'd

" To closer conflict ; shield to shield advanc'd

" Sustain'd the clashing tumult of the fight :

" Eteocles, with presage of success,

" Call'd to his aid the wily discipline

" Learnt in Thessalia, from the pressing toil .

" Withdrew his left foot backward, guarding well

" His body, with his right advancing wheel'd

" Oblique, and plunged his sword deep in his bowels,

" Driven to the chine.   Th' unhappy Polynices

" Stood writhing with his tort'ring wound awhile,

" Then fell, the blood fast welling from the wound.

" And now the victor, as secure of conquest,

" Threw down his sword to strip him of his arms,

" Heedless of him, and on the spoil intent ;

" A fatal oversight : he breathing yet,

" And grasping in his dreadfull fall his sword,
" Scarce rais'd it as he lay ; Eteocles
" Stooping receiv'd it in his heart.   Thus both
" Together fell, together lie in blood,
" Biting the ground, the conquest undecided.

" CREON.

" O Œdipus, with friendly grief I mourn
" Thy ills : the god hath ratified thy curse.

" MESSENGER.

" Yet give me hearing, whilst I speak of ills
" Added to ills.   Expiring on the earth
" Her sons were fall'n, when the unhappy mother,
" Attended by her virgin daughter, came
" With zealous speed : soon as she saw their life
" Fast-flowing from their wounds, with shrieks she cried,
" Too late, my sons, too late to succour you
" I come : then clasping each, o'er each she mourn'd,
" Wailing the painfull care with which her breasts
" Nourish'd their infancy.   Their sister too,
" Companion of her griefs, with sighs address'd them,
" Ye dear supporters of your mother's age,
" My much loved brothers, how have you betray'd
" My virgin hopes !   With pain his gasping breath
" Eteocles drew, but at his mother's voice
" Stretch'd forth his hand moist with the dews of death :
" He utter'd not a word, but with his eyes
" He spoke to her in tears, signal of love.
" But Polynices, yet alive, his eyes
" Cast on his sister, and his aged mother,
" And spoke these words, Destruction on our heads
" Is fall'n, O mother ; yet I pity thee,
" My sister, and my brother stretch'd in death :
" A friend, though made a foe, is yet a friend.
" O thou, to whom I owe my birth ; and thou
" My sister, in my native earth entomb me,
" And pacify th' exasperated state.

" Be this at least of my paternal soil

" My portion, though the royal seat be lost.

" Let thy dear hand, my mother, close my eyes ;

" (And with his own he drew it to their lids)

" Now farewell both ; the shades of death surround me.

" Thus each expiring their unhappy lives

" Resign'd together.   When the mother saw

" This dire event, impatient of her grief

" From her dead son she snatch'd the reeking sword,

" And did a deed of horror ; through her throat

" She thrust the steel, and on their much loved bodies,

" Each in her arms embracing, lies in death.

" Strait to the strife of words the armies rose ;

" We claim'd the conquest for our chief, and they

" For theirs ; amidst the leaders stern debate

" Was kindled ; these contend that Polynices

" First won th' advantage with his spear ; and those

" That victory for neither had declared,

" Where both were slain.   Then from the bick'ring troops

" Antigone withdrew : they rush'd to arms.

" The sons of Thebes had providently sate

" Reclining on their shields : prevention then

" Was ours, and sudden on the Argive host,

" Not yet accoutred in their arms, we fell ;

" And none sustain'd th' attack, but hasty rout

" And flight fill'd all the plains ; the blood of thousands,

" That fell beneath the spear, flow'd on the earth.

" Thus were we victors in the fight ; and some

" The trophy'd image raise to Jove ; whilst some

" Snatch from the Argives slain their shields, and send

" The spoils to grace the town ; others attend

" Antigone, and this way bear the dead,

" To share the last sad office of their friends.

" Thus on one part the state in her success

" Rejoices, on one part bewails her loss.

" CHORUS.

" No more the ruin of this royal house

" Pierces our ears ; our eyes may now behold

" Advancing to these gates th' unhappy three,
" That sunk together to eternal night."

Doctor Donaldson argues very fairly that Euripides' parents must have been wealthy, or, says he, "They could not have placed their son for his education under the extravagant Prodicus." But we also have it that Aristophanes insinuates that Euripides' mother " was a seller of herbs," and Theopompus affirms it as a fact. Now, I think there is no necessity to place much reliance upon this statement for the following reasons :—In the first place, the lady might have distributed medicinal herbs, from philanthropic motives, gratuitously ; or she might have cultivated them (for sale) in her gardens, in like manner as people of wealth in the present time do pines or melons. I look upon Theopompus's remark as having been sarcastically made for some purpose of his own, or it may be a mistake altogether, as we have none of his works preserved entire, and the allusions to the circumstance by Aristophanes are mere satire. But, be it true or not that Euripides' mother " was a seller of herbs," it is a fact assumed by all that he was not neglected, for he undoubtedly received an excellent education ; and it is asserted also as a fact that he attended lectures given by the " renowned Anaxagoras," the " learned Prodicus," and the " refined Protagoras;" and we are further told that Euripides gained two victories in the Eleusinian and Thesean athletic games, when he was only seventeen years old. Amongst his several accomplishments, he was considered a clever artist, and some specimens of his painting were exhibited at Megara. The first tragedy he wrote was the "Peliades," which was exhibited in the year 455 B.C. We have no trace of this play beyond the fact recorded, nor was our author successful on this occasion ; but he gained the first prize in the year 428 B.C·

with his tragedy "Hippolytus," which I will have the pleasure of treating upon by-and-bye. From the year before named, 455 B.C., when Euripides first exhibited his writings, until he produced the tragedy of "Hyppolytus," we have trace of only one success; this was thirteen years previously, viz., in the year 441 B.C., when he gained a prize; but it is not authentically stated which of his tragedies he then exhibited.

Our poet was signally unfortunate in his selection of wives, for he was married twice and both the ladies were faithless to him; their names were Chœrila and Melito. It was supposed that through these misfortunes he retired to Macedonia; here he wrote his tragedy of the "Bachæ;" and he died in the year 406 B.C. Donaldson repudiates the recorded cause of his death; for, says he, "If he had died the violent death as related, Aristophanes (who was his enemy) would certainly have described it." I do not, for my part, see the force of this argument, which is but an hypothesis; and without better proof I am not disposed to repudiate a statement which has been recorded by several eminent writers. The doctor finds fault with this poet for that he was "too great a rhetorician." Surely this was a fault in the right direction, if a fault at all. I think the learned doctor here used a term he did not mean; for, if he meant to disparage the orator, I am inclined to think he intended to say he was pedantic in his mode of writing his sentences. Had he so expressed himself, there might have been some reason in his remark; but I do not hold with the idea that a man is in error for being rhetorically correct; besides which, the doctor concludes by inferring that it was this particular qualification in our poet which makes his works esteemed greater than either Æschylus or Sophocles. This surely is an hypothetical conclusion, if ever there was one, showing clearly that even so great a man as the

renowned Donaldson is sometimes fallible.   It was for
this particular excellence so paramount in Euripides, that the
"immutable Quintilian" wrote in his praise. The doctor says
that Euripides was the inventor of prologues ; and he winds
up his description of him in anything but a cheerful or res-
pectful tone, somewhat tinged with a spice of bigotry of his
own.   Upon the whole I consider Euripides is uncharitably
treated by the talented, but unscrupulous Dr. Donaldson.
—Here I finish my eighth lecture.

LECTURE IX.

In addition to the tragedy of the "Seven Chiefs against Thebes" by Æschylus, there are traces of three others by him alluding to this same subject; yet, although we have ample proof that they were in existence, from a variety of circumstances and frequent allusions to them, to us they are entirely lost, and we know of no means how to discover even a remnant of them. The subjects of these tragedies were Laius, Œdipus, and the Sphinx.

I am glad now to inform you that I feel myself more at home with my author, in his tragedy of the "Seven Chiefs against Thebes," than I did in that of the "Supplicants." In this play before me, he improves, but he does not resume that lofty genius which I discovered in his "Prometheus Chained." The action of this tragedy is laid within the gates of Thebes, where Eteocles is preparing to defend the city. Outside the walls the army from Argos (headed by Polynices and his six chiefs) is encamped. The chorus consists of the Theban ladies, who have assembled before the temple, and are clinging to the statues of their heathen gods, imploring their protection. Here Eteocles enters, and rates them for giving way to fear, instead of animating their husbands and brothers to acts of bravery and heroism. Relative to this tragedy, Potter remarks, that he is "sorry

Euripides finds fault with Æschylus for occupying the chiefs when they ought to have been in action." I am very sorry Mr. Potter makes this remark, for this reason : Euripides, in my opinion, proves himself the best judge of the three. He was not only correct in pointing out the error Æschylus had fallen into, but he proves himself right by producing the same effect in his own "Phœnician Virgins" in a much more consistent manner. Potter again alludes to this (strongly prejudiced) in favour of Æschylus, and he finds fault with what Euripides has done in the Phœnician Virgins most ungenerously. He says that Euripides fails by introducing Antigone at the top of the tower, to describe the encampment before the city, and that "we are disappointed." I don't see this : the only disappointment I feel on this head, is that a man of talent like Potter should have fallen into so egregious an error. I will explain to you why I am so positive in my opinion. In the play I am now going to treat upon, I find a most inconsistent character introduced,—a soldier, who is made by Æschylus to know and do a great deal too much ; for, to have accomplished all he is represented to have gone through, he must have been endowed with capacity enough for half a regiment. This man is represented without any distinctive mark, as to rank ; therefore we can treat him merely as he is termed,—a "soldier," not as an officer, as Potter describes him. The soldier says :—

"Illustrious King of Thebes, I bring thee tidings
"Of firm assurance from the foe ; these eyes
"Beheld each circumstance."

The fair inference, of course, is that he is wearing the uniform of the besieged army ; yet, he is represented as having been amongst the enemy, and seems to know everything concerning them, most minutely—so much so, that he even describes the armorial bearings displayed on the shields of six of the chiefs—and to know that the shield of the seventh chief is plain, not displaying any device at all.   He relates that the officers and soldiers deposited their little presents (as last remembrances to their friends) into the car of Adrastus, which was to convey them back to Argos ; how they " dropped a tear," that "no remorse was on their countenances," and how their souls were " glowing with rage."   He describes their lionlike valour, their eagerness for battle, and how he left them round the urn, casting lots to ascertain which gate each of the several chiefs should be appointed to make the attack on the city. He says that they are still gathering—that he saw the dust from and heard the snorting steeds,—that he saw the foam fall so thick from them, that, like dew, it whitened the fields ; and that his is the " faithful eye" with which he will hold the watch ; and that, through the information which he will afford, no danger shall surprise the city.   The word " faithful," which the soldier is made to use, means vigilant.

Did you ever listen to such bombast as all this ? Now, just look at the absurdity and impracticability of so much coming under the observation of one man, and that man a spy—the variety of circumstances he states he was an eye-witness of whilst present in the enemy's camp.   Take also into consideration the vast area of space he must have traversed to have gained all this knowledge, the time it must have taken, and the improbability of free transit, then you'll come to the same conclusion that I have, and you'll agree with me in thinking that Euripides was correct in pointing out the error that Æschylus had fallen into, and I think you'll not blame me for endeavouring to set Mr. Potter right in the matter.   By-and-bye I will show you how entirely correct Euripides is in his plan to gain the necessary information of the enemy's position; but I will reserve doing this until I come to that part of the tragedy where the description takes place.   Men who write for the public must expect to be criticised, and I dare say I myself shall come in for my share of gentle hints.   We are none of us infallible, so I trust that "the noble army of solemn critics" will be gentle in their onslaughts upon an humble and inoffensive individual like myself.   One thing I promise : I will give my opinions unbiased and conscientiously ; for if I discover errors in one author I will point them out as freely as I do in another : there can be no occasion for duplicity nor deception in an instance of this description.   One more remark respecting Potter's logic : he says that "Æschylus is unjustly censured for delaying the time in describing the chiefs, when they ought to have been in action.   It was necessary that Eteocles should be well informed what Argive prince assumed his station at each gate, that he might know what Theban chief to oppose against him."   What a strange idea is this, what a "lame and impotent conclusion" to come from a talented man like Potter ; it must have been downright prejudice on his part, it could not have been anything else.   Now, mark well to what I am about calling your attention.   To begin with, there is nothing to show how it could affect Eteocles, particularly, who the chiefs were. He must have felt convinced the enemy would select their best men to direct the attack, and it is equally certain that he would choose the best of his own leaders to defend his own position, let his opponents be whomsoever they might ; wherefore then was there any necessity to be so very fanciful upon this point as Potter is.   After all he betrays himself, for he admits that "it is a sacrifice of reason."   He calls it "propriety for sake of boldness of description."   I really think such reasoning shows a want of propriety, and an excess of boldness, on the part of the asserter. He says, " it is but candid to consider Eteocles as a commander, receiving intelligence, and giving his orders, to an officer who goes to execute them, whilst he himself is arming for the battle." Why! he gives no orders at all here, nor does he even make the soldier a reply. Potter says, " Were it not so, the reader of taste would rather be indulgent to some little impropriety." Here we have it. These very words of Potter's, prove that he was arguing by mere caprice, and against his own convictions. He began by making an assertion in favour of the works of one author, which (as he proceeded) he found he could not substantiate; and, instead of going back, he struggled on, and in the end found fault with the works of another author, in which he was equally in error. It is the most unfair piece of criticism I have ever read in my life. He excuses Æschylus for a positive error, by insinuating a similar mistake in Euripides, where none exists; and as he proceeds he turns round and (indirectly) admits that he has been arguing without his host. To confirm all this, he quotes P. Brumoy as being of a different opinion. Well indeed might Brumoy differ from Potter in this instance, for Potter actually differs from himself. In point of fact the whole of his preface to the play of the " Phœnician Virgins " is a mass of contradictions.

The characters represented in this tragedy are Eteocles, a Soldier, a Herald, Antigone, Ismene, and the Chorus.

SCENE.—*City of Thebes, near the great Temple.*

I will commence this play by reading the first scene to you.

" ETEOCLES.

" Ye citizens of Cadmus, it behoves
" The man, that guides the helm of state, to speak

Q

" What the sad times require ; nor suffer sleep
" To weigh his eyelids down.   For if success
" Attends our toils, to the good gods we bow,
" The authors of the blessing : Shou'd misfortune,
" Avert it Heav'n ! befall, Eteocles
" Shall hear his name alone wide thro' the city
" Insulted by each tongue, that vents its spleen
" In mutinous reproach, or loud laments :
" From which may Jove, the guardian of our state
" Defend the sons of Cadmus.   But this hour
" Call on you all, whether your flow'ry spring
" Yet wants the prime of manhood, or your age
" Puts forth its firmest strength, t'exert your pow'rs,
" Well it becomes you, to defend the city,
" The altars of the gods presiding here,
" (Ah, never may their honours be effac'd !)
" Your children, and this land, your common parent,
" And dearest nurse, whom her fost'ring soil
" Upheld with bounteous care your infant steps,
" And train'd you to this service, that your hands
" In her defence might lift the faithful shield.
" E'en to this day indeed the gods incline
" To favour us ; and so long immur'd
" Within our rampires, each bold work of war
" Hath prosper'd in our hands.   But now the seer
" That listens to the flight of birds, and thence
" Forms in his præscient mind the sure presage,
" Guiltless of fire, from their oracular wings
" Draws his deep skill, and warns us that the pow'rs
" Of Greece, combin'd against us, in the night
" Advancing, meditate the dark assault.
" Haste all then to the walls, haste to the bulwarks
" With all your arms, fill ev'ry tow'r, secure
" Each pass, stand firm at ev'ry gate, be bold,
" Nor fear th'assailing numbers : Heav'n is with us.
" Meanwhile on ev'ry quarter have I sent
" T'observe their forces, and descry their march :
" By these not charg'd, I trust, in vain to watch,
" Inform'd I guard against the wiles of war.

" Soldier.

" Illustrious King of Thebes.   I bring thee tidings
" Of firm assurance from the foe ; these eyes
" Beheld each circumstance.   Seven valiant chiefs
" Slew on the black-orb'd shield the victim bull
" And dipping in the gore their furious hands,
" In solemn oath attest the god of war,
" Bellona, and the carnage-loving pow'r
" Of terror, sworn from their firm base to rend
" These walls, and lay their ramparts in the dust ;
" Or dying, with their warm blood steep this earth.
" Each in Adrastus' car some dear remembrance
" Piled to their distant parents, whilst their eyes
" Drop'd tears, but on their face was no remorse.
" Each soul of iron glowing with rage
" Of valour, as the lion when he glares
" Determin'd battle.   What I now relate
" Sleeps not, nor lingers : round the urn I left them,
" By lot deciding to what gate each chief
" Shall lead his forces.   These against select
" The best, the bravest of the sons of Thebes,
" And instant at the gates assign their stations.
" For all in arms the Argive host comes on
" Involv'd in dust, and from the snorting steeds
" The thick foam falls, and dews the whiten'd field.
" Be thine the provident pilot's gen'rous care,
" Guard well the town, e'er yet the storm assails it ;
" E'en now the waves of war roar o'er the plain :
" Seize then this fair occasion, instant seize it.
" My faithful eye this day shall hold the watch,
" That, well inform'd, no danger may surprise thee.

" Eteocles.

" O Jove, O Earth, O all ye guardian gods ;
" And thou dread curse, the fury of my father,
" Of fatal pow'r, O rend not from its roots
" This ruin'd city by th' insulting foe
" Trampled in dust, her sweet Helladian tongue

" Silent, and all her sacred fires extinct !
" Ah, never let this land, this town of Cadmus
" Bend her free neck beneath the servile yoke !
" Protect her, save her ; as you share her honours
" I plead : a flourishing state reveres the gods.

" CHORUS.

" Woe, woe, intolerable woe !
" Fierce from their camps the hosts advance,
" Before their march with thund'ring tread
" Proud o'er the plain their fiery coursers prance,
" And hither bend their footsteps dread :
" Yon' cloud of dust that choaks the air,
" A true tho' tongueless messenger,
" Marks plain the progress of the foe.
" And now the horrid clash of arms,
" That, like the torrent, whose impetuous tide
" Roars down the mountain's craggy side,
" Shook the wide fields with fierce alarms,
" With nearer terrors strikes our souls,
" And thro' our chaste recesses rolls :
" Hear, all ye pow'rs of heav'n, propitious hear,
" And check the furies of this threat'ning war !
" The crouded walls around
" Loud clamours rend the sky ;
" Whilst rang'd in deep array th' embattled pow'rs
" Their silver shields lift high,
" And, level with the ground
" To lay their rampir'd heads, assail our tow'rs.
" What guardian God shall I implore ?
" Bending at what sacred shrine
" Call from their happy seats what pow'rs divine,
" And suppliant ev'ry sculptur'd form adore ?
" The time demands it : why then, why delay ?
" The sound of arms swells my affrighted ear.
" Hold now the pall, the garlands, as you pray.
" Hark ! tis the rude clash of no single spear.
" Stern God of war,
" Dost thou prepare

" Thy sacred city to betray ?

  " Look down, look down ;

  " O save thine own ;

" Nor leave us to the foe a prey :

" If e'er thy soul had pleasure in the brave,

" God of the golden helm, hear us, and save !

" And all ye pow'rs, whose guardian care

" Protects these walls, this favour'd land,

" O hear these pious, suppliant strains ;

" Propitious aid us, aid a virgin band,

" And save us from the victor's chains !

  " For all around with crested pride

  " High waves the helm's terrific tide,

  " Tost by the furious breath of war.

And thou, great Jove, almighty sire,

" Confound with foul defeat these Argive pow'rs,

  " Whose arms insult our leaguer'd tow'rs,

  " And fright our souls with hostile fire.

  " The reins that curb their proud steeds 'round,

  " Rattle, and death is in the sound :

" 'Gainst our sev'n gates seven chiefs of high command,

" In arms spear-proof, take their appointed stand.

  " Daughter of Jove, whose soul

  " Glows at th' embattled plain :

" And thou, by whom the pawing steed arose,

  " Great monarch of the main

  " Curb'd by thy strong control ;

" From our fears free us, free us from our foes !

  " On thee, stern Mars, again I call :

  " Haste thee, god, and with thee bring

" The Queen of Love, from whose high race we spring ;

" If Cadmus e'er was dear, defend his wall !

" Thou terror of the savage, Phœbus, hear,

" In all thy terrors rush upon the foe !

" Chaste virgin-huntress, goddess ever dear,

" Wing the keen arrow from thy ready bow !

  " Hark ! fraught with war

  " The groaning car,

" Imperial Juno ! shakes the ground ;
   Fierce as they pass,
  " The wheels of brass,
Dear virgin-huntress! roar around :
" The gleaming lustre of the brandish'd spear
" Glares terribly across the troubled air.
  " Alas my country ! must these eyes,
  " Must these sad eyes behold thy fall ?
  " Ah, what a storm of stones, that flies,
  " And wing'd with ruin smites the walls !
  " O Phœbus ! at each crouded gate   .
  " Begins the dreadfull work of fate ;
  " Each arm the thund'ring falchion wields,
  " And clashes on the sounding shield.
  " O thou, whose kind and matchless might,
  " Blest Onca, thro' the glowing fight
  " Obedient conquest joys t' attend,
  " All our sev'n gates, dread queen, defend !
  " And all ye mighty, guardian pow'rs,
  " That here preside, protect our tow'rs :
  " Nor the war-wasted town betray,
  " To fierce and dissonant foes a prey !
  " Ye gods, deliverers of this land,
  " To whom we stretch the suppliant hand,
  " Hear us, O hear our virgin pray'r,
  " And show that Thebes is yet your care !
" By ev'ry solemn temple, ev'ry shrine,
" Each hallow'd orgie, and each right divine,
" Each honour to your pow'r in rev'rence paid,
" Hear us, ye guardian gods, hear us, and aid !

" ETEOCLES.

" It is not to be borne, ye wayward race :
" Is this your best, is this the aid you lend
" The state, the fortitude with which you steel
" The souls of the besieg'd, thus falling down
" Before these images to wail, and shriek

" With lamentations loud ?   Wisdom abhors you.

" Nor in misfortune, nor in dear success,

" Be woman my associate : if her pow'r

" Bears sway, her insolence exceeds all bounds ;

" But if she fears, woe to that house and city.

" And now, by holding counsel with weak fear,

" You magnify the foe, and turn our men

" To flight : thus we are ruin'd by ourselves.

" This ever will arise from suffering women

" To intermix with men.   But mark me well,

" Whoe'er henceforth dares disobey my orders,

" Be it or man or woman, old or young,

" Vengeance shall burst upon him, the decree

" Stands irreversible, and he shall die.

" War is no female province, but the scene

" For men : hence, home ; nor spread your mischief here.

" Hear you, or not ?   Or speak I to the deaf ?

" CHORUS.

" Dear to thy country, son of Œdipus,

" My soul was seiz'd with terror, when I heard

" The rapid car roll on, its whirling wheels

" Grating harsh thunder ; and the iron curb

" Incessant clashing on the barbed steed.

" ETEOCLES.

" What ! shou'd the pilot, when the lab'ring bark

" Scarce rides the swelling surge, forsake the helm,

" And seek his safety from the sculptur'd prow ?

" CHORUS.

" Yet therefore to these ancient images,

" Confiding in their sacred pow'r, I ran,

" When at the gates sharp sleet of arrowy show'r

" Drove hard ; my fears impell'd me to implore

" The blest gods to protect the city's strength.

" ETEOCLES.

" Pray that our tow'rs repel the hostile spear.

" CHORUS.

" This shall the gods—

" ETEOCLES.

" The gods, they say prepare
" T' abandon us, and quit the vanquish'd town.

" CHORUS.

" Ah, never, whilst I breath the vital air,
" May their blest train forsake us ; nor these eyes
" Behold destruction raging thro' our streets,
" And in fierce flames our stately structures blaze !

" ETEOCLES.

" Let not these invocations of the gods
" Make you improvident ; remember rather
" Obedience is the mother of success,
" Wedded to safety : so the wise assure us.

" CHORUS.

" Yet in the gods is a superior pow'r,
" Which often in afflictions clears away
" Th' impenetrable cloud, whose sullen gloom
" Sharp misery hung before our darken'd eyes.

" ETEOCLES.

" The victim, and the hallow'd sacrifice,
" When the foes menace, are the task of men ;
" Thine, to be silent, and remain at home.

" CHORUS.

" That we possess our city yet unconquer'd,
" That yet our tow'rs repell th' assailing foe,
" Is from the Gods : from them our voice calls down
" Further success : why shou'd this move thy anger ?

" ETEOCLES.

" It does not, virgin : No : your pious vows
" I blame not.   But be silent ; lest thy fears,
" Swelling to this excess, dismay our youth.

" CHORUS.

" Affrighted at the sudden din of war,
" And trembling with my fears, with hasty foot
" I sought this citadel, this sacred seat.

" ETEOCLES.

" If haply now your eyes behold the dead,
" Or wounded ; burst not forth in loud laments :
" For blood and carnage is the food of war.

" CHORUS.

" Distinct I hear the fiery-neighing steed.

" ETEOCLES.

" Whate'er thou hear'st, it asks not thy attention.

" CHORUS.

" The city shakes beneath th' enclosing foes.

" ETEOCLES.

" Be satisfied ; to guard it is my charge.

" CHORUS.

" I fear : the clash is louder at the gates.

" ETEOCLES.

" Peace ; nor distract the city with thy cries.

" CHORUS.

" Ye social pow'rs, leave not our walls defenceless.

" ETEOCLES.

" Woe on thee !   Canst thou not bear this in silence ?

" CHORUS.

" God of this state, save me from slavery !

" ETEOCLES.

" Me wou'dst thou make a slave, and all the state.

" CHORUS.

" All-pow'rful Jove, turn on the foe the sword !

" ETEOCLES.

" Heav'ns, of what quality are women form'd ?

" CHORUS.

" Wretched, as men are, in their country's ruin.

" ETEOCLES.

" Still wail thy country ?   Still embrace these gods ?

" CHORUS.

" Wild with my fears, I speak I know not what.

" ETEOCLES.

" Would'st thou indulge me in a light request ?

" CHORUS.

" Speak it at once, quickly shall I obey.

" ETEOCLES.

" Be silent, wretch ; nor terrify thy friends.

" CHORUS.

" I will ; and with them bear what fate decrees.

" ETEOCLES.

" I praise thy resolution.   Clasp no more
" These images ; but stand apart, and ask
" Happier events ; entreat the friendly gods

" To aid us. Hear my vows ; then instant raise
" The heav'n-appeasing Pæan, whose high strains
" Of solemn import, 'midst her sacred rights,
" Greece pours symphonious ; strains, that raise the soul
" To gen'rous courage, and fix'd disdain
" Of fear and danger. To the guardian gods
" Whose tutelary pow'r protects our fields,
" Protects our crouded streets ; to Dirce's fount ;
" Nor thee, Ismenus, will I pass unhonour'd ;
" If conquest crowns our helms, and saves our city,
" The hallow'd sacrifice shall bleed, and load
" Their smoking altars ; this victorious hand
" Shall raise the glitt'ring trophies, and hang high,
" To grace their sacred walls, the rich-wrought vests,
" Spoils of the war, rent from the bleeding foe.
" Breath to the gods these vows : but let no sigh
" Break forth, no lamentation rude and vain :
" Weak is their pow'r to save thee from thy fate.
" My charge shall be at our sev'n gates to fix
" Six of our bravest youth, myself the seventh,
" In dreadfull opposition to the foe ;
" E'er yet the violent and tumultuous cry
" Calls me perforce to join the fiery conflict."

I have read rather more of this play right off than I have
in any other instance, or am likely to do in future. I have
done so because I thought it advisable to let you compare
the scene with 'my opening remarks.   There is one thing
certain : no one can deny Æschylus the credit for having
portrayed the obstinacy of woman's character in the most pro-
voking light.   It seems strange that our poet should just
have selected the king to do the work which would have
been more in character had it been done by the priests.   I
think that Euripides would have been equally correct had
he censured Æschylus for this waste of time, as well
as his " Chief " business.   The idea of a King (with his

city surrounded by an enemy) standing at parley with
a lot of women, instead of starting at once to muster his
forces! Potter says he might have been buckling on his
armour; if so, he was a precious long time about it. One
can understand very well such a scene as this transpiring;
but the king is not in his right place. The language used
by Eteocles is exceedingly trite, very philosophical, and as
much like a model moral philosopher's lecture to a lot of
obstinate grown-up girls as one can well imagine, but
as unkingly as any poet could possibly conceive. Only think
now for yourselves, the king leaving his soldiers without
any generals (for he has not yet appointed them), cutting
into the temple after a lot of ladies, and addressing them in
the following language (for this is the true meaning of what
he says) : Is this inconsistent waywardness on the part of
you women the only assistance you can afford the state? Is
this the encouragement you give your husbands and brothers
to defend your country? 'Tis entirely void of wisdom. This
teaches me a lesson: for I see women are not fit associates
for men, either in trouble or fortune; for if they happen to
have influence over us, they immediately presume upon it,
and there is no limit to their insolence ; or, if they become
distracted with fear in the hour of danger, they are certain to
create more difficulty, and add inconvenience to misfortune :
all this is occasioned by the usage of society, in permitting
women to mix with men. You have no business here ; be off
home with you, and spread no more mischief. Do you hear
me, or are you deaf? Rather an uncourteous way, this, to
address the gentle creatures, we must admit ; but I suppose
ladies then were sometimes refractory, same as they are now-a-
days. It does not seem that he had much influence over them
to induce them to hold their tongues, although he was their
king; for all his ravings seem to be to intimidate them to

sing small, down to piano key, or even somniferous in their breathing. He showed a strong desire to shut them up altogether; and had he determined to do this, no place could have been more opportune than where they were, in the great temple, within the city walls. I wonder he did not do so, and set a strong guard to protect them where they were, no place more appropriate or secure. He ridicules their clinging to the statues of the gods, and draws the following very consistent analogy. He says: What you are doing here, clinging to these images, is like the pilot of a vessel praying to its figurehead, instead of remaining at the helm to steer her safely through the storm. Don't waste too much time there invoking the gods, but be obedient, for "obedience is the mother of success." This is something similar to a passage in Shakspeare, "Thy wish was father, Harry, to thy thought;" we also sometimes hear that "wit is the mother of invention." The Greeks (particularly Aristophanes) frequently drew these aphorisms, and they are often very happy hits. Eteocles tells the ladies that their duty is to go home and remain silent. I don't blame you for being pious, but be silent. I will make it my business to guard the city, therefore don't distract or dismay our soldiers. Be silent. Woe on thee; can'st thou not listen and keep silence? Gracious heavens! there's no reasoning with women. That's right, still yell out. And then (sarcastically) he says, "Woud'st thou indulge me in a light request?" Upon which they say, "What is it?—we'll obey." "Then be silent," says he, "and don't terrify your friends." You must please not to misunderstand me in my explanation. Eteocles does not make the comparison to the figurehead of a vessel irreligiously; for it must be borne in mind that these ornaments were frequently effigies of some god these people worshipped. The continuation of Eteocles' admonitions runs thus: I praise you for coming to the resolution that you'll make no more noise. Leave the images alone, and stand aside; pray silently; then suddenly raise the pæan; after which, I will go and appoint six chiefs to watch the towers, and the seventh I'll see to myself. I will just explain to you the meaning of this word pæan; for 'tis of great signification, and most material to the Grecian Poets. It means a triumphal song, mostly sung as a chorus in the temples on high feast-days and other joyous occasions. Eteocles tells the ladies to sing with the double object of cheering his own soldiers and chilling the ardour of his adversaries. The poetry of a pæan consisted of a foot of four syllables. There are several kinds: one is what is called a trochee and a pyrrhic—this is one long, and three short syllables;—another is, two short, a long, and a short syllable; then there is a third, which is a short, a long, and two short syllables—this is iambus and a pyrrhic;—the others are called a pyrrhic and a trochee, and a pyrrhic and iambus. I will now read to you the soldier's address to Eteocles; he says:—

" Now I can tell thee, for I know it well,
" The disposition of the foe, and how
" Each at our gates takes his allotted post.
" Already near the Prætian gate in arms
" Stands Tydeus raging ; for the prophet's voice
" Forbids his foot to pass Ismenus' stream,
" The victims not propitious : at the pass
" Furious and eager for the fight, the chief,
" Fierce as the dragon when the mid-day sun
" Calls forth his glowing terrors, raves aloud,
" Reviles the sage, as forming tim'rous league
" With war and fate. Frowning he speaks, and shakes
" The dark crest streaming o'er his shaded helm
" In triple wave ; whilst dreadfull ring around
      The brazen bosses of his shield, impress'd
" With this proud argument. A sable sky

" Burning with stars ; and in the midst full-orb'd
" A silva moon, the eye of night, o'er all
" Aufull in beauty pours her peerless light.
" Clad in these proud habiliments, he stands
" Close to the river's margin, and with shouts
" Demands the war, like an impatient steed,
" That pants upon the foaming curb, and waits
" With fiery expectation the known signal,
" Swift as the trumpet's sound to burst away.
" Before the Prætian gate, its bars remov'd,
" What equal chief wilt thou appoint against him ?"

Here begin the errors spoken of by Euripides, for which Mr.
Potter so unmercifully chastised him. Now, says this leger-
demain, aspiring individual, I can tell you all, for I know
everything that is transpiring in their camp exactly—how
their soldiers are stationed, how many there are at each gate,
and every movement of their whole host. At the Prætian
gate stands Tydeus ; he is in a desperate rage because the
prophet has forbidden him to cross the Ismenus stream ; he
is reviling the soothsayers for being so timid in mixing the
fates up with the war ; when he speaks he frowns, and his
plume of three dark feathers shades his helm; the very bosses
on his shield are ringing from the blows struck on them by
Tydeus during the excitement of his argument. He then describes the weather, and says that Tydeus is standing near
the river's edge, all agitation and excitement for the fight to
begin. Now mark, this is only the beginning of what he
knows, and what he saw.

As I promised you I would describe the seven chiefs,
I will do so, as I go on. Tydeus was one of them. He
was son of Œneus, King of Calydon. He left his father's
kingdom on account of a murder ; or, as some say, an acci-
dental death. The statements are various. One is, that he

murdered his brother, Olenius; another, that he killed his
uncle, Alcathous; and a third, that he slew a friend acci-
dentally. At all events, whether it was through one or
other of these events, we find him dwelling at Argos,
married to Adrastus's daughter, Deiphyle, and sworn
friend to his brother-in-law, Polynices. Now, soon as it
was decided to go to war with Eteocles, Tydeus was chosen
to take the challenge. He went to Thebes for this purpose,
and not being pleased with his reception, he challenged
Eteocles and all his officers each to single combat. We
are told that he vanquished them all; but it is not stated
how many of the number he killed, nor how Eteocles
came off so free. It is quite certain he was not killed, and
it is equally clear that he soon appointed a fresh set of
officers, to replace those who had been placed *hors-de-combat*
by Tydeus. I, myself, am disposed to think that the chal-
lenges were never accepted, Eteocles not wishing to give the
chance to his opponents to say that he violated the sanctity of
a flag of truce. We are further informed, that on Tydeus's
return from Thebes to Argos, he was waylaid by fifty Thebans;
that he killed forty-nine out of their number, and only spared
the fiftieth, that he might return to Thebes, and tell of his
comrades' deaths. Tydeus was mortally wounded before
Thebes, by Melanippus, but he also killed his adversary;
and as they lay on the ground, Tydeus was so savage, that
he tried to gnaw Melanippus's brains out of his skull.
Tydeus was buried at Argos; and his monument was still
standing there at the time Æschylus wrote this Tragedy.
Now, having described one of the chiefs, I must resort to
my precious soldier again. He says :—

" May the gods crown his valiant toil with conquest.
" But Capaneus against th' Electran gates

" Takes his allotted post, and tow'ring stands
" Vast as the earth-born giants, and inflam'd
" To more than mortal daring : horribly
" He menaces the walls ; may Heav'n avert
" His impious rage ! vaunts that, the god assenting
" Or not assenting, his strong hand shall rend
" Their rampires down ; that e'en the rage of Jove
" Descending on the field shou'd not restrain him.
" His lightnings, and his thunders wing'd with fire
" He likens to the sun's meridian heat.
" On his proud shield pourtray'd, a naked man
" Waves in his hand a blazing torch ; beneath
" In golden letters, I WILL FIRE THE CITY.
" Against this man. But who shall dare t' engage
" His might, and dauntless his proud rage sustain ?".

The first line of this speech,—

" May the gods crown his valiant toil with conquest,"

applies to Menallippus, whom Eteocles has appointed to
guard the Prætian gate, against Tydeus.   The chorus
having called a benediction on Menallippus's head, the
soldier says, before he alludes to Capaneus,

" May the gods crown his valiant toil with conquest."

Now, to describe Capaneus, who has taken his post to
attack the Electran gate, the soldier says, He is of tremendous
stature, and endowed with more than mortal courage. He is
desperate in his rage, and he declares, whether the
gods favour him or no, his own hand shall rend the
rampires down.   (Rampire is synonymous with ram-
part.)   That even Jove (were he on the battle-field)
should not prevent him consummating this feat.   The
soldier then minutely describes the device displayed on

R

Capaneus's shield, which is a naked man, waving a blazing torch, the motto being, I WILL FIRE THE CITY. Capaneus was an Argive, a son of a nobleman named Hipponous; and his wife was Evadne, a daughter of Iphis, sometimes called Iphicles. She was a lady of Argos. She threw herself upon her husband's burning ashes; he being struck by Jupiter with thunder, because he declared he would breach the Theban wall, in spite of Jove. Evadne was also consumed, her ashes mingling with her husband's. These frequent sacrifices of life, by wives, is accounted for, from the belief that when they destroyed themselves, they were reunited to their husbands after death. Ladies, don't you follow Evadne's example; rather try how a neat widow's cap becomes you. Besides, who knows what may take place in a year or so. Don't you know the old motto, *nil desperandum?* Besides, it is a certain fact, I have heard it expressed myself, by young ladies, many times, that widows mostly go off again before maidens do. To be candid with you, I must say that I prefer maidens, particularly where widows are blessed with a lot of pledges of their former affection. I have always been an advocate for giving all ladies a fair chance in their turn; and I tell you candidly, I do not think it is exactly the thing, pretty widows taking advantage of young bashful maidens, by designedly displaying their features through tantalising pieces of lace, or muslin, crimped or goffered up, for the express purpose of destroying somebody else's peace of mind. Now, to my friend the soldier again. He tells Eteocles that the next chief he noted down was Eteoclus. You must please not to confound this chief's name with that of the King of Thebes. The king's name terminates " les," whilst the chief's here alluded to, finishes " lus." Eteoclus was an Argive, and a most valiant youth. In this battle he was killed by a son

of Creon, whose name was Megareus.   The soldier who saw
so much, and describes so minutely what he saw and
what he heard, says, that Eteoclus was posted at the Neis
gate; that the device on his shield was a man in armour,
with a ladder, fixing it against a wall; and that there
were letters plainly marked under the figure thus: NOT
MARS HIMSELF SHALL BEAT ME FROM THE TOWERS.
Then he says, " At the next gate stands Hippomedon; he
is named from the martial goddess (meaning Minerva). I
(the soldier, of course), heard his thundering voice.   I
saw him and his massive shield, which struck me with terror;
the image displayed being A TYPHEUS HUGE, disgorging
from his foul enfouldered jaws, in fierce effusion, wreaths of
dusky smoke, signal of kindling flames: its bending verge
with folds of twisted serpents bordered round."   This device
was so terrific to view, that it alarmed our valiant soldier.
Hippomedon was son of Nisimachus; he was killed by
Ismarus, a son of Acastus.   Now, again to my soldier, of
redoubtable energy.   At the Northgate, he says he saw the
fifth bold warrior, near to Amphion's tomb.   He swears by
his spear, which is more dear to him than his God, and
though Jove himself opposed him (they have most of them
proclaimed in a similar manner), he will level these walls to
the ground.   And this very young fellow has a beard which
is little more than down on his chin.   I suppose it was such
a beard as is sometimes designated an incipient camel's hair
brush.   Ah! says the soldier, his shield shows marks of
hard fighting, for all he's so youthful.   The device on it is
a sphinx, and the mangled body of a Theban. The motto is:
'GAINST THIS LET EACH BRAVE ARM DIRECT THE SPEAR.
He has come all the way from Arcadia.   His name is Parthenopæus.   He is no hireling, but fights for Argos, in
return for hospitality rendered him by Adrastus.   This

chief was son of Meleager, and was killed by Amphidicus, son of Talaus. The sixth and seventh chiefs are, Amphiaraus, at the Omolæan gate ; and your brother, Polynices. Amphiaraus has a shield which is plain. Your brother's shield bears two devices —one, a warrior blazing in golden armour, the other a modest female emblematic of Justice. The inscription is : YET ONCE MORE TO HIS COUNTRY, AND ONCE MORE TO HIS PATERNAL THRONE I WILL RESTORE HIM. Polynices is swearing fiercely, and fired with rage, to meet thee sword to sword to kill thee, then die himself; but if he takes you alive, he will exile you, same as you did him. I need not relate anything further now respecting Polynices; that has already been done at the commencement. Amphiaraus was son of Oicleus; it has been stated that Apollo was his father. His mother was Hypermnestra ; but we are not informed if she had this son by Apollo before she was married or no. Amphiaraus was married to Eriphyle, sister to Adrastus. He was an astrologer, and knew that he would be killed at this fight, so he secreted himself, but Polynices induced Eriphyle to tell where her husband was. Amphiaraus, when discovered, went to the war, but, previous to starting, he charged his son, Alcmæon, to destroy his mother immediately it became known that he himself was killed. He was not slain in the battle; but, attempting to retire therefrom, he was swallowed up by the earth. Upon the news of this reaching Argos, Alcmæon destroyed his mother, in obedience to his father's injunctions.

Speaking of Choruses in the ancient plays, why! here are two in this,—the Theban ladies, and my friend, the soldier,—the indomitable and everlasting soldier. For, now the fight is over and he has no more reports to

make to Eteocles, he commences a fresh course of information, to the other Chorus.   He says :—

" Have comfort, virgins, your fond parents' joy ;
" The city hath escap'd the servile yoke,
" And the proud vaunts of these impetuous men
" Are fall'n : the storm is ceas'd, aud the rough waves,
" That threaten'd to o'erwhelm us, are subsided.
" Our tow'rs stand firm, each well-appointed chief
" Guarded his charge with manly fortitude.
" All at six gates is well : but at the seventh
" The god, to whom that mystic number's sacred,
" Royal Apollo, took his awful stand,
" Repaying on the race of Œdipus
" The ill-advis'd transgression of old Laius."

The last line, of course, alludes to poor Laius's misad-
venture in getting drunk, and forgetting the oracle's warning.   The soldier tells the ladies that the city is saved,
but that both the brothers have fallen, each by the
other's hands.   The sons of Œdipus are both dead.   This is
cause for lamentation, also for joy : joy for the safety of the
city, but lamentation that the chiefs have fallen.   These two
brothers, when alive, inherited all the steel-mines in Scythia;
yet, for all this, now they are dead, they shall neither of
them occupy more space than is enough for a grave; or,
as Hamlet says, " The length and breadth of a pair of
indentures."   You see our soldier was a philosopher too ;
but, thank goodness, we have done with him.   The last
scene but one is recited by the Chorus, Ismene, Antigone,
and the Herald.   It is all in verse, and descriptive of what
you already know.   I will, therefore, finish this Tragedy
with a short scene, by the Herald and Antigone.

" HERALD.

" My office leads me to proclaim the mandate
" Of the great rulers of the Theban state.
" Eteocles, for that he lov'd his country,
" They have decreed with honour to interr.
" To shield her from her foes he fought, he fell,
" Her sacred rights rever'd, unstain'd with blame,
" Where glory calls the valiant youth to bleed,
" He bled.   Thus far of him am I bid to say.
" Of Polynices, that his corpe shall lie
" Cast out unburied, to the dogs a prey ;
" Because his spear, had not the gods opposed,
" Threaten'd destruction to the land of Thebes.
" In death the vengeance of his country's gods
" Pursues him, for he scorn'd them, and presum'd
" To lead a foreign host, and storm the town.
" Be this then his reward, to lie expos'd
" To rav'nous birds, unhonoured, of the rites
" That grace the dead, libations at the tomb,
" The solemn strain, that 'midst the exequies
" Breathes from the friendly voice of woe, depriv'd.
" These are the mandates of the Theban rulers.

" ANTIGONE.

" And to these Theban rulers I declare,
" If none besides dare bury him, myself
" Will do that office, heedless of the danger,
" And think no shame to disobey the state,
" Paying the last sad duties to a brother.
" Nature has tender ties, and strongly joins
" The offspring of the same unhappy mother,
" And the same wretched father.   In this task
" Shrink not, my soul, to share the ills he suffer'd,
" Involuntary ills ; and whilst life warms
" This breast, be bold to show a sister's love
" To a dead brother.   Shall the famish'd wolves
" Fatten on him ?   Away with such a thought.
" I, tho' a woman, will prepare his tomb,

" Dig up the earth, and bear it in this bosom,
" In these fine folds to cover him. Go to.
" I will not be oppos'd. Fruitfull invention
" Shall devise means to execute the task.

" HERALD.

" I charge thee not t' offend the state in this.
" Rage soon inflames a people freed from danger.

" ANTIGONE.

" Inflame them thou, he shall not lie unburied.
" Long have they strove to load him with dishonour.
" Great were his wrongs, and greatly he reveng'd them.
" Vengeance, the meanest of the gods, will do
" What she resolves ; spare then thy tedious speech,
" And be assur'd that I will bury him.

" FIRST SEMICHORUS.

" With what a ruthless and destructive rage
" The Furies hurl their vengefull shafts around,
" And desolate the house of Œdipus !
" What then remains for me ? and how resolve ?
" Can I forbear to mourn thee, to attend thee
" To the sad tomb ? Yet duty to the state,
" And reverence to its mandates, awes my soul.
" Thou* shalt have many to lament thy fall ;
" Whilst he,† unwept, unpitied, unattended,
" Save by a sister's solitary sorrows,
" Sinks to the shades. Approve you this resolve ?

" SECOND SEMICHORUS.

" To those, that wail the fate of Polynices,
" Let the state act its pleasure. We will go,
" Attend his funeral rites, and aid his sister
" To place him in the earth. Such sorrows move

---

* Eteocles.   † Polynices.

" The common feelings of humanity ;
" And, where the deed is just, the state approves it.

" FIRST SEMICHORUS.

" And we with him, as justice and the state
" Concur to call us. Next th' immortal Gods,
" And Jove's high pow'r this valiant youth came forth
" The guardian of his country, and repell'd
" Th' assault of foreign foes, whose raging force
" Rush'd like a torrent threat'ning to o'erwhelm us."

In this tragedy, by Æschylus, the poet provides Antigone assistance in the performance of the sacred duty she imposes upon herself, by making the Theban ladies sympathise with her, and declare that they will go and attend the funereal rites, and assist her in placing the body of Polynices in the earth. But in the tragedy of " Antigone," by Sophocles, which will follow this in my Course of Lectures, the author makes Antigone perform the task alone, without any aid whatever.

END OF FIRST SERIES.